THE DEFIANT

THE DEFIANT

by

M. QUINT

Illustrated by Lily Padula

MᶜSWEENEY'S
SAN FRANCISCO

McSWEENEY'S
SAN FRANCISCO

Printed in the United States.

ISBN 978-1-936365-54-8

10 9 8 7 6 5 4 3 2 1

www.mcsweeneys.net

for Namwali Serpell

"*If we find ourselves with a desire that nothing in this world can satisfy, the most probable explanation is that we were made for another world.*"

—C.S. Lewis

"*Trust no one but your crew—least of all the sea.*"

—Sir Francisco Ventana
(translated from the Spanish)

1

EARLY THAT MORNING, just before the strange mist began to fall, Gabriel was startled awake by the feeling that someone was touching the inside of his throat. It wasn't painful, exactly, not like a bump or a burr, but it definitely wasn't normal. And it didn't seem to be going away.

Lying on his back, Gabriel swallowed once, twice, trying to dislodge the alien feeling. It didn't work. Wiping the crust from his eyes, he sat up and gave his neck an exploratory poke. Nothing. Nothing on the outside, at least. But the feeling didn't change, and it was all the weirder for its consistency—for the steady pressure that didn't shift. Still, he could swallow just fine. And after giving a cautious "HA HA HA," he found that his voice was normal, too.

Throwing back the covers, Gabriel swung his bare feet onto the icy floor, stood up, and stretched his arms high above him. Yawning, he surveyed the room. To his left, three sleeping boys were nestled into nooks, snoring gently. As Gabriel picked his way across the room, he took care not to wake them. Sleep was precious in homes like this one, where space was so tight, and nobody valued it more than he did.

Taking soft steps toward the door, he lifted a long leg over a tiny curled body blocking his path. It was the new boy, the one who'd just arrived yesterday. He was huddled around himself like a pill bug.

It's getting crowded again, Gabriel thought. Never any space, and now even less.

He glanced down as he moved over the boy, anxious to avoid stepping on the sleeper. It took him a moment to register what he saw; when he did, his whole body seized. There, tucked under the new boy's arm, was Gabriel's book.

It was the one about the boy swept out to sea in the belly of a giant peach. Gabriel stood frozen, staring down at the worn lavender cover, his mind flooded with memories of all the times when crawling inside that peach had been the thing that saved him. Gabriel loved to read, loved the aloneness it allowed him; just seeing his book outside his possession—this book about a boy like himself, a boy without parents—made a black panic swell in his chest. He had to get it back.

He waited a moment more and then, with the clean swoop of a seagull diving for fish, Gabriel dipped a long arm down and plucked the book from the thief. He would fight for it if he had to, but for now he held his breath.

The new boy did not stir.

Quietly, Gabriel stepped back toward his bunk, holding the book tightly in his hands. Now there was the problem of what to do with it.

There were only so many places to hide something in the small room.

He considered the mattress on the bottom bunk, his bunk, thinking he could tuck the book beneath it, but underneath the mattress was the first place someone would look. Where could he hide something without making it seem like he was trying to hide it?

He thought. He looked. And then, all at once, a truly ingenious plan popped into his head.

Climbing across his bed, Gabriel gently—very gently, so as not to warp the pages—placed the book in the crevice between the mattress and the wall. He did his best to make it look careless, haphazard, the book not completely hidden but not on display either. That had been his mistake: putting the book on his shelf, where it had been clear that it was valuable to him. If he hid it more thoroughly now, the snoop would know for sure that it really was worth stealing. But no one ever took anything it seemed like no one else wanted. Gabriel had learned this lesson well. The moment you showed you cared—that's when the things that mattered were taken away.

Propped on his knees, Gabriel surveyed his work. He'd left one corner of the book peeking out, but it was barely distinguishable from the smudged grey wall behind it. Not bad, he thought. Then he let out the cough he'd been holding in, muffling the sound with his hands.

The strange prickling in his throat had grown into an itchy fury. He coughed again, harder this time. What was happening to him? Hand to his throat, he gave a last glance at the book and began to move across the room once more.

Something was odd about the sky that morning; it was a grey, foggy day, and looked almost as if it was about to rain, but streaks of white sunlight still burst through the clouds. Gabriel stood at the window a moment, squinting at the bright haze outside. Weird weather, he thought, as he pulled the door open and padded down the dusky hallway to the bathroom. He didn't think much more of the strange light in the sky. There was something really odd going on in his throat, and that's where his focus was fixed—at least until he reached the door to Angelica's room, and realized that it was ajar.

Angelica. The only girl in the group home. Her door was open just enough to reveal an edge of paisley bedding and half of the antique cage that housed Rodney, her giant black bird. Despite himself, Gabriel craned his neck to peek farther in.

The bird was awake. The disgusting thing was perched on its branch, gnawing at its mangy feathers. Gabriel recoiled, backing up into the hallway, trying to avoid the creature's notice, but he must have jostled the door somehow, because now it opened even wider, and Rodney, as if in response, began to thrash his wings, stirring the stale air in the room. An awful stench smacked Gabriel's nose. It was like pond scum and rotting fruit; for a moment, he thought he'd be sick. He hated Rodney, hated how he stank like something dying and snipped at Gabriel whenever he came close—but mostly he hated how the bird's screeching caws seemed to echo the nasty things Angelica said.

He took a breath, afraid to make another move. The bird whipped its head up and swiveled it sharply, its black eyes boring two holes straight into the stunned boy. Gabriel could only stare as Rodney's beak slowly opened, revealing a wormy, twitching tongue. He knew it would be just seconds before the piercing squawks started, alerting Angelica to his intrusion. And if that happened…

He didn't hang around to think about the trouble he'd be in. Quick as he could, Gabriel scurried down the dark hallway, not stopping until his hand gripped the knob of the bathroom door.

It was locked. Ordinarily he would have waited quietly for whoever was inside to finish up, but he was eager to put another barrier between himself and the gnarled bird. Plus, the strange thing in his throat had grown even more irritating since he'd gotten out of bed, more prickly and scratchy and rigid. It was as if he'd swallowed a tiny starfish. What was going on? He didn't feel sick otherwise, but this certainly wasn't good. Gabriel rubbed his neck and swallowed hard. He had to find out what was happening to him.

Lifting a long-fingered hand, Gabriel gave one tentative rap on the door and stepped back, waiting for a voice to acknowledge his knock. Instead, the door flew open, banging loudly against the wall, and Gabriel rocked back on his heels, shocked. Looming in front of him was the pinched, scowling face of Angelica.

"What do *you* want?" she hissed.

"I… I… um…" Gabriel stammered.

How had he not seen this coming? The open door must have meant that she wasn't in her room, he realized now, so of course he'd run into her here. But this was the first time Gabriel had ever seen Angelica awake this early. It was also the first time since Wednesday that she had spoken to him at all. Usually she treated him as if he barely existed, like

a shadow, which was entirely okay with him. When he did attract her anger, it felt like hot oil splattering against his skin.

Gabriel and Angelica were both fifteen—beyond that, they were different in every way imaginable. Where Gabriel was dark, Angelica was fair, with sour-cream skin and a thin ribbon of straw-colored hair that she loved to coil into ridiculous styles. (This morning, she had spooled it on top of her head in a series of tight knots, which made it seem as if her ruddy scalp were sprouting cacti.) While Gabriel was tall and long-limbed, with a lanky frame that made him curl inward like a comma, Angelica was small and scrawny. And while Gabriel was quiet, Angelica was very, very loud.

Angelica was also, by dint of being a girl, the only denizen of the group home who got her own room. This stirred a deep envy in Gabriel. The privacy! The endless time to sit and think! He could hardly imagine it. His whole life had been one big fight for space, for quiet, for a safe spot for his things. He'd long ago stopped hoping for someone to take him in, for a real home, for an end to the constant moving from one facility to the next—his daydreams, as of late, were focused on one simple wish. To be alone.

Since he'd gotten to the group home, he hadn't found even one minute of solitude. Angelica had quickly noticed his desire for quiet, sensing his envy of her precious space, and had made it her mission to disrupt whatever peace he tried to eke out. If he was reading a book, she'd blare the TV. If he was sleeping, she'd talk on the phone in her loudest voice, just outside his door. When he'd first arrived, Gabriel had been placed in the same small school as Angelica—the Greenly

School—and this unasked-for association had, for whatever reason, bred an ugly resentment in the girl. Over the last few months, she had made it her business to make his life miserable. Now, as Gabriel stood toe-to-toe with Angelica, her arms akimbo, her face twisted, he marveled that such a tiny person could scare him like this.

"What do you *want?*" Angelica spat again.

"I—I just—I." Gabriel kept floundering for a point, shifting clumsily, trying to put a little more distance between the two of them. He would have put an ocean between them if he could. There was no point in mentioning his throat, even if he could have remembered it just then—Angelica wouldn't have cared. There was no point in saying anything at all. With no ready answer, he could only stand in the hallway, gawking dumbly.

"Well, if you're done bothering me," Angelica said, sneering at Gabriel, and finished her thought by slamming the bathroom door in his face.

2

TEN MINUTES LATER, slogging through a bowl of stale cereal, Gabriel tried to make his mind go blank. He had returned to his room and made himself ready for the day, retrieving his backpack and finding some almost clean clothes, and now he sat in the kitchen, silent.

Slowly, from deep down inside, a familiar sadness had begun to creep up through him like a thorny vine. He felt it twisting its way through his body now, stretching thick misery into every corner. Chewing his cereal, forcing the flakes past the thing in his throat, he did his best to push the sadness back down to where it had come from.

It was safer to keep his feelings hidden, he knew—to conceal them from people like Angelica, who would only use them against him. He shoved his sadness and anger down, feeling the darkness condensing until it was just a hard, angry ball spinning in his chest. He was seething, but he told himself to think of nothing. If you thought of nothing, then you didn't risk thinking of the bad things, or, most dangerous, of—Gabriel's stomach turned. He had a few happy memories stored away, too, but letting them surface was even worse.

For a moment he saw himself shrieking at the water's edge, lifted by his father's powerful arms. He couldn't make out the face, but he could remember the arms, the darkly curling hair, the thumbprint birthmark… And just as the water soaked him, the ocean—

Gabriel's spine sprang straight. He sat very still. The ocean. Something was pulling at the base of his brain—something he was supposed to remember. He gasped. The field trip! How had he forgotten? And now he was late and he hadn't even—no! His head fell forward into his hands. He had forgotten his permission slip—Ms. Inez had reminded him every day that week, and now the trip was here and he still hadn't done it. What was wrong with him? Why couldn't he manage to remember the easiest thing?

It had nothing to do with his memory, of course. He'd had a dozen chances that week, a dozen times when he'd practically had the slip in one hand and a pen in the other; the problem was that Gabriel dreaded asking Ms. Baxter, the woman who ran the group home, for any help at all. Just being in the home already seemed like an imposition. Most days he felt like any minute he might be told to pack up and leave.

It had happened before, more than once. Gabriel knew to be cautious, to keep his head down, to ask for nothing and try his best to be invisible. But he had to go on this trip.

They had been studying the explorers in school for the entire month—it had all been leading up to this day. He had even started going to the library after class to study the few books on ships and sailing that the Greenly School carried, so he'd be able to recognize the different parts of the vessel when he finally saw them: the masts, the main, the lines. He had to do something. There was no way he was going to miss a chance to see the long-lost ship of Sir Francisco Ventana.

"Hello? Anyone home?"

Angelica rapped a fist against the back of Gabriel's head. He'd been so distracted by his thoughts that he hadn't noticed her creep up behind him. Now he turned, startled, to find her pinched face just inches away. He felt the anger inside him bubbling up again, but he clenched his fists and pushed it back down.

It was a familiar trick, one Angelica had used a lot when he first got to the home: she'd rile him up, and if he said anything at all, she'd yell for Ms. Baxter. Then he'd be the one in trouble, because Angelica did not hesitate to lie. But he wasn't going to fall for it now. He wasn't going let Angelica make him miss the day he'd been waiting for. That was what she wanted, he knew, and he wouldn't give her the satisfaction.

Ducking around her, Gabriel abandoned his breakfast and hustled down the hallway until he came to a stop in front of Ms. Baxter's bedroom door. He took a deep breath, picturing himself actually standing in Ms. Baxter's bedroom, imagining the words he would have to say. He knew Ms. Baxter didn't hate him like Angelica did, but she didn't particularly like him, either. It didn't matter. Failure, in this moment, would make every day of his life in this house more miserable than the one before it. He had to see that ship.

"Why are you standing there like that?"

Gabriel jumped back from the door and reeled around. There was Angelica again, just behind him, her ugly mouth mangled in the shape of a smile. Rodney was there too, dirty claws gripping the skin of Angelica's bare shoulder. When the girl cocked her head, the fat black bird cocked its head, too.

"Are you eavesdropping?" Angelica said, taking a step closer.

"No, I—"

"I'm going to tell," Angelica said, cutting him off. "We don't need a spy in this house. I'm going to tell Ms. Baxter you're a spy and then she'll kick you out and you'll have nowhere to go." She smiled sweetly and batted her blonde lashes. "How does that sound?"

Gabriel didn't speak. He didn't move. But deep in his chest, the hard ball of anger started to spin. And as it spun, it expanded and grew hot, and before he knew it, his body had shot forward of its own volition, pushing past Angelica and her awful black bird. But the hallway was too narrow, his legs too long, and he couldn't get by without roughly bumping against her. Instantly, the spooked bird flew off her shoulder, beating its wings in a crazed flurry.

Angelica didn't make a sound, but Gabriel realized what he'd done, what the consequences would be. He felt his bones turn leaden.

"I—I didn't mean to—" he started, but he couldn't think of the words with Rodney's squawking and flapping blurring his thoughts. Why had he let her provoke him? He could usually push the anger down. How did she still find ways to get the best of him like this? Fixed where he stood, Gabriel watched as Angelica slowly reached one arm up above her head. The raven dug its grimy talons into her thin wrist. The girl and the bird looked at Gabriel with the same dark joy. When Angelica finally spoke, her voice was eerily calm.

"You hit Rodney."

"I didn't!" Gabriel cried.

"Oh yes, you did." Angelica spat back, her voice rising. "You did. You hit him."

"I hit the wall!"

"You hit Rodney!"

"Please, stop!" Gabriel was begging now. "I know I shouldn't have—"

"You are in *so much trouble*!" Angelica shrieked, banging on the door in front of them. "Ms. Baxter! Ms. Baxter! Gabriel tried to kill Rodney!"

Gabriel stood there numbly as the door began to open. He knew that in just seconds Ms. Baxter would be there in the hall, grilling him about what he'd done. It would be his word against Angelica's, and his word never counted for anything. He had to get out of there, permission slip or no. There was nothing left to do now but escape.

Racing through the early purple light, the houses whizzing past him in a blur, Gabriel was glad for once that he lived in the flattest part of the city—the fog-covered hills reserved for the rich would have only slowed his speed. Overhead, the sky was still swirling strangely, but Gabriel barely noticed. He tried to let the rhythmic slap of his feet against the pavement drown out all thoughts of how he'd ruined his chance to see the *Defiant*. He ran on, through the Mission District, past the rainbow fruit stands outside the groceterias, past the gaping black mouths of the abandoned theaters, past the lines of skinny, smoking artists outside the coffee shops. Gabriel saw none of it. He had just one thought now, circling through in his head: Find Esme.

3

SHE HAD HALF a mile to go, but she was beating her best time by four seconds. Sweat ran in rivulets down the girl's face, pooling hotly in her armpits and at the small of her back. She burst through the foggy morning, rounding the edge of the gritty field and sprinting toward the finish line. Her thick, powerful legs were not the typical limbs of a runner, but she had trained them into champions. Today she would make it.

Crossing the chalk, doubled over, the girl hurled her wrist up toward her face to peer at her watch. A cold shock of disappointment slammed into her. Two seconds late.

"Aw, man!" Esme hollered across the empty field. She collapsed onto the ground, not even bothering to brush away the gravel digging into her knees. It was only 7:15, but Esme had already done a hundred sit-ups, thirty pull-ups, and twenty-two lunges. If it were up to her, she would have tried to beat her mile time again, but, because she was thirteen years old, she didn't get to decide how to spend her mornings. She had twenty minutes to get to school.

The Greenly School was tiny—a dingy two-room facility above a restaurant supply store on Mission Street. The school had only one class, with three teachers and, all mixed together, a couple dozen kids ranging in ages from ten to fifteen. It was a last-chance school—a place for kids who, for one reason or another, had been told they couldn't make it somewhere "normal." Esme had never thought she'd wind up at a place like that. She'd never loved school, but she'd always done okay. Not great, but okay. Then her dad had died, and it had all begun to seem so pointless.

But running, that she loved. And she was good at it—very good. So why did she have to go to school at all, instead of dedicating herself to the thing that let her excel?

As she sat in the dirt, Esme absently moved her thumb across the wide strawberry birthmark spanning the soft stretch of skin below her left ear. It was a habit she fell into whenever she was caught by troubled thoughts. Something about the mark always being there, the dependability of it, made her feel calm. But she hated the way the red splotch looked, just like she hated her upturned nose, the freckled paleness of her skin, her limp cinnamon-colored hair, and, most of all, her short muscular body. The only part of herself that Esme didn't mind so much were her eyes. They were a vivid mossy green, and arched into happy horseshoes when she smiled.

Esme was not smiling now. She felt defeated.

Sitting on the wet track, glumly picking gravel from her knees, Esme

looked up and noticed the strange sky for the first time. It was an odd sort of overcast, spanned with bright silver swirling clouds. At the far rim of the track, the leaves on a few thin trees shuddered in the warm autumn wind. Everything was very quiet, very still. Far off, Esme could hear the low din of garbage trucks making their rounds. What time was it, anyway? She looked down at her watch and cringed. Late. Just like her running time. If she didn't hurry, she'd miss first period. They were only a month into the school year, and Esme already led the class for tardies.

With a long sigh, she picked herself up and started the short walk back home, dragging her feet as she went. Passing the rows of drab, crumbly houses, Esme tried to catch a glimpse of the people inside. She didn't know her neighbors, rarely saw anyone coming or going, but she often wondered who they were. Families, eating breakfast together? Lonely old ladies? Kids like her?

Her house sat in the distance, a dumpy box with such small windows that, even on the sunniest days, the inside stayed dim. Technically Esme lived with her Aunt Stevie, and with whatever sulky boyfriend her aunt had decided should move in (before said boyfriend quickly decided to move out). But mostly Aunt Stevie was gone, and Esme lived in the house alone.

Esme hated being alone.

The first time Aunt Stevie hadn't come home for dinner, Esme had been living there for a month. They were both getting used to the new arrangement. This was two years ago, right after Esme's dad had died.

She'd never known her mom, and her grandparents were all gone, so Stevie had been the only option. It was understandable, she told herself that first night, that Stevie didn't know she was supposed to make sure her niece had dinner every single evening; her aunt didn't have any kids herself. So Esme just poured herself a bowl of cereal, went to bed after eating it, and tried not to worry.

It started happening every few days after that. Esme would watch as the clock ticked past seven, then eight, holding out hope for as long as she could, until her growling stomach urged her to go in search of whatever might remain in the cupboards. She'd make herself some oatmeal or just eat a jar of tomato paste and tell herself that this sort of thing was normal. But when several days in a row began to go by with no sign of Aunt Stevie, the food began to run out. Then Esme would go to bed with no dinner at all.

She was tired all the time, and her jeans started to sag off her hips. Esme told herself that she was doing okay, that things were just fine, but truthfully she was consumed by worry. It was only when she was running that her worries seemed to quiet. When she didn't eat, though, running made her dizzy.

She had heard about food stamps on television, but had never actually known anyone who used them. She didn't want to ask Ms. Inez; she worried that would get her aunt in trouble. So one day Esme waited after school until she was sure the computer would be free. Then she found the website, printed out the paperwork, forged her aunt's signature, and mailed the forms in. When the laminated card appeared in the mail a few weeks later, Esme squirreled it away under her mattress.

She didn't know why, but it seemed important to keep the card hidden from Aunt Stevie.

Esme was meticulous about rationing her money each month. She found a strange pleasure in monitoring her expenses, and made long charts detailing what she would buy, how much it would take, and how long each card would last. When her aunt appeared, gushing with a thousand excuses—her mean boss kept her late! She got into a huge fight with Gerald!—Esme always told her not to worry, that it was fine. She had considered asking her aunt to leave something for groceries, but she knew that money was tight. Esme didn't want to be a burden. If Aunt Stevie made her leave, after all, where else could she go? Who else did she have?

Esme looked up again as she approached the house. The sky was blustery, schizophrenic, bright rays piercing through the swirling clouds. A few drops fell around her, one grazing the tip of her nose. Great, Esme thought. Rain. She kicked at a rock, miserable about the prospect of being cooped up inside all day without even a chance to play basketball at recess or—Esme halted mid-step. All at once, she remembered what day it was. The field trip! And she was so late!

Well, she wasn't going to miss this. She would run.

Esme sprinted down the block, then took the steps two at a time, banging open the front door and bursting inside. "Stevie!" she called out, hoping against all odds that her aunt was home and might be able to give her a ride to the Marina. But the house was silent. It'd have to be the bus.

Scanning the dark living room, Esme spotted her backpack on the old recliner and snatched it up. She bolted down the hallway, kicked open the door to her room, and picked up a pair of jeans and a T-shirt off the floor. She shoved the clothes into her pack—she'd have to change out of her running gear later—and raced back into the living room. Then, grabbing the lone squishy black banana from the fruit bowl, Esme bounded back to the front door, flung it open—and just missed colliding with the lanky boy in the doorway.

4

"YOU'LL BE *FINE*," Esme repeated for the millionth time that morning. She'd spent the whole bus ride to the Marina trying to convince Gabriel he'd be allowed to come along on the field trip without a permission slip. But the distant look on his face made Esme feel pretty sure she wasn't having much luck.

"What's Ms. Inez going to do?" she said. "Send you back?"

Gabriel just shrugged and turned to stare out the window, a black curtain of hair hiding his face. He'd barely said a word to her the whole ride. This isn't working, Esme thought.

Ever since Gabriel had shown up at Greenly, Esme had had a careful curiosity about the new boy. He was quiet but not shy—something she had never noticed in anyone else—and she'd found herself watching him when she was sure he wouldn't notice. There was something about him that drew people in, that made them want to be around him, some respectful kindness in the way he spoke, a certain attention he paid you. He made people feel special. But even though the students at Greenly liked him (no small feat, for a new kid), Gabriel didn't seem to be especially close to anyone. He mostly ate lunch alone.

Esme had decided, after much consideration, that Gabriel was a truly awkward-looking boy. Attached to the end of his stringy arms were thick, wide hands, and on his face a broad nose stood out among his otherwise delicate features. But his teak-toned skin was smooth, his tawny eyes long-lashed and heavy-lidded. He wore his dark hair long and was constantly brushing it out of his eyes. He was the mirror image of his mother, although neither of them knew that.

They had been partnered for a lab in science a few months back, Esme and Gabriel, but he hadn't spoken much then, either. Once, when she was handing him a beaker, their hands brushed, sending a shock of sparks up her arm. But she definitely wouldn't call them friends.

She'd been pretty surprised when he'd shown up at her door that morning, asking for her help. She'd listened, loaned him money for the bus, and then, once they'd boarded, watched him fall silent again. When the bus came to a stop in a roundabout along the water, the two of them exited wordlessly and began the short walk to the dock where they'd been told to meet their teacher.

It was strangely empty in the Marina that day; no tourists freezing in their summer shorts, no crowds bunched together to gawk at the clusters of barking seals. The only sounds Esme heard were the deep creaks of the moored ships in the distance, rocking in slow unison in their slips, and the occasional sad cry of a seagull overhead. As they walked toward the dock, Esme wondered if she should keep trying to get Gabriel to talk—if something were bothering her, *she'd* want someone to talk to. But Gabriel wasn't like her or anyone else she knew. She was still trying to make up her mind when she noticed the small boy darting toward them. He was waving both arms wildly as he ran, and as he skidded to a stop before them, his hands still danced in the air above his head.

"Hey, where you guys been?" he said. "Why're you so late?"

Carlos hadn't caught his breath yet, but he was already pelting the pair with questions. He was the youngest student at Greenly—tiny, even for a ten-year-old—and always seemed on the verge of exploding. His short, spiky black hair shot out from his head as if he'd stuck his thumb in an electrical socket, and his clothes were usually one size too big for his frame. He was one of those kids whose feet were always dancing. Unlike most of the Greenly students, he lived with both his parents, and in one of the nicer parts of the city—he'd been sent to Greenly two years ago, after an unfortunate accident involving a fire at his last school. Everyone whispered about it, but no one knew exactly what had happened.

Carlos looked up expectantly, raising himself up and down on the balls of his feet. "Where you been?" he repeated, eyes bulging for an answer. Esme glanced at Gabriel, but he seemed not to register the question. He was looking out at the water, a faraway expression on his face.

"Gabe!" Carlos shouted. "Where *were* you guys?"

Gabriel shook his head and looked down at the boy, seeming to notice him for the first time. He was about to respond when a shove from behind sent him tumbling.

"You two on a date?"

Gabriel spun around. Quincy's feline eyes sparkled back at him, the challenge in them unmistakable. With one hand the boy smoothed the tight braids that spanned his head.

"ARE YOU?" Carlos whispered.

"Looks that way, huh?" Quincy said, and smirked.

Gabriel didn't know much about Quincy Hunter—just the same stuff everyone knew. He was cutting and quick, and had been sent to Greenly for an accumulation of petty offenses: stealing, cheating, truancy. The clincher—the thing that had used up his last chance anywhere else—was kidnapping his old principal's prized poodle. Quincy had sworn he'd just wanted to walk the dog around the block, but the poodle had gotten off leash and taken off into the woods. A week later Quincy had landed at Greenly. Still, he seemed to have a good, solid family—he lived with his mom and two older brothers, Mike and Marcus. The twins were legends, star soccer players, both headed north to Washington in the fall to play college ball. Gabriel had often wondered what that must be like, to have not one but two big brothers looking out for you.

"Are you Gabe's girlfriend now, Es?" Carlos pressed her.

"Yeah, Es, are you?" Quincy echoed, grinning.

Gabriel watched Esme's pale freckled face flush a deep red. He'd had enough of this.

"Cut it out," he warned, glaring at Quincy, who spread his hands wide in mock innocence.

"Just keeping things interesting. Someone's gotta."

"Oh, really?" a small dark-haired girl grumbled, nudging her way into the group. "And what's so boring about us?"

"Whatever, Rose." Quincy laughed, waving her away.

The girl took a step closer to Quincy. She put her hand on her hips. "I *said*"—she drew out the word a beat longer than necessary—"What's so boring about us, huh?"

Quincy looked down at her, then rolled his eyes. "You know what I meant," he said.

"Uh-huh, I do," Rose huffed. Then she turned and, looking up, half-asked, half-declared, "We're not boring, right, Gabe?"

Gabriel peered down at the girl scowling up at him. He knew the look was not unkind—it was just the face Rose typically wore. He noted the dark circles under her eyes and wondered if she was unwell, or just suffering from lack of sleep. He knew she had to help out in her parents' store most days—he'd seen her there early one Sunday morning, sweeping the front walk. She was scratching at the cast on her left arm now, the arm she'd broken over the summer in an attempt to show her older brother she could stand on the handlebars of her bike, just like him. (She couldn't.)

Rose Chen was the youngest girl at Greenly, a year younger than Quincy and one older than Carlos. She had a small heart-shaped face, a crown of dark, glossy hair cut in a short mop, and a mouth that turned down slightly at the corners, so that she seemed to wear a perpetual pout. The story of how she'd ended up at Greenly was something of a legend. Apparently, while running the mile during PE, Rose had asked her old gym teacher if she could stop and get some water; the teacher had said no, and told her to keep running. Rose, in response, had kept running on into the night, dodging every effort to catch her, and even after she had finally been brought to ground she had refused to drink a single drop. For the next week. She wound up in the hospital, near kidney failure.

The doctors told her parents she had a "borderline personality disorder," a description Rose found hilarious and used often, with pride. As soon as the hospital released her, her old school sent her straight to Greenly.

"Are we, Gabe?"

"Huh?"

Rose shook her head impatiently. "Tell Quincy we're not boring."

But before Gabriel could respond, Quincy cut in. "I didn't even say anything, Rose. Gabe, tell her I was just messing around."

Gabriel looked back and forth between the two of them. They were both staring at him expectantly, and Gabriel felt the familiar urge to disappear. One hand wandered up to his throat, where he could feel the prickle returning. He sighed. He didn't want to play peacemaker. Why did they always look to him for that? Couldn't he just walk away and leave them to their little fights? He glanced toward the dock, looking for an escape route.

A woman, fragile as a sparrow, was standing at the far end. Beside her stood a very large boy. Without another word, Gabriel began taking long strides toward them. The rest of the group fell in line behind him and followed along.

5

AS THE STUDENTS spilled down the dock, Ms. Inez took a deep breath, readying herself. It was going to be a long day, she knew, but it would be fine. She could do this. A low buzz issued at her hip, startling her, and she reached into her purse for her phone.

Guide is running late. Start without him.

"Great," Ms. Inez muttered. It was a message from her boss, Principal Leibowitz. Ms. Inez looked down at her phone again, moving to check her email, but stopped herself. Tucking the phone back into her bag, she smoothed her skirt with nervous fingers, scanned the approaching group, and did a quick count: Esme, Carlos, Quincy, Gabriel, and Rose. More than half the class hadn't shown up, but maybe that wasn't such a bad thing. It would make the group easier to manage, at least—no small task with the Greenly kids.

"Hey Ms. Inez!" Carlos called, running ahead. "I found Esme and Gabe! Did we miss the boat?"

Ms. Inez opened her mouth to answer, but the large boy beside her spoke first.

"That ship's been around for half a millenium," Baron said. "I highly doubt it will matter if we're a few minutes late."

Ms. Inez sighed. Baron was always making haughty remarks like that, always provoking the other students. It was hard to not let his attitude get under her skin. But she tried her best to be understanding—she knew Baron's home life was less than ideal, with his dad, his only parent, working that big-deal job in Silicon Valley. She knew he must be left alone a lot. And, of course, Baron couldn't have an easy time being as big as he was. Ms. Inez had tried to schedule a conference with Baron's father, but Mr. Worthwright hadn't returned any of her calls. She made a mental note to try to reach him again next week.

For now, Ms. Inez shot Baron a pleading look, which he met straight on. Though he was only twelve, Baron was nearly the same height as the willowy teacher. He had tree-trunk legs and an enormous belly that hung out heavily over his beltline. His eyes were small and perfectly round, their whites bright against his dark walnut complexion and rimmed with the oval glasses that made him look like a particularly chubby owl.

"Glad you could join us," Baron called to the approaching group.

"Oh, sorry," Quincy shot back. "Didn't mean to interrupt your date."

He'd just made this joke, but Rose and Carlos still giggled, and Ms. Inez felt Baron tense beside her. She put a hand on his shoulder, but the boy shook her off.

"Shut up, Quincy," Baron said.

"Excuse me?"

"You heard me."

Quincy took a step toward Baron, but as he did, one foot caught the other, and he stumbled.

"Smooth as always," Baron said, and smirked.

"Why don't you just eat another candy bar, fatty?"

"Hey!" Ms. Inez took a shaky step in front of Quincy. "Cool it, okay?"

Quincy was about to fire back when a shrill voice cut him off.

"Well, look who made it after all!"

The students turned to see Angelica walking up the damp dock behind them, the black bird bobbing on her shoulder. Instinctively, Gabriel hunched his shoulders and looked to the planks below him. Angelica narrowed her eyes at him, then turned to Ms. Inez and smiled sweetly.

"Sorry I'm late, Ms. Inez. Had to get my permission slip signed before I left." She waved the small piece of paper toward the teacher, who plucked it away and tucked it into her bag.

"That's fine, Angelica," she said. Despite her best efforts, Ms. Inez had never warmed to the girl. There was something off about her, something cold in her eyes that made the teacher feel strangely afraid. And she hated that ugly black bird.

"I thought we talked about bringing Rodney to school?" Ms. Inez said.

A darkness flickered across Angelica's face. When she spoke, though, her voice was sugary.

"But Ms. Inez, we aren't *at* school. I didn't think this counted."

"Angelica," Ms. Inez said, and sighed. "The rules are important."

Angelica nodded, her eyes wide. "Gabriel gave you his signed slip, then?" she cooed.

Ms. Inez blinked a few times, surprised. She'd completely forgotten about Gabriel's permission slip. Now she was on the spot. She couldn't break the rules so blatantly in front of her students, could she?

As it turned out, she never had to make that choice. The tight row of uniformed kids marching down the dock completely stole the group's attention.

"Who're they?" asked Carlos.

"I'm not sure," Ms. Inez replied slowly. This was not what she wanted. Her students were supposed to be the only ones touring the ship today—she had planned it that way. The Greenly kids did not typically play well with others, especially others like the ones making their way toward them now. Ms. Inez squinted, trying to recognize the uniforms: pale blue, with red triangle-shaped insignia on the breast pockets. The kids were all different ages, like the Greenly group, but they weren't laughing or chatting like her students usually did. They moved forward silently, in one straight line. After another moment, Ms. Inez stepped from behind her class to greet the stout curly-headed man whom she took to be their teacher.

"Hello there," the man called out. His voice was not unkind, but he didn't smile, either. Behind him, the uniformed students stood shoulder to shoulder. "Looks like we've got a mix-up on our hands," he said, casting an appraising eye over the Greenly kids.

"I'm—I'm sorry?" Ms. Inez stuttered in confusion.

"You all are here for the *Defiant* tour, I assume?"

"Yes, we're the Greenly School," she replied. "Are you the guide?"

As soon as she'd said it, Ms. Inez realized the ridiculousness of her question. Somehow the stout man managed to chuckle without altering his expression.

"Ha! Gosh, no. No. Not the guide. Bob Franklin. We're the St. Perpetua sailing team. Come to see the ship ourselves. Got a twelve-thirty tour. You?"

The man's clipped speech flustered Ms. Inez, and she fluttered her hands by her side as she replied.

"We're scheduled for twelve. But—but the guide seems to be late."

"Well then," Mr. Franklin said, "I'll just take my kids along the marina, check out some of the other ships, let you all have some space."

And with that, the man turned on his heel and began walking away, his sailing team in tow.

Ms. Inez looked back at the Greenly kids. They had stayed remarkably quiet throughout the exchange—in fact, they'd seemed silenced by the presence of the St. Perpetua kids. Ms. Inez turned again, back toward the sailing team, and saw that the last two girls in their line were lagging behind. Before Ms. Inez could wonder why, the smaller of the girls called out, "Do you smell something, Hannah?"

The larger girl looked over her shoulder and wrinkled her nose.

"Oh yeah," she replied. "I definitely smell some trash."

Then, with a quick flip of their ponytails, the girls turned their backs to the Greenly kids and skipped to catch up with their group.

Ms. Inez felt her heart split. She didn't want to look at her students; she was too afraid of what their faces would show.

"Ms. Inez?" Carlos said, breaking the silence. "I don't smell trash."

"She meant you, you idiot." Quincy spat on the wet wood at his feet. The other kids were looking at the water, or the sky, or anywhere but at the sailing team fading into the drizzly distance.

"Hey, now—" Ms. Inez warned.

"She meant you, too, Quincy," said Baron.

Before Ms. Inez could stop him, Quincy flew past her shoulder, lunging for the larger boy. The two of them collided and fell to the dock, shouting and pulling each other's clothes as the other students looked on, stunned—all of them except Angelica, who stood a bit away from the others, arms crossed and grinning. Ms. Inez was about to intervene when Esme shot forward, shoved her strong arms between the boys, and pulled them apart.

"You really gonna ruin this for everybody?" she said when they stood, giving them each a hard look.

The boys bowed their heads.

"Come *on*, you guys!" Carlos whined. "I want to go on the boat!"

Ms. Inez looked from Quincy to Baron. Then, willing her voice bright, she faced the other students and smiled.

"You guys ready?"

"Yeah!" Carlos and Rose shouted back.

She turned to the boys.

"You two ready?"

The boys nodded glumly.

"Okay then!"

And with that, Ms. Inez began walking briskly down the wooden ramp toward the slip where the ship was docked. The students followed, quiet once again.

Overhead, jagged fingers of light pierced the gloomy clouds. A warm wind swirled the briny air as hazy mist wrapped them up in a pale, damp veil, blurring the seascape ahead. For a moment, passing through the vapor, the students couldn't see anything. Then a gust of wind parted the mist, and the *Defiant* rose from the water before them.

Gabriel had seen hundreds of pictures of old explorers' ships in library books, but nothing could have prepared him for what he saw now. The *Defiant* rose so high from the water that Gabriel couldn't even see the deck. It was much longer than he'd imagined, too—the ship's wooden body stretched out well beyond the slip, curving up slightly on either end. It was incredible. Gabriel wanted to go aboard so badly his scalp was tingling.

The great sailing ship had been rediscovered five years ago, buried in the ocean floor south of Cuba, remarkably intact considering how long it had been submerged. Last seen afloat sometime around 1465, the *Defiant* had been built and captained by Sir Francisco Ventana, the famed explorer (or rogue, depending on whom you asked). The ship had been dragged to the surface and ferried to Norway, where it had been painstakingly restored before being towed five thousand miles to San Francisco. The plan was for the *Defiant* to become a permanent attraction here, and when Ms. Inez had gotten wind of this, she'd immediately called the city tourism board and convinced them to let her students

aboard for free, before the public opening. It had taken some prodding, but eventually she'd won the day.

"Everyone!" Ms. Inez clapped her hands twice, and the students turned in her direction. As if on cue, a single streak of white light cut across the sky, and a moment later a low rumble moved across the water.

"Lightning!" Carlos cried out. "Is it going to hit us?"

"Don't be stupid," Baron scoffed, gesturing up at the tall wooden mast. "Lightning hits the highest points available."

"Don't call me stupid," Carlos huffed.

"Then stop saying stupid stuff."

"Okay, okay," Ms. Inez cut in, and looked up nervously. The sky above was strange, unlike any she could ever recall seeing. Huge churning storm clouds were gathering above them now, intermittently breaking up to reveal a pale tangerine light. The mist was turning to a drizzle; if they didn't go aboard soon, they'd all be soaked. Where was the guide?

Ms. Inez decided to forge ahead. "You all remember from your reading that this was the ship of Sir Francisco Ventana," she said, and then paused, realizing she didn't know much more than what she'd already told her students in class. She was going to have to improvise. "It is, as you can see, it's a very, um, complicated ship—"

"Actually," a low voice boomed, "it's not."

6

MS. INEZ TURNED. Her breath caught. She was standing face-to-face with a most peculiar-looking man.

He was incredibly tall, and so thin that his spine seemed to bow with the effort of holding up his unusually large head. A shock of red hair curled in tight spirals around the borders of his long, pale face, and a rough front tooth peeked out from between his thin lips. He could have been twenty or fifty—he had one of those unknowable faces.

"Oh, great, our guide's here!" Ms. Inez said a little too loudly. She was still a bit flustered. "You are our guide, right?"

The man said nothing, but dropped his large head ceremoniously. When he looked up, Esme noticed that his eyes were the same clear grey as the water.

"We're the Greenly—" Ms. Inez started, but the man was not interested in letting her finish.

"I apologize for being late. We had a bit of a reception here last night to celebrate the arrival of the *Defiant*."

"How fun!" cried Ms. Inez. The man gave her a quizzical glance, as if the idea of a party being fun was plainly absurd.

"Yes, well, I was just tucking a few leftover things away in the hold below deck."

"What's a hold?" Carlos shouted back excitedly at the man, who ignored the question entirely.

"My name is Lewis Farn," he said instead. "And I will be your guide today."

"He looks like Ichabod Crane," Esme whispered in Rose's ear. The small girl dissolved into giggles. Farn shot her a daggered look, and she instantly quieted.

"If you'll follow me," Farn said, and turned on his heel, walking off with long bowed steps to where the *Defiant* was moored to the slip. Without the slightest hesitation, the man leapt up the steep gangplank, expertly making his way up to the deck. The students looked at Ms. Inez for instruction. She didn't see that there was anything to do but follow.

They found Farn standing beside the great mast in the center of the *Defiant*'s wooden deck and hurried to cluster around him. Only Gabriel hung back, drifting toward the front of the ship, to what he knew to be the prow. He needed a moment to take in the enormity of what he felt. There was a strange warmth on the bottom of his feet, for one thing; it wasn't uncomfortable at all, but it definitely puzzled him. It was almost like heat was emanating from the heart of the ship itself. The *Defiant* bobbed gently on the waves, and Gabriel sensed that the hull was expanding and contracting, as if the ship were breathing. Gabriel closed his eyes. Deep creaks issued from the *Defiant*'s shifting body, a sound almost like a low chuckle. He knew it was ridiculous, but he couldn't shake the feeling that the ship was alive.

"Gabriel!"

The sound of his name tore him from his thoughts. He opened his eyes to find Ms. Inez waving him back toward the group. Farn was just beginning his speech as Gabriel shuffled his way over. The man spread his hands wide as he talked.

"Welcome aboard the ship built by the great captain Francisco Ventana—the *Defiant*. As you all should know, Ventana was a sea captain, privateer, navigator, renowned pirate, and politician. He was second-in-command of the Spanish fleet of 1450, and thusly subordinate only to the Queen of Spain herself. His exploits were legendary. He was—"

"What sort of exploits?" Carlos interrupted.

Farn paused thoughtfully. "Well, you've heard that Ventana stole the Safire Peacock from the Portuguese Duke and delivered it to the Queen with her morning toast and tea?"

The students shook their heads, unimpressed.

"Maybe you'd be more interested in Ventana's famous rescue of the kidnapped nephew of Seville's most famous magician, the Great Barbacini?"

The students stared at him blankly. Farn took a step back, unwrapped the scarf from around his neck, and cleared his throat.

"How about the time Ventana was thrown overboard by his first mate—the mutinous Andre le Dix—only to survive by befriending two pure white dolphins who delivered him back to the *Defiant* alive and ready for vengeance?" Farn finished all in one breath, then gasped for air.

"Really?" Carlos's eyes shimmered.

"That's made up," said Quincy.

"Actually, " said Baron, "dolphins are quite sociable animals, and—"

"Who cares?" Quincy sneered.

"Boys, boys," said Farn. "Believe what you will. But it's all quite true. Ventana was a hero to the Spanish but a pirate to the English, to whom he was known as El Tiburón. Can anyone tell me what *tiburón* means?"

"Shark," Baron said, stifling a yawn.

"Very good. Now, contrary to what your teacher, Ms.—" Here, Farn made a lazy gesture toward Ms. Inez.

"Inez," the teacher replied, pursing her lips.

"Right. Well. Contrary to what Ms. Inez may have led you to believe, the *Defiant* is decidedly *not* a complicated ship. It was designed—" Farn stopped speaking and touched a long finger to his brow. "Well, let me back up a moment." Adjusting his stance slightly, spreading his legs apart, Farn steadied himself against the rocking ship and continued.

"First, it is important to know what kind of a ship the *Defiant* is."

Like two wires touched together, the answer sparked in Gabriel's mind: *Caravel.*

"Anyone?"

Farn surveyed the group. Gabriel felt the answer pulsing in his brain, tingling on his tongue, but he didn't release the word. He wouldn't. He had spent weeks studying for this trip; as much as he may have ached to show his expertise, the nautical knowledge he'd gained was too precious to put at risk. As soon as you let on that a thing is important to you, he thought, that's the moment it gets taken away.

It had happened to him a hundred times. His clothes, his books. His sister. Gabriel would never make that mistake again. The smart move was to keep the important things private, to tend and grow and protect them like a tiny garden. To never show you cared.

"It's a caravel," Baron said, his voice dripping with boredom. Farn nodded approvingly.

"Correct, young man. The *Defiant*—"

"Hey, aren't ships supposed to have girls' names?" Rose said loudly.

"Yes, my dear. Very smart. They are. And the *Defiant* is actually the *Beatriz*. We believe the ship was named for Beatriz de Luna, a cousin of the Queen. But Ventana and his crew always referred to the ship as *la Desafiante*. And so we call her the *Defiant* to this day."

"That's dumb," Rose grumbled. "They should call it *Beatriz*."

A shadow fell across Farn's face. He bent down toward Rose.

"Do not refer to the *Defiant* as dumb, if you don't mind."

Rose scowled, but didn't reply. Farn straightened, and clapped his hands once to get back on track.

"Now, where was I? Oh, yes! The *Defiant* is a caravel. The exact origin of the caravel design is a matter of much debate—there are many theories, but no conclusive evidence to confirm them. We know from Portuguese records that caravels were being used as fishing vessels by the thirteenth century. The Portuguese tried to keep the design a secret, but, seeing as Ventana was Spanish, clearly they had little luck." Farn allowed himself a laugh, but when no one joined in he quickly turned serious again.

"The caravel was favored by the great explorers—Columbus, for one, as well as Ventana. They preferred the ships because of their lightness and maneuverability—a boon on their long, dangerous sails. And yet the design was almost entirely lost. In fact, before the *Defiant* was rediscovered, there was no actual physical evidence that the caravels had existed at all."

"So how'd you know so much about it?" Quincy jeered. Ms. Inez shot him a warning look. Farn coughed and cleared his throat, clearly displeased by the interruption.

"Before the *Defiant* was restored—and I should add that it is still undergoing restoration—it was possible to trace the existence of the ship only through historical accounts, shipbuilding documents, anthropological studies, and archaeological recreations. But perhaps I'm getting ahead of myself." Farn paused, his grey eyes flickering around the ship appraisingly. "Though the *Defiant* may seem like an impressively large ship to you, it is not nearly as large as the sailing ships you may know from your history books—the great galleons with their many sails and armored bodies. No, the *Defiant* is sleeker, more streamlined—just this one large mainsail attached to the middle mast, and those two smaller sails at either end. At its fundamentals—pay attention, now—the *Defiant* weighs fifty-five tons, is sixty-five feet long, nineteen and a half feet wide, and fifty-six feet high. Some of its features include…"

As Farn went on detailing the *Defiant's* measurements, Gabriel found himself retreating further and further into his own thoughts. It wasn't that he wasn't interested—he knew all this basic stuff already. The other students, for once, seemed absorbed by what they were hearing, or at least resigned to it. While their attention was focused on Farn, Gabriel slowly edged his way back, peeling away from the group. He began walking the circumference of the ship.

He figured it would take him about three minutes to return to the spot where he'd started. As he walked, Gabriel tentatively tested his knowledge, eager to see if the weeks in the library had paid off. There was so much to take in, so much he didn't know, but the words started popping into his head: the gentle slope at the front of the ship was the bow, the three great posts rising up from the deck were the masts. The long needle-nose pole shooting out from the prow was the bowsprit. And though the sails were lashed to the masts with thick lines—shuddering now in the wind—Gabriel could picture exactly how they would look unfurled, the three triangles tilted back at an angle, spread wide like the longest feathers on a bird's wing. Just like in the books.

"Look up!" Farn cried, snapping Gabriel back to attention. He had almost completed his lap around the deck, having passed the entrance to the hold and the rowboat perched against the rail and the strange glass case that sat toward the stern, but he was still a few feet off from the others. Farn pointed upward, and the students tipped their heads back to gaze up at the tops of the masts, wobbling beneath the dark clouds. Lateen rigging, Gabriel's brain shouted silently.

"Lateen rigging!" Farn boomed. "*Triangular sails*. The most impressive innovation, in my opinion, in nautical history. Prior to their invention, in the fifteenth century, the standard square sails permitted sailing only *before* the wind. But the triangle shape allows the sail to take

43

the wind on *either side*, thereby enabling the vessel to sail into the wind, immensely increasing the ship's speed and maneuverability."

Farn was on the verge of delving into greater detail when Quincy yelped and sprang forward. "Ow!" he cried, rubbing the back of his neck.

Ms. Inez leapt toward Quincy and wrenched his hand away. She peered down, squinting. "I don't see anything," she said, puzzled. She looked back at the group. "What happened? What's going on here?"

Quincy whipped around, his feline eyes flashing. "Someone yanked my braid," he snarled. "Trying to pull it out of my head or something. Someone..." Quincy narrowed his gaze at Rose, who was failing to keep down a smirk. "Someone short."

The small girl let out a surprised, nervous giggle. "Wasn't me," she said.

Quincy took a step forward and lowered his twisted face toward hers. Rose stopped smiling and curled her lip.

"I said, *it wasn't me.*"

Quincy stood there glaring. Then, just as he seemed to be turning away, he raised a hand and jabbed Rose hard in the forehead with his index finger, snapping the girl's head back.

"Quincy!" Ms. Inez cried, lunging forward and yanking Rose away. She looked down at the tiny girl, expecting tears. But Rose just rubbed at the growing red mark on her forehead with her cast and muttered, "Is it lunch yet?"

"Yeah, this is BOR-ING," Angelica singsonged. Ms. Inez shot her an angry look, but the girl blinked back innocently.

"It is not lunchtime yet, guys," Ms. Inez sighed. "Not for another hour."

In response, Rose shrugged and turned away. Sheepishly, Ms. Inez glanced over toward the guide, who was staring at the kids like they were a pack of wild monkeys.

"I'm sorry, Mr. Farn," she said weakly. "Please. Continue."

"Well, I—" Farn stuttered, gathering himself. "Well, let's see. I was talking about... yes. Okay, then." Farn raised himself to his full height and went on.

"So, the seagoing explorers wanted to travel farther and farther, to explore new lands and discover new peoples. And as their appetite for adventure increased, so too did the changes in the geometry of their caravels. Skilled craftsmen were called upon to cater to the needs of the most ambitious explorers, and ships like the *Defiant* were often built to precise specifications."

"Such as?" Baron asked, pushing his glasses back up onto the bridge of his nose.

Farn was quiet a moment, thinking. Then he smiled wryly at the large boy. "Well, in Ventana's case, he designed it so he could sail with only six people."

"Why?" Carlos asked. "Is that low?"

"Well," Farn said, and smiled. "Typically, a caravel would be manned by upwards of twenty men. But because there were only six people in the world Ventana trusted to crew his ship, he built the vessel to ensure he'd never have to employ a man who might turn mutinous."

"That means someone who murders him," Rose hissed in Esme's ear, slicing an index finger across her throat. Esme laughed and shoved her away.

"Did anyone ever get murdered?" Angelica asked eagerly. The wind whistled a little louder, stirring the thin spines of her blonde hair.

"Yeah, were they murdered?" echoed Carlos.

"There was fighting on the ship, yes, of course." Farn nodded. "But no one was ever killed aboard the *Defiant* by another man's hand. Ventana was exceptional at controlling his crew."

"What's that?" Carlos pointed just above Lewis Farn's right ear. Farn glanced back and then turned to Carlos, smiling.

"That, my curious friend, is the original anchor of the *Defiant*."

"I thought anchors were supposed to be in the water when the boat wasn't sailing," Quincy said, his face skeptical. "To keep them in one spot."

"Yes, that's true," Farn said, and nodded. "And there actually is an anchor weighting this boat down right now. But the original anchor here hasn't been properly examined since the *Defiant* was rediscovered. We don't know if its mechanisms are still operational, or if it needs to be repaired or reweighted in some way. So we are using a new anchor, a modern one, in the meantime. And you see this here?" Farn pointed to a large orange cylinder strapped to the other end of the ship. "We are using a counterflotation instrument to account for the additional weight of the double anchor."

"Genius," said Baron.

"I don't get it," Rose grumbled.

"It's probably fine now," Baron said, "but when the new, second anchor is eventually lifted from the water, the ship will struggle because it wasn't designed to support that much extra weight. So that tube helps keep it floating."

"Precisely!" Farn clapped Baron on the shoulder, grinning.

"Hey!" Carlos called out. Somehow he'd slipped away without Ms. Inez noticing, and was standing at the top of the staircase that led, it seemed, down into the ship. "Can we go down here?" he hollered.

The students crossed over to Carlos and gathered around. The passageway gaped like the mouth of a cave, a low, hollow noise rising up from the blackness, but Lewis Farn, not breaking stride, took the steps two at a time and disappeared into the darkness below. The kids looked up at Ms. Inez. It was fine. It was fine! This was all part of the tour. And yet, something about following Farn into the unknown seemed unwise.

"I don't want to go down there anymore," Carlos whimpered. "It's too dark."

All at once, Ms. Inez jerked into action. "Nonsense!" she twittered. "There's nothing to be scared of. Come on." And with that, the teacher sucked in a breath and began the descent. The children had no choice but to follow.

7

"APOLOGIES," FARN SAID, his low voice bouncing through the cavernous space. "I forgot my flashlight."

He was holding a candle high, sharp shadows cutting across his face and around the dim hold. The children huddled together at the bottom of the stairs.

"I hope you can see something of the magnificent construction down here. Though actually, *not* being able to see it is even better. It nicely represents what the crew of this ship might have experienced themselves. Now, everyone stay close and follow me this way."

"It smells like dirty old vegetables down here," Rose muttered to Esme. As they picked their way through the darkness, the girls tried not to step in one of the dozens of soggy puddles covering the floor. Rose was right; there was a strange odor. It was the heavy musk of salt and wood and decay, a smell that made breathing difficult. Esme struggled to shake the feeling that the walls were closing in on them.

Farn was pointing to the wall beside him. It was affixed with wide horizontal planks about two feet apart. Carlos put his hand on the rough, soggy wood.

"Are those bunk beds?"

"Indeed they are," Farn replied. "This is where the crew slept in a storm, or if they wanted to get away from the elements. Or when they were ill. There was little room for the men down here, so mostly they made do with sleeping above deck, which was always uncomfortable, of course. Now, all of you, come over here."

The group shuffled blindly behind Farn until he stopped again. Bending over, he held his candle out, casting light into a low, large cubbyhole.

"This area is called the hold. It's where the cargo was kept. Food rations, spices—anything that needed transporting. But most impor tantly, this is where the water was stored, in great wooden casks."

"But it's so small," Ms. Inez said.

"Yes, you're right," Farn replied. "Sailors on ships like the *Defiant* were always at great risk of dehydration, or worse. They couldn't store nearly as much water as their larger counterparts. And here," Farn swept his hand to the right, "we've installed a few temporary shelving units for storage."

The shelves were nearly bare except for a few scratchy-looking blankets, an emergency kit, three cardboard boxes, and a small hammer.

"These shelves would not have been part of the original ship, and will be removed immediately after the renovations are complete," Farn concluded.

Quincy took a step toward Farn, his eyes catching the orange light. "Where's the captain's cabin?" he said.

"Ah!" Farn cried, delighted. "Good eye, my boy. Actually, Ventana didn't believe in separating himself from his crew. He slept in a bunk alongside them or, more often, on the deck above."

"So the whole ship is just these two big open spaces?" asked Esme. "Above and below?"

"Indeed it is," Farn replied.

"How'd they have any privacy?" said Rose.

Farn let out a short, sharp laugh. "With pirates and sharks and squalls and a million other dangers, privacy was really the least of their concerns. Privacy, she asks me!" Farn shook his head in amazement. "Now, we should head back up above deck before this candle burns out on us."

Back on deck, Farn opened the floor for any questions. Instantly, Carlos's hand bolted into the air.

"Yes?" Farn said, and sighed. "You. Go ahead."

"How do we know all the stuff you told us is right?"

For a moment, Farn looked taken aback. "Well," he replied carefully, "the Institute for Nautical Archeology issued an extensive report on the excavation and restoration of the *Defiant* that you are welcome to read yourself." He crossed his arms defensively. "But even before that, studying these great ships has been my life's work. Of course, examination of various documents and manuscripts can help describe the practice of Iberian shipbuilding, but regular records weren't kept until the sixteenth century—long after the *Defiant* had already been lost. In this ship's time, such information was safeguarded in the minds of skilled masters who passed on their traditions orally, from generation to generation. Their secrecy ensured that their knowledge would not be stolen by competitors. They left nothing in writing, except for—"

"Hey!" Rose called out. "What's Gabe looking at?"

Farn turned. Without anyone noticing, Gabriel had slipped away from the group again, and was now standing before the great glass box he'd passed by before. It nearly reached his chest.

"Ah," Farn smiled back at Rose. "Perfect segue, my dear. Let's go have a look."

The students scrambled across the deck, eager to see what Gabriel had found. They crowded around the box, jostling each other to get a better look. And there, inside the case, resting on raised blocks, was an enormous, ancient book. It lay open at its center, a long length of deep crimson satin resting in the spine like a tongue. Long, fluid curls of ink swept and dipped across the pages, dancing along in a bold hand.

"What is it?" Esme breathed.

"The Codex Mare." Farn's grey eyes glittered as he spoke the name. "I was—"

"What's it do?" Carlos cried. "Why's it in that box? Who wrote it?"

"Carlos, please," Ms. Inez said sternly. "Let Mr. Farn finish his talk."

"I just—"

"This isn't your personal tour," Quincy said hotly. Ms. Inez held up a hand.

"Everyone can ask questions at the end." She turned back to Farn. "Please, go on."

Farn gave the teacher a tight smile, then turned to the students. "It was Ventana himself who wrote it," he said. "It's part journal, part instructions for operation and maintenance of the *Defiant*. Its latter third is composed entirely of maps—from Portugal down past Africa through the South Atlantic, up across South America through the Pacific and into the New World."

"That's here—America," Carlos whispered to Rose.

"I *know that*," Rose snapped.

"Ventana's maps," Farn continued, "chronicle which islands he found along the way had reserves he could use—meaning food and fresh water." Farn tapped the glass with a crooked index finger. "I hope you children realize what an enormous privilege it is to actually *see* the Codex Mare in real life. Until 1992, historians could not even say absolutely whether the Codex was real, or simply legend."

"Why not?" Rose and Baron said together.

Farn let the tension build in the air for a few more seconds, then went on, his words echoing the thought running through Gabriel's head.

"It was missing for nearly four hundred years!"

"Where was it?" Carlos cried out.

Quincy rolled his eyes. "*Missing*, moron."

"Now, now," Farn warned, "that's a fair question." Carlos stuck out his tongue at Quincy, but Farn ignored them both. "There *are* some theories as to its whereabouts during that time. It's believed that the Codex was secretly passed from hand to hand among Spanish sailors in the hundred years after Ventana's death in 1468. This was done to maintain control of Ventana's routes. After that it seems that the Portuguese and Germans had it for a time—possibly the British, too. We can infer this from the inscriptions on the back inset page, where those in possession of the Codex wrote their names. But the names stop at 1601, and there are no records of its use after that until it was discovered in 1992, in the wine cellar of an old Spanish monastery."

Standing on her tiptoes, Rose looked up from the Codex and frowned. "I can't understand it."

"That's because it's in Spanish," said Baron, adjusting his glasses.

"But I can't read Spanish," Rose grumbled.

"Gabe can," Esme offered.

Gabriel didn't move. Silence wrapped around the deck as all eyes fell on him. Esme was just about to repeat herself when Angelica cackled, "*Muy bien.*"

"I wouldn't laugh, young lady," Farn said, his low voice rolling across the deck. He peered down at Angelica.

"Why's that?" she mumbled, casting her eyes away from Farn's stern look.

"In Ventana's time, there was no more coveted item than the Codex Mare. Rival explorers fought fierce battles for its possession long past Ventana's death."

Angelica looked up cautiously at Farn. "Why?" she asked.

"The Codex contains all the secrets of the great seas," Farn replied, his face serious and drawn with purpose.

"You couldn't sail without the Codex back then?" Carlos breathed, his nose pressed against the glass case.

"Of course it was possible to sail without the Codex," Farn said, turning toward the younger boy. "But explorers often perished along those dangerous journeys, drifting into deadly waters or perilous islands. Or they might have failed to find land at all, and simply starved to death. It was Ventana who blazed the path from Portugal to the Americas and back again, sailing it more times than any other explorer. He documented the route thoroughly. The Codex holds that documentation."

"The other explorers died?" Angelica's eyes glistened and grew wide. Farn nodded gravely.

"But with the Codex in their possession, they had a secret weapon: Ventana's knowledge of the seas."

Farn let the silence that followed hang in the air a moment before shattering it with another loud clap.

"Now. Navigation! Who knows how Ventana knew where he was sailing? How he found his way."

"The stars?" Quincy said tentatively.

"Exactly! Yes!" Farn did a little hop in the air and whirled toward Quincy. "But *how?*"

Quincy gave an indifferent shrug. Farn was poised to press the question when a loud sigh broke out from behind him. He turned to find Baron, eyebrows raised, lips pursed.

"They used Polaris. The North Star. Because of the earth's rotation, the stars appear to travel across the night sky in circular arcs. Except for the North Star. That stays fixed. Making it an ideal point of reference by which to navigate." Baron grinned and looked around eagerly, awaiting his ovation.

Rose was rubbing the red bump on her forehead. Ms. Inez was fiddling with her phone. Angelica was making kissy lips at Rodney. And Gabriel was bent over the glass box, Carlos just beside him, bouncing on his toes. Nobody was paying any attention to Baron at all.

"So what's it say?" Carlos said. "C'mon, Gabe, read the words!"

Gabriel felt his face grow hot. He had spoken Spanish with his parents when he was small, but that was a long time ago. The script in the book was almost unrecognizable. He coughed once, trying to shift the prickle in his throat. No luck. Maybe he could pick out enough to gather a basic understanding of what the pages said. Brushing the hair from his eyes, he leaned his long body still closer to the book before him.

"Well," he began slowly, "he starts out talking about something that broke. They need to fix something in order to steer the ship. But I don't know what." Gabriel looked up. "Sorry. I don't know what that one word means."

"That's okay," Ms. Inez said, urging him on.

Gabriel looked back to the Codex. The shifting clouds above were casting strange patterns on the surface of the glass, making it harder to see. "Then he starts talking about going east, about needing to get to an island. He needs to get there fast."

"Why?" Carlos asked. "Why does he need to?"

"I don't know." Gabriel shook his head. "The page ends there."

"Can we turn the page?" Carlos pleaded. Farn smiled back at him indulgently.

"I'm afraid not. The Codex must be kept under glass in order to preserve its delicate pages, and to keep it safe from the elements." He lifted his hands to the dark sky as if to demonstrate.

Gabriel frowned. "But that doesn't make sense. I mean, didn't Ventana write it so people would know how to—"

Before he could finish, a blinding flash—more brilliant than a hundred bolts of lightning—exploded above them, and the students looked up just in time to see a bright pink blaze rip across the sky.

8

"COMETS!" ROSE CRIED, but they all knew it was something else. Something was happening—something unnatural.

For a moment, everything went deathly still, like the air itself was holding its breath. The kids felt a sick churning in their bodies. And then the world collapsed into chaos.

As they watched in stunned horror, the dark waters beneath the *Defiant* began to move. Slowly at first, then faster and faster, angry, white-capped waves were battering the ship, pummeling its ancient wooden frame from every direction. The ship lurched, and the seething waters sprang up in a series of huge, gushing towers. Somewhere down below, the thick chains attaching the ship to its anchor snapped like shoddy string. Free from the weight, the ship keeled sharply to the right, flinging everyone aboard violently across the deck. The students clamored to grab on to anything that would keep them from being tossed overboard into the dark frothing waves. The sea raged, swelling and folding in on itself, hurling the *Defiant* high up into the spray before slamming it back down with a terrible crash.

Gravity seemed to give way. The straight lines that governed the city's distant buildings were eclipsed. The ocean peaked and collapsed beneath them, and the students were hurled across the deck once more. Through their screams, they could hear the faint barks of what must have been drowning seals. Fish leapt from the water and rained down over their heads. It was as if the sea had come to a boil.

There was no shelter from the freezing water that crashed down, burning their eyes and coating their mouths. Sputtering, retching, Gabriel pawed the saltwater from his face, desperately trying to make out any sign of the others. It was hopeless; the roar of the crashing sea was deafening now, overpowering every other noise. He had managed to grab hold of a large wooden barrel, but his eyes were raw, and his arms already felt like streams of fire were snaking through them. For a moment he imagined just letting go, letting himself be swallowed by the angry ocean. Then, all at once, he heard it. Someone was screaming his name.

"Gabe! Gabe!"

The voice was close. Gabriel searched frantically for its source, but the blinding waves kept crashing down, threatening to sweep him away.

"Gabe!"

There she was, right in front of him. Esme was clinging to the base of the forward mast, struggling to keep her grip on the slippery wood. Without a second's thought, Gabriel shot out a long arm and grabbed hold of her ankle, locking it tightly in his grasp.

As soon as she felt his grip, Esme lunged toward something else. Rose was just on the other side of the mast, eyes filled with terror. Esme seized her wrist.

"Grab Carlos!" she screamed. "And don't let go!"

Amid the waves, Rose managed to grasp the collar of Carlos's shirt. Carlos, in turn, held tight to Baron's hand. Baron wrapped his legs around Quincy's middle, completing their human rope.

When Gabriel saw they were all connected, he felt a tiny prick of hope. Esme, Carlos, Rose, Quincy, Baron—Gabriel's stomach dropped sharply. He searched the deck frantically, blinking hard, trying to wash out the salt even as he was pummeled by the waves. He thought he saw movement. He looked again. It was unmistakable. There was Angelica, tucked and shaking beside the *Defiant*'s small wooden rowboat.

"Angelica!" Gabriel shouted, the wind battering around him. She looked up, and Gabriel was paralyzed by the expression on her face: it was the purest fear he'd ever seen. Instinctively, he reached out, but as soon as he did, he felt his grip on Esme's ankle begin to loosen. Angelica was a good ten feet away; she was clawing for his hand, searching his face with pleading, terror-filled eyes. Her look made his chest grow cold. But there was just no way to reach her without letting go of Esme. A moment later, as the giant wave crashed down and swept Angelica overboard into the black water, Gabriel knew that she had seen him hesitate and pull back.

Someone was screaming. It took the stunned boy a minute to realize it wasn't Angelica, but Rose.

"Ms. Inez!" she cried hysterically. Gabriel whipped around just in time to see their teacher and Mr. Farn lifted by another wave and bucked overboard themselves, down into the water below. They had been trying to get to the students, he realized, but it had been a catastrophic choice. Gabriel clung to his barrel, trying to locate Ms. Inez in the churning waves, but all he saw were strange slashes of pale blue against the dark swirl. The slashes surfaced and then disappeared, writhing in the black water. When Gabriel realized what he was looking at, his breath froze. It was the sailing team—the kids they'd met earlier. They had been flung from the dock, and now they were thrashing against the pounding sea.

"Ms. Inez!" Rose screamed again. But it was too late. She was already gone—they were all gone—swallowed by the monstrous storm.

Still calling her teacher's name, Rose began hurling herself toward the rail, struggling against Esme, who had her by the wrist. Carlos, Baron, and Quincy had made their way to the mast. Rose, unencumbered, kicked at Esme hard, desperate to free herself from the other girl's grip.

"Rose, please!" Esme begged. "You have to hold on!"

Beneath them, the ancient wooden boards began to groan, chatter, and bend. The *Defiant* trembled harder and harder, vibrating in such an uncanny way that Esme felt sure it would explode. Instead, a great burst of water shot up beneath them, lifting the boat and all upon it into the air. We're dead, Gabriel thought; the ship is going to splinter on impact. But when the *Defiant* hit the frothing waters again, it skidded across the surface and somehow stayed upright. In another moment, it had come to an uneasy standstill.

Struggling to his feet, Gabriel coughed up a mouthful of seawater and spat it out onto the deck. He wiped back the black strands of hair plastered to his face and, through burning eyes, looked out across the water, trying to gauge where they were. As best he could tell, the ship was now about a mile from shore. He looked back at the tangle of kids on the deck and did another quick count: Esme, Rose, Baron, Quincy, Carlos. It wasn't everyone, but it was a miracle any of them had survived at all. The *Defiant* was still intact. And they were alive.

9

"ARE WE GOING to die?" Carlos whispered.

"I—I think so," Baron stuttered back. "I think we're definitely going to die."

On the deck of the *Defiant*, the kids were clustered in a tight huddle, bound together in collective shock. They could hardly breathe, and no one dared to move. It felt like the smallest disruption might trigger another geyser burst, or cause the *Defiant* to break apart beneath them. They stayed that way, bunched together, shivering in their wet clothes, until Esme felt something strange above her left eye. Carefully, she let go of Carlos, untangled her other arm from Quincy, and brought her hand to her left eyebrow, surprised to feel a welt rising there. She felt no pain at all. When had she hit her head? And on what? When she pulled her fingers down, the blood coating them seemed to belong to someone else.

Esme looked up. Above them, the sky looked like a mirror painted black and then cracked with a ball-peen hammer—rays of white light cutting through the dark swirling cloud cover. A faint pink hue rimmed the blackness. It was an evil, unnatural sky, and Esme quickly looked away. Huddled right below her, Rose sobbed violently.

"Ms. Inez," she wailed, burying her face in the crook of her casted arm. "She's gone!"

"Rose, Rosie," Esme said softly, over and over, trying to comfort the girl. "Come on, Rose."

"Angelica, too." Carlos burst to his feet, his voice strained with panic. "There's no way she could swim in those huge waves!" Rose looked at him, sucked in a ragged breath, and began crying even harder.

"They both drowned!" she cried.

"And that guide," Baron said, his voice dazed, far away. "Farn. He went over too. They all drowned."

"We don't know that," Esme shot back quickly. She tried to sound uncertain, despite her own belief that their teacher, their guide, and their classmate were all most likely dead. She had to maintain a brave face for the littler kids, she knew. Reaching out, she pulled Rose close to her and held Carlos tight, pointing at the calm waters surrounding the ship.

"Look," Esme urged. "Look at the water. It's over."

It was true that the sea had stopped churning, the waves lessened to mild chop. The sky above was still swirling, but the heavy mist had begun to lift. And the *Defiant*, from what they could tell, was still whole. The six of them could barely stand for the shaking of their legs. Off in the distance, they saw, great plumes of thick black smoke blocked out the entire city.

"My house!" Quincy cried. "My *mom*!" He covered his mouth with his hands. Heavy tears began streaming down his cheeks.

"I want to get off," Carlos whispered, squeezing his eyes shut.

"We can't," Rose replied, her voice robotic now. She was staring straight at the black smoke. "Everything's on fire. We're trapped."

"Why did this happen to us?" Carlos looked around at the other kids desperately. His eyes settled on Gabriel, searching his face for any hint of an answer.

"Gabe," Carlos pleaded. "Why?"

"You ask *him* why?" Quincy cried. "Why?" He let out a high, hysterical laugh. "What even happened here? Do you know, Carlos? Does anyone?" Quincy's eyes grew wide and panicked. He sprang forward and grabbed Baron by the arm. "You!" he cried, pushing his face right up to Baron's. "You always have an answer for everything. What happened?"

"I—" Baron stuttered, struggling to free his arm from Quincy's grip. "I don't—it might have been a meteor," he said weakly.

Quincy stared at him a moment, then looked away in disgust. "They're all dead," he muttered. "All of them."

At this Rose began to convulse so hard that Esme thought she might choke.

"Quincy," Esme said sternly. "We don't know anything yet."

"Are you kidding? Look around you!" Quincy cried, gesturing wildly toward the black smoke. He began rocking back and forth, shaking his head. "Was it a bomb?" he yelled. "Were we attacked?"

"Yes, yes yes, that's plausible," Baron said. He started nodding furiously, but then changed course. "Wait, no no, no, no, that can't be right."

He faltered. "Wait, yes. I mean, impossible." Baron took a deep, shuddering breath and hung his head. "I don't know," he whispered.

"Are we at war?" Carlos cried, grabbing onto Gabriel's shirt. "Are we?"

Gabriel stared back at Carlos, dazed. He felt like something must have hit his head; his thoughts were all coming too slowly.

"I don't know," he said. "Could a bomb do that to the water?" He looked around the deck until his eyes found what they were searching for. "Es?"

But Esme didn't answer. She was rigid, still as a statue, blinking out at the water, her arms wrapped tightly around Rose. Confused, Gabriel touched her lightly on the back. "Es?" he repeated. Still she did not move. She must be in shock, he thought.

And then, instead of speaking, Esme let go of Rose and raised one shaking arm before her. Gabriel turned, following her gaze out across the waves, until his eyes met the thing that had made Esme turn to stone.

10

THERE, IN THE very near distance, rocketing toward them with tremendous speed, was a huge, white-capped wall of water. As if on cue, another pink bolt erupted across the sky above them. It was all too much, all happening too fast, and as the giant wave cast its shadow over the ship, Gabriel closed his eyes again. It was over.

But instead of being overwhelmed by water, Gabriel felt himself being lifted up. The *Defiant* had become part of the swell. The ship rose fifty feet in the air, then stopped, suspended on the crest of the wave. For a moment, everything was sickeningly still. Then slowly, slowly, the wave began to crumble, and the kids' stomachs all lurched with the *Defiant* as it plummeted down.

The ship shot forward so fast that everything beyond it was lost in a blur of greyish blue. The movement gave Gabriel new energy— they were alive, still. The end was not assured. But just ahead, no more

than half a mile off, a cluster of black crags, jagged as barbed wire, tore sharply from the frothing sea. The *Defiant* was heading directly for them.

Gabriel struggled to think. He looked up at the sails furled tightly around the masts: no use. He began to panic, flinging himself across the deck, pulling at lines and cranking winches. "Help me!" he screamed. But the others were all too stunned to move.

Flailing, Gabriel yanked at a length of rope coiled on the deck, leading to the head of the main sail; he couldn't budge it one inch. Even if he could manage to release it, what would that do for them? The sails would be torn apart by the waves; he had no idea how to control the ship.

His mind was a blank. It was like someone had cut all the wires that connected Gabriel's brain to itself. It might have stayed that way until the *Defiant* smashed into the rocks if not for the white streak that caught the corner of his eye. The back of a massive white shark had crested the water, no more than a hundred yards away. A moment later the waters burst open and the shark's head emerged, jaws yawning wide as it flung a fat grey seal high into the air. The helpless animal let out one piercing cry, freezing Gabriel where he stood. He watched as the seal began to fall, writhing in terror.

And then another white shark, even bigger than the first, rose from the sea, baring rows of razor teeth, and clamped its jaws down around the smaller shark's head, dragging it down into the heaving sea and ignoring the seal entirely.

Gabriel shut his eyes tight against this new horror. What he had just witnessed was beyond his comprehension. Had he imagined it? He had definitely seen the monstrous sharks emerge, one after the other;

and if the boiling sea had made them insane, it had probably done the same for everything else in the ocean. Gabriel could picture it clearly: the peaceful grey whales catapulting their enormous bodies up from the water, crashing against the rocks; the black and white killer whales snatching up seals and sharks, flinging the bloody bodies into the air before gleefully ripping them apart; other, darker things butchering the killer whales in turn, black blood thickening the waters.

Someone was shaking him by the shoulders. His eyes sprang open to find Esme looking up at him. The instant he saw her face, he understood that there was no time to waste imagining the end—he needed to do *something*. She was counting on him to save everyone. And he could, he knew he could. If there was just someone who could help him—

Instantly, the wires in Gabriel's brain reconnected with a jolt. Leaping past Esme, he hopped over Rose and pushed Carlos out of his path until he was standing before the long glass case. Somehow it had survived the storm. He didn't feel the glass cut into his elbow, just the heavy Codex in his hands. The binding smelled of dust and dead animal; the parchment was worn, but sturdy. He looked down at the giant book and prayed that it would tell him how they might be saved. He flung the pages wildly, until his eye fell upon a diagram of the anchor. It was as if a star had burst in his brain.

Dragging Baron off the ground, Gabriel heaved the Codex into his hands and started shouting directions. The others followed his commands as best they could, Rose running to grab the hammer from the hold and Quincy producing the pocketknife he had brought with him to the ship. They all hacked at the rope Gabriel had chosen, those who had no tools using their teeth, gnawing away until the thin cord that secured the orange flotation cylinder to the side of the ship snapped and the huge buoy fell away. The students gave a short, triumphant shout.

Gabriel's plan made sense: by cutting loose the buoy, they would change the balance of the ship, and alter their course. But would it really work? The *Defiant*, despite the lost weight, was still dead set for the rocks. The students held on to whatever was close, preparing for the impact. A cold dread leaked through their bodies. They were nearly upon the crags now, so close they could hear the cries of the seals atop them. The six kids reached for each other and held tight, trying not to scream.

Then, slowly, almost imperceptibly, something began to shift. The tilt was so small they barely felt it, but as the *Defiant* barreled forward, as the barks of the seals grew louder, the ship eased over onto its side. At the last possible moment, with mere inches to spare, the ship heeled just far enough to scrape past the jagged rocks and continue out into the still waters beyond.

For a few minutes, nobody dared to move. Then, one by one, the students staggered to their feet and turned to stare in amazement at the black ridges in their wake. It was impossible, but it was true. They hadn't been dashed against the rocks. They had made it. Gabriel's plan had worked. Overwhelmed, the kids fell to their knees. They were all in shock, exhausted and undone. Their wet bodies shivered in the bitter air, but in their stupor they barely felt the cold.

They had lost their teacher. They had lost their homes. They were lost at sea. Now that the immediate danger was over, nobody knew what to say, or what to do. Hot tears poured down Quincy's cheeks. Baron was sick again and again over the side of the ship. Rose and Carlos held each other, shaking. Esme lay sprawled across the deck while Gabriel, sitting a bit apart from the rest, hugged his knees to his chest and closed his eyes. After a time, the students curled up together and fell into a dark, fitful sleep, until Gabriel was the only one awake.

Alone at the rail, he looked out at the gently rippling waters, marveling at the sea that had long since calmed. The sun was just lowering toward the horizon, splashing rosy hues across the sky and fading up into the bruised violet night. He found it hard to believe that just that morning he had woken up in San Francisco, ready to live out another normal day. He tried to wrap his mind around all that had happened and shook his head in disbelief. His home was gone. The five kids asleep behind him might as well be the only people left in the world. Tomorrow could bring more pink flashes, more giant waves. As for tonight, Gabriel was standing at the prow of a ship he could not sail, drifting across the endless ocean.

11

THE FIRST TWO days at sea, the kids were convinced that they'd be rescued. They cast their voices into the wind, desperate for someone to hear them, to help, but the ocean swallowed their cries so completely that soon they gave up trying. Meanwhile the ship was still drifting, leaving them at the mercy of whatever conditions befell them. They roasted in the sun by day, then huddled together shivering at night. Seasickness, awful and absolute, wormed through their bodies. Despite their empty stomachs, they all spent long hours retching over the side of the ship. (All of them, that is, except for Quincy, who turned out to have a particularly strong sea belly.)

They slept in shifts, always making sure two people were awake at any given time. What difference that pair could make if any real danger came was unclear, but it seemed like the smart thing to do. And more often no one actually slept, plagued as they were by hunger, sickness, and fear.

They were still only a few miles from shore. Everyone was desperate to get off the ship, to land, but they knew that this was impossible. It wasn't the distance; it was the fires.

The flames were violently beautiful, especially at night, when they lit the borders of the ocean with ragged light. They seemed to spread across the whole broad edge of the city. At first, despite the choking smoke that seared their lungs, Gabriel prayed the *Defiant* would keep hugging the rim of the shore; the idea of being cast farther out to sea was still more frightening. He figured that as long as they could see land, there was hope of being rescued. But how much of the land was on fire? Just the coast? The whole city? No one knew.

And despite his desperate study of the Codex, Gabriel knew he could not sail the *Defiant*. The sails were lashed to the masts. The rusty, ancient anchor that might have kept them in place looked as if it could also rip a hole in the ship, if they released it incorrectly. He couldn't risk it. And so on the third day, when the winds gathered and began to push the *Defiant* away from the flames, Gabriel could only hang his head and resign himself to the mercy of the ocean.

The children saw their share of wonders and horrors as the ship made its way through the waters. Great rotting carcasses of whales and sharks floated by, ribs bleached white from the blazing sun. Sometimes schools of dolphins appeared alongside the ship, their metallic bodies springing from the water like dimes tossed up by the sea. When the red and blue remnants of a downed airplane appeared in the sea ahead, Gabriel and Esme ushered everyone below deck; they didn't want the other kids to see dead bodies. Through it all everyone kept watch for dry land.

"First island we see, that's where we stop," Quincy kept repeating. Rose and Carlos, scared and seasick, echoed his refrain. But Esme had reservations. They couldn't just stop *anywhere*.

"It'll sap our strength to row from the ship to an island," she argued. "And suppose we get there and there's no food, no fresh water? Then we're stuck."

"I'll take my chances," Quincy grumbled.

As for Gabriel, he couldn't help wondering if he should have fought harder to keep them from drifting away from San Francisco. He knew this was crazy—the shores were on fire. But their families—his sister— might still be out there, somewhere. And yet try as he might, he couldn't see any way to reach them. They had no way to steer the ship, no orientation out here where the waters stretched on forever.

Day turned to night and back to day, and still the *Defiant* drifted on through the fickle waters. One morning the sea would be magical, the easy waves all gilded crests and glimmering spray, puffball clouds idling overhead; the next, the ocean would be brooding and fitful, pale spume and dark currents swirling, briny winds moaning like mourners for the dead. The *Defiant* ambled on without route or guide, the aimless drift casting a sort of thin desperation over the children aboard.

But worse than the drifting—worse by far—was the hunger. Every moment of every day, they were painfully hungry. Even in their fitful dreams they felt it: the vicious gnawing in their guts. They had been smart at first, rationing out the lunches they had brought for the field trip into tiny, shared bites: a chip here, a soggy half banana there. But the food was close to exhausted after only a few days. On the other hand, they had discovered several gallons of water in an emergency earthquake kit someone had had the foresight to stash below deck, and in what felt like a miracle, the "leftover things" from the ship's opening party Lewis Farn had mentioned stashing in the hold turned out to be several dozen containers of soda and fancy mineral water (as well as a few streamers and tinfoil stars that were of no use to them at all). They were learning to live with the hunger, but without those precious drinks, the students knew they would be dead within days. Even that haul wouldn't last them long—no more than two or three weeks, at most.

As the days passed, the students scoured the ship for food. They rooted among the musty stacks of wooden crates in the galley below deck but found nothing. They lifted heavy coils of damp rope, which lay curled in corners like giant sea snakes. Nothing. They pried up soggy boards with the hammer, breathing in the dank, mossy ancient-seawater smell that filled the dark bowels of the ship. Still nothing. The *Defiant* was not a working ship; it hadn't been sailed in centuries. There wasn't one can of beans aboard, nor a single tin of sardines.

On the morning of the sixth day, Esme told everyone to gather on deck with everything they had. Gabriel, Quincy, Baron, Rose, and Carlos arranged themselves before her, backpacks in hand, awaiting instruction. Esme, in turn, pulled a small yellow notebook from her back pocket and opened it to a blank page.

"We need to take stock of our supplies," she said. "Call out what you've got. Everything. Rose, you first."

Because it had been a field-trip day when they packed, the students had taken far less with them then they would have ordinarily—and

Rose, Baron, and Carlos had all lost their backpacks in the chaos of the pink flash. When the tallying was through, Esme's list looked like this:

7 pencils
3 pens
1 highlighter
6 three-ring binders (plus paper)
3 notebooks
1 ruler
Half packet of cinnamon gum
Stopwatch
Calculator (broken)
Pocketknife
3 backpacks: black, blue, green.

Clothing:
Gabriel: Blue hoodie, black T-shirt, jeans, socks, blue sneakers (size 11)
Esme: White T-shirt, black sports bra, jeans, jean jacket, black
    socks, sneakers (size 8)
BONUS: Running shorts, yellow T-shirt, white socks, grey
    sweatshirt
Baron: Button-up blue plaid shirt, navy wool jacket, khakis, brown
    loafers (size 13)
Quincy: Gold Warriors jacket, grey T-shirt, black thermal shirt,
    blue zip-up hoodie, jeans, white socks, black sneakers (size 8)

Rose: White down jacket, green and blue striped long sleeved shirt,
    purple corduroy pants, green socks, blue Velcro shoes (size 5)
Carlos: Red windbreaker, white long-sleeved shirt, blue T-shirt,
    jeans, white socks, red sneakers (size 7).

That inventory done, Esme went down below deck to record all
that they had inherited.

On the shelf:
1 small hammer
3 nails (rusty)
2 wool blankets (scratchy)
5 wooden crates
1 large glass jar
1 cardboard box
1 roll of twine
1 long white candle (used)
1 book of matches (5 matches)
11 cans of soda (4 Coke, 4 7UP, 1 root beer, 3 ginger ales)
24 large bottles fizzy water
Party decorations

Contents of emergency kit:
Pack of Band-Aids (17 total)
Roll of cotton gauze
Spool of white medical tape

Iodine

Bottle of aspirin (25)

All in all, it wasn't very much—far less than Esme had expected. She closed her yellow notebook and tried to tamp down the swell of fear, rubbing at the red splotch on her neck to calm herself. It didn't help. In the darkness, Esme swooned. It was too close down here, the air too thick and rank. Everything in her body told her to escape. She sprang toward the stairs, taking them two at a time, and burst back up onto the deck, startling the others. They were still hovering over the spilled contents of their backpacks—all their worldly possessions. Esme, silent, began to gather the heap of goods together, sorting the lot into two separate backpacks and leaving the third one empty.

"Hey, that's mine!" Quincy cried when he saw his red binder going into Gabriel's green pack. Quincy grabbed for it, but Esme yanked it away.

"Nothing is *yours* anymore. Everything belongs to the group now. Even our clothes."

"Our *clothes?*" Carlos repeated, touching the sleeve of his favorite blue shirt.

"Yep," said Esme. "Wear what's yours for now, but be prepared to swap, if we need to. We'll keep all our stuff together on the shelves below deck."

Quincy stared down at the tangled loot. Then, before anyone could stop him, he lunged forward, plucked out a piece of shining silver, and clutched it to his chest.

"Not giving up my knife," he declared. "My brothers gave me that."

"Quincy," Gabriel started, his voice a low warning. But Esme held up a hand. She was too tired to stop a fight right now. She could talk to Quincy later about the knife, convince him how important it was to keep everything together and safe. Right now, she still had one more uncomfortable topic to discuss with the group.

They needed a system for the bathroom. Things were getting bad. For the past few days, she had tried to avert her eyes every time one of the boys perched teetering on the side of the ship; meanwhile Rose, even more dangerously, was somehow only going at night, climbing up on the rail when she had the cover of darkness. On the open deck above, in the close quarters below, no one was ever completely hidden from view. There was absolutely no privacy, just as Farn had said, and now their collective embarrassment was getting to be too risky all around.

We'll bring up the glass jar, Esme told the group. We'll keep it above deck, but under the rowboat. Everyone would know to avert their eyes from that one spot. They would rotate who emptied it each day. It wasn't perfect, but it was the best they could do right now.

By the second week, weary and defeated, the students began to despair. They had seen no new shores, no signs of any other ship on the water. They spent long hours lying around in silence, trying to save their energy; they sprawled along the deck when the sun had gone down or stacked themselves up on the three rough bunks in the cabin below, arms across their faces to shield them from the endless drips of filthy seawater seeping through the wooden boards above. In that inky, dank cabin, rocking, always rocking, they struggled to find something like sleep—some momentary relief from the awful, endless hunger. Rose fainted nearly every time she stood. Quincy, already skinny to begin with, now looked like something half-dead. The xylophone ridges of his spine were visible through his shirt. The children were terrified by what this meant for him, and for them—they were sunburned and starving and they knew that if they didn't figure something out, they would not survive another week.

It was under the banner of this blinding desperation that Quincy made the first terrible mistake.

12

HOW QUINCY AND Carlos managed to heave the rowboat up and over
the side of the ship was unclear. It wasn't a big boat—only about twelve
feet long, and made of a lightweight, caramel-colored wood. It wouldn't
have been a challenge for two adults to lift, but Quincy and Carlos were
half-starved kids, hardly at the peak of their strength. Yet somehow,
fueled by a manic desire, they had found the vigor to send the small
boat sailing over the side of the *Defiant*.

The plan Quincy had sold to Carlos went like this: they would push
the boat over into the water, and then one of them would jump overboard
and swim to it. The boy left on deck would toss down the oars and then
jump overboard, too. On the *Defiant*, they were slaves to the currents;
on the rowboat, Quincy thought, they could strike out on their own
and find land. Carlos had been skeptical at first, but he too wanted off
the ship. In the end, it didn't take much arm-twisting to convince him.

The morning before, Quincy had told Gabriel that he could stand at the helm alone overnight, just to give Gabe and Esme a break. Gabriel, wary but exhausted, had agreed, and Quincy took up the post just as the sun was dipping down. Hours later, in the grey light of dawn, he crept down to where the others were sleeping and woke Carlos.

They knotted a thick rope around the metal ring on the rowboat's nose so that it wouldn't drift away before they could swim to it. Both boys tingled with excitement as they urged the craft overboard. They were going to save the day, they thought. It was a foolproof plan.

The instant the boat began to fall, Quincy realized what a grave miscalculation he'd made. He'd assumed the rowboat would fall the fifteen feet to the water in a nice, even drop, but the boat wasn't balanced; it tipped in the air as it fell, landing on its side with a crunching flop. The boys watched, horrified, as the rowboat settled on the surface, scooping up a huge gulp of water in the process, and began to slowly sink down. There was no way it could hold that much water and stay afloat.

"We're going to lose the rowboat!" Carlos cried, not understanding that Quincy had already leapt past him. In another moment, the older boy had disappeared into the water.

Gabriel woke to Carlos screaming into the cool morning. Eyes glued to the waves, the boy kept on yelling until the other kids came running up from below. "Quincy!" Carlos cried, pointing to the boy clinging to the sinking rowboat.

Gabriel didn't hesitate. Grabbing a nearby coil of rope, he circled a length around his waist and secured it with a knot. Then, positioning his feet against the ship for leverage, he hurled the other end of the rope

down into the water. Quincy let go of the rowboat and swam the few feet over to where the rope had landed. But when he took it, he seemed unsure of what to do next.

"Tie it around your waist!" Esme hollered down.

"But the rowboat," Quincy called back weakly.

Gabriel bent over the side of the ship and locked eyes with the boy below. "Quincy. Tie the rope. Now."

In another five minutes, a dripping Quincy was being yanked back over the rail and onto the rough deck. Before he had a chance to say a word, Rose gave him a single hard slap across the top of his head. Then she wrapped her good arm around his shoulders and held on tight.

"I'm—I'm sorry," Quincy sputtered, more surprised by the hug than the slap.

"What were you thinking?" Esme cried.

Quincy peeled Rose off and stood up shakily. As he glared back at Esme, his stupor vanished. Then, all at once, he balled his fists, shook his head wildly side to side, and screamed into the sky.

"I want OFF! I need to get off this ship! Don't you get it? I was just trying to get us to land. Just trying anything—"

"We all want to get off," Gabriel snapped back. "And you nearly sabotaged the one chance we have."

"Not to mention nearly killed yourself doing it," Baron added, shaking his head in disgust.

"I know," Quincy said. His breaths came slower now, and his voice dropped a register. "But we have no plan. We have no idea where we are. We could have tried to get off back by the shore, when we could still see it."

"The shore was on fire," Baron replied evenly. "We couldn't land there."

"I know, but—"

"We will get off as soon as we find a place we can survive," said Esme. "An island with food. And water. Until then, you just have to deal with being on this ship like the rest of us."

"As for right now," Gabriel said, "we need to get that rowboat back onboard." He bent down and picked up the length of rope still attached to the nose of the boat below. When he gave it a yank, it pulled taut in his hands.

"All of you," Gabriel said. "Grab on. "

13

IT TOOK THEM five hours. Lined up along the rope, single file, the kids heaved and pulled with all the strength they could muster, but again and again someone would slip or let go in exhaustion and the boat would crash back down into the water. They had all but given up when, somehow, they were able to summon the last of their strength and pull the dead weight of the rowboat back onto the *Defiant*. The kids stared at it in amazement. They couldn't quite believe they'd really done it.

It was Carlos who went and sat in the rowboat first. Baron joined him, and then so did Rose and Esme and Gabriel, until only Quincy remained standing on the deck, alone.

"Come on, Q," Esme said, and beckoned. But Quincy didn't budge.

"Let him be," Gabriel said softly, but Esme was already climbing out.

"What is it?" Esme sighed when she'd approached.

"You're gonna be mad," Quincy whispered.

"I'm already mad," she said, and shrugged. "So just tell me."

"I lost the knife. My pocketknife. I lost it in the water. You said to give it to you and I didn't and I lost it."

Esme felt her face grow hot. This—this was exactly why she'd told him to give her the knife! She opened her mouth to say as much, but then stopped. What was the point? Quincy had lost the one thing he had that was important to him. He'd let everyone down. Nothing she could say would make him feel any worse.

"I'm not mad," Esme said gently. "I'm just sorry it's gone. But there's nothing we can do about it now."

Quincy nodded slowly. He rubbed his forearm roughly over his eyes once, twice. Then, together, the two of them climbed into the rowboat. After she'd taken an empty seat, Quincy plopped down beside her. To her surprise, he let his head fall heavily onto her shoulder. She felt his body swell before it emptied in a great *whoosh*.

"If I were home right now," Quincy said softly, "first thing I'd do is take a long, hot shower."

The rest of the group nodded, skin tingling at the thought.

"If I were home right now," Carlos said, "I'd have my mom make me a hundred cheeseburgers. A thousand!" At the word *cheeseburger*, each mouth onboard began salivating. (Except Rose's. She was a vegetarian.)

"I'd be riding my bike," Rose said. She glanced down at her cast. "Riding from my house along the beach. I really miss that."

"I know what you mean," Esme said. "I miss running."

"You could run here," Baron offered. Esme glanced around the small circumference of the deck. "Take me about a minute a lap," she said, and laughed. "But yeah, I guess I could try."

They stayed sitting in the rowboat until the sun began to set, casting its bonfire colors across the sky. They talked about home, about what they missed most and what they didn't miss at all. They talked about food and school and Ms. Inez. But mostly, they imagined what it would be like the first time they set foot on dry land again. It was still early when they finally fell silent, not a star to be seen yet, but they were all ready to collapse. Gabriel volunteered to stay at the helm, but the rest of the kids persuaded him that it was okay to leave the ship unmanned for one night.

It was decided that Baron and Rose would sleep up on deck, with the blankets. The others shuffled down below, crawled up onto the hard bunks, and waited for sleep to take them.

Curled up on the bottom bunk in the hollow darkness of the cabin, her hipbones digging into the hard wood beneath her, Esme struggled to think. A low sound issued from just above, like air being letting out of a tire—Gabe's breathing. Esme shifted, feeling her face glow warm. Despite her best efforts to squash it, she couldn't quite ignore the sparkling thrill she felt from being this close to him in the dark.

Esme propped herself up and peered around the cabin. It seemed like the others were asleep, but it was so dark that she couldn't really be sure. She lowered her voice.

"Gabe," she whispered.

No answer. She tried again, a little louder this time. "Gabriel? You asleep?"

A rustling, then a whisper. "No, I'm not asleep."

"I'm worried," Esme said.

Silence. Had he heard her? Esme lay in the darkness, fidgeting. There was something else she'd wanted to say, something she wasn't sure how to bring up. But then the words were coming out of her.

"I—I've also wanted—well, I'm sorry, Gabe. About Angelica. I know you weren't close, but you lived in that—that place. Together."

The wood creaked as Gabriel shifted on the bunk above.

"Do you know why Angelica was in that home—why she was at Greenly?" he said, after a time.

"No—not really," Esme stammered. "I guess I heard something, but I don't think it could be true."

"Why not?" Gabriel said.

"It was too… just too…"

"Too what?" Gabriel let the question hang, but Esme couldn't think of what to say. So Gabriel went on, his voice low and even.

"Did you know Angelica had a family? Living in the city?"

"I—no," Esme stuttered in surprise. A family? Why would Angelica have been in the foster home, then? Before she could ask, Gabriel went on.

"A mom and dad. And a little brother." Gabriel lowered his voice. "The brother starts waking up in the morning with bruises. The parents can't figure it out. They get worse and worse, but the kid—he's real young, only two or so—he can't tell them what's going on. Then one day, the kid falls down some stairs. Breaks a leg. His sister was there."

"You don't mean," Esme whispered. "She wouldn't. She was cruel, sure. But she wouldn't. Would she?"

"You know everything I know about it."

Then Esme asked the question she knew she shouldn't ask. "You're not sorry Angelica died, then?"

"I never said that," Gabriel said sharply.

Esme cringed, and covered her face with her hands. Silence poured around them.

"Gabe?" Esme finally managed. "How are we going to do it? How are we going to get out of here?"

Her skin was bubbling and electric, her heart beating double time. Esme lay there in the blackness, listening to the steady, shallow breathing above her.

Gabriel said nothing.

14

THERE WAS, IN fact, an idea that Gabriel had been turning over in his mind, wisps of a plan gathering like storm clouds. He hadn't brought it up, because he wasn't at all sure how to pull it off yet, but the fear in Esme's voice made it clear that they had to do something. And so, the next day, just as the sun began to lower in the sky, Gabriel called the other kids together above deck and made an announcement.

"We've got to try and fish."

The others considered this a moment. Then Rose spoke up.

"But we don't have any fishing poles," she countered, scratching a clump of plaster off her rotting cast.

Carlos shifted foot-to-foot. "Yeah, how're we gonna fish without poles?"

"Also," Rose said, "I'm vegetation."

"I hate fish," Quincy grumbled.

"Who cares, you two?" Esme shot back at them. "Would you rather starve?"

Gabriel pushed the hair from his eyes and sighed. "Come on, guys. I'm sure there's a way to—"

"We don't need actual poles." Baron, who had been quiet until then, took a cautious step forward, his face drawn and serious. "I've fished a lot before. With my dad." He looked up. "I think I can figure this out."

"What do we need?" Gabriel asked intently.

Baron pushed his glasses up on his nose, thinking. "First we need to find something to use for a line."

"Like what?" Carlos sprang up on his toes. "What can we use?"

Without hesitation, Gabriel crossed the deck in a few long strides and disappeared down the stairs. When he emerged a few moments later, he was holding the long coil of twine. This he presented to Baron, who examined the thin rope for a minute, yanking on it to test its strength. Then he nodded.

"This will work."

The other children watched rapt as Baron unspooled nearly twenty feet of the stuff, wrapping one end around his massive forearm. Next he plucked a bobby pin from Rose's hair and, bending the metal into a *U*, fashioned it into a hook. And then, despite the weak protests of the others, Baron took the last bit of meat from the last half of a baloney sandwich they had all been sharing, bite by bite, and skewered it onto the end of the hairpin. It was crazy—using the last of their food for bait—but what else were they going to do? Nobody dared to say aloud what they all knew: if this didn't work, they were going to starve.

"Won't be long now," Baron breathed as he carefully lowered the length of twine down into the water below. They waited.

An hour passed. Then another. Baron was still and sturdy as an oak, eyes trained upon the calm slate water. The rest of the kids grew restless and moved on to other distractions. But Baron stayed at the rail, unwilling to abandon his post. Gabriel watched from a distance, not wanting to disturb the other boy's concentration. When the first stars began dotting the sky, he walked over to where Baron was hunched, back rounded like a boulder.

"Maybe you should take a break," Gabriel offered.

But Baron didn't respond. Gabriel tried again, this time placing a hand on the boy's thick shoulder.

"We can try again later."

Baron did not look up, just shook his head slowly, side to side.

"Wait," he murmured. "Just wait."

With a heavy sigh, Gabriel straightened up again. He looked over at Rose, who was curled against the main mast, fast asleep, and then quickly turned away from the thinness of the girl's arm. It was hardly bigger than a broomstick now. Gabriel let his long body sink to the ground. It's no use, he thought, and closed his eyes against the setting sun, the endless sea.

Please, he thought, as he drifted off. Please don't let me dream about water.

There was a thump and then a terrific yelp. Gabriel leapt to his feet, spinning wildly; he'd gotten up just in time to see Baron tugging a giant silver fish over the side of the ship and onto the splintered deck. Gabriel gasped. It was beautiful—the most wonderful thing he'd ever seen.

The others, alerted by the commotion, didn't hesitate. They fell on the fish's flapping body and began tearing into its gummy pink flesh with their teeth, like a pride of lions over a kill. Shoving great chunks into their cheeks and crunching through the toothpick bones, they licked fat from fingers slick with blood. With each salty bite, they could feel their minds begin to clear—their strength returning. They laughed between swallows, giddy to feel full again.

All at once, Rose reeled back and pointed down at the ravaged fish.

"What is *that?*" she asked, scrunching her face.

The students peered down. Blinded by hunger, they had ripped open the fish so fast that they'd almost missed it. There, buried among the blood and flesh, was another fish. They could all tell the tuna hadn't eaten the smaller creature; it wasn't in its stomach, or in any way digested. It was perfectly whole, connected loosely to the surrounding muscle by a sticky gossamer coating that looked like spider webbing. And instead of glinting silver like the tuna, this second fish was an electric pink.

Esme looked to Gabriel for an answer, but he just shrugged.

"Who knows?" he said.

It was as good a response as any. Besides, they were still starving. Without any more discussion, the students lowered their heads and tore into the pink fish as well.

15

FOR THE REST of the week, day and night, breakfast, lunch, and dinner, the children caught fish and ate fish. Under Baron's instructions, they each learned how to use a chunk of flesh from the last catch as bait, casting their lines into the water and gradually reeling them in when something bit. The sea bore up so much that they began drying long strips of fish in the sun, turning it into jerky to save for later, in case the fish stopped biting. For now, though, the haul was so good that the kids could hardly stomach one more bite.

Sometimes, instead of fish, Baron would pull up a long string of seaweed, the other end of which was sometimes tangled around something else. They found a few planks of driftwood that way. They scrubbed the wood as best they could, drying it in the sun, and began to use to clean planks for plate.

*   *   *

Their hunger quelled, their days became consumed by endless discussions about the day the sea had exploded. Everyone agreed the pink bolts they'd seen rip through the sky were at the heart of it—they had to be—but they all had different ideas about just what those pink flashes were.

"It could be any number of things," Baron mused. "But I think it was a natural occurrence—most likely the result of global warming, or a combination of—"

"No way!" Quincy shot to his feet. "Did you not see that insane wave? It was definitely a nuclear attack. Probably from Mexico, I bet."

"Don't be an idiot," Baron scoffed. "First of all, Mexico doesn't have nuclear weapons. Secondly, they're our allies. Third—"

"It was aliens!" Carlos said, leaping up next to Quincy. "There's nothing else that could make the ocean crazy like that, right, Esme?"

"I'm with Baron. I think it was probably some freakish natural occurrence. Some sort of..." Esme trailed off.

"Maybe an asteroid hit the water?" Rose offered.

"Maybe," Esme said, and shook her head. "Maybe. But who knows?" She turned to Gabriel. "What do you think?"

Gabriel shrugged. It wasn't that he didn't have thoughts about the pink flashes; he just didn't see the point in playing guessing games. And the way everyone always looked to him for answers—it made him uncomfortable. He didn't want to talk. He wanted to act.

After another day or two of these debates, Gabriel began to slip away below deck. There, alone at last, he would lift the Codex Mare off the highest wooden shelf and quietly study its ancient pages. It felt like the only source of solid information he had.

Hour after hour, Gabriel sat bent over the tome, head bowed as if in prayer. The great book filled his entire lap with its heavy bulk. Its weathered brown cover was peeling at the cracked spine, but otherwise it was in surprisingly sturdy shape. The very first page had a bold inscription: *Codex Mare*. Gabriel would stare at that title, fingering the crimson ribbon, foolishly hoping this ritual would somehow prime him to understand what followed.

As Farn had said, the first hundred pages of the Codex were devoted to Ventana's personal entries. The man had not kept a daily diary; instead, he had simply recorded events of note in a sweeping, swirling script. The last entry, dated March 15, 1467, was only one sentence, which Gabriel rendered into English after some effort:

Trust no one but your crew—least of all the sea.

There, the section ended.

After the diary came an overwhelming stretch of pages filled with details of the *Defiant* herself. There were illustrations, showing parts of the ship that had been rejiggered, or broken and fixed; there were also chunks of text with what seemed to be instructions for things like what to do if the *Defiant* ran aground or acquired a hole in its hull. Gabriel didn't understand much of it, beyond the sense the pages gave that Ventana had customized nearly everything on the ship to match his specifications.

But it was the next hundred pages, the section devoted to maps, that was the most dizzying. There seemed to be no standard for how the charts were drawn or what they might contain. Some were rough sketches, while others were highly detailed; others offered close-ups of just one bit of land, or just one section of beach. Still other maps charted huge swaths of territory, from Spain to Africa, or from Africa to Mexico.

Without question, though, Gabriel's favorite part of the Codex was the final section, the one that Farn had failed to mention. The last two hundred pages were filled with intricate drawings of Ventana's life at sea. There were birds, thousands of birds, and fish and sharks and dolphins, and barnacles of every shape and size. Gabriel loved to study these small sketches, to imagine all the things Ventana must have encountered. The drawings seemed more pleasure than necessity at first, but Gabriel was coming to understand that, for Ventana, everything about the sea had its own clear purpose.

There were no people sketched in the book. Only animals and islands, in all their variations.

Finally, on the very last page of the Codex was the list that Farn had told them about—the names of all those who had possessed it. The page began with the largest inscription: *Francisco Ventana*. There were eleven other entries, and at the end of each study session, Gabriel would run his finger down them, whispering each name aloud:

> Alfonso de Hortega
> Bartolomé Quiroga
> Ruy Sanches de la Mobellar
> Domingo Corvacho
> Joham Gonçallvez
> Hanns Schweissguth

Thomas Barnysdale

Velasco Lopes de Coronel

Ana de Jesús

Antonia de Santa Maria

Sabastian de Olano

Gabriel imagined this last name to be that of the monk who had hidden the Codex away in a cellar. Somehow this felt right to him.

The other kids, for the most part, were more than happy to leave the Codex to Gabriel. Only Baron came close to matching Gabriel's level of obsession. Whenever he could pry the tome away, Baron would sit hunched over the maps, pencil in hand, carefully tracing their lines, all his focus trained on figuring out where in the world the *Defiant* had traveled back then, as if this might possibly tell them something about where they might be heading.

Esme felt fine about leaving the book to the two boys, mostly. She hated sitting still and studying more than anything. But Gabriel's increasing interest in spending his time alone with the Codex was beginning to worry her—if it lasted much longer, the group might start looking to her, the next oldest, to take charge. And that was something she definitely did not want.

These thoughts streamed through Esme's mind as she ran circles around the deck, stopwatch bouncing in her pocket. She felt guilty about using the watch—she knew she should save the battery—but Esme was addicted to timing herself. Three hundred laps in an hour was her record so far.

She was a real puzzle to herself, in many ways. She had no issue with stepping forward when no one had asked—she didn't hesitate when it came to breaking up a fight or keeping track of rations. So why did she shy away from making decisions when it seemed like the others might expect it of her?

It was more or less the same conundrum that had landed her at Greenly. It wasn't that she hadn't been doing her work, like everyone said. She did all her work! Always! She just hadn't been able to actually hand it in. The teachers at her old school had been baffled. Esme Simons wasn't a star student, they knew, but she certainly got a C or better on every test. She was clearly studying. So where was her homework?

Her homework, completed to the very last question, had generally ended up buried in the woods next to her house, though Esme couldn't tell them that. It was too weird. Sometimes she'd let the papers go in the little stream by the track, watching them float away, carried by the current. But that felt like littering in a way that burying didn't.

Only Ms. Inez had ever suspected what was really going on. Esme had wanted to explain, to confess everything to the kind, nervous teacher; she just hadn't found the right words. And now it's too late, Esme thought sadly, slowing her pace to a walk. Now that world is completely gone.

Of course, Gabriel didn't know any of this. He had no idea how terrified Esme was of being tapped to lead. He simply took on the Codex as a natural extension of his old habits: reading and being alone. And he took his studies seriously, closely guarding the time when he could sit and read undisturbed. But eventually the others, curious about his long absences, began to follow him below deck. And though he preferred to study alone, Gabriel appreciated their interest—it made him feel that the responsibility the book conferred wasn't resting solely with him. And so, with everyone gathered around, Gabriel, having by then wrestled his way to a rough understanding of many of the book's passages, began to read the Codex aloud.

He'd begin with the fun parts—the stories of Ventana's adventures—before switching over to the section on the *Defiant*. Gabriel insisted that everyone needed to learn as much as they could about the ship; while they already knew some of the more basic terms (deck, sail, mast), the kids could all use a little more know-how. Gabriel wanted them to learn the correct way to call out directions at sea, the proper names of all the ship parts they might come into contact with. He turned these study sessions into a game, mixing up information from the Codex with bits and pieces he'd picked up in the Greenly library. He'd call out a question, and the kids, split into two teams, would compete to answer.

Gabriel: If I'm pointing toward the back end of the ship, that direction is called...

Rose: Aft!

Gabriel: And that part of the ship is called?

Quincy: The stem. I mean, stern! Stern!

Gabriel: Right, the stern. Esme, same two questions, but for the front?

Esme: The direction in front of us is fore, and the front of the ship itself is the prow. Or, wait, or the helm!

Gabriel: Correct! The basket at the top of the main mast? The place you sit in to look out for land?

Rose and Baron (in unison): The crow's nest!

After just a few sessions of study, the students could all recite the points of sail—the boat's course in relation to the wind's direction. They knew that starboard was the ship's right side, facing forward from the stern, and that port was its left. They knew that changing course from starboard to port was called tacking, and that the small metal spools used to pull in or let out the lines attached to the sails were the winches, and that when your sail got loose from the winch or you lost your wind, you said your sail was luffing. If the wind was too strong, you would reef the sails—bring them in, make them smaller—because if you had less sail area to hold the wind, you could save them from being overpowered.

Of course, these things were only words to them now. The sails themselves were still strapped tightly to the masts, not reefed or luffing or doing anything at all.

Gradually, though, as he read the Codex and walked the deck, Gabriel began to understand how thoroughly Ventana had altered the *Defiant*'s design. He had added a series of blocks, ropes, and winches running to the center of the deck to reduce the need for crew movement; and unlike its larger, more fragile predecessors, which were easily overwhelmed by a strong shoal or current, the *Defiant*'s wide beam and deep keel seemed to make it not just faster but more powerful as well. Most crucial, as Farn had said, were the triangular sails. They had given the *Defiant* the ability to do something never before possible: sail into the wind.

Ventana seemed fascinated by the wind; he spoke of it dancing, breathlessly characterizing its temperament like it was a living thing. Gabriel decoded the old captain's advice line by line, racking his brain until each word offered up its proper meaning.

Though the wind may be fierce, you must ALWAYS face in her direction to raise your sails.

To find out where she is coming from, you must face the wind head-on. Turn your head slightly, this way and that. You will feel her on each side of your face, upon each cheek. When she touches the tips of both ears at the same moment, that is the direction from which she blows.

If the wind blows wildly, you may feel your ship is moving too fast, on her side, overwhelming you. Though you may be afraid, DO NOT lower your sails! You must cut through the water, and when your sails are set perfectly to catch the wind, your ship will be steady.

Still, there was so much Gabriel didn't understand. Again and again he would find himself staring blankly at a page, unable to progress past a particularly difficult section. At those times he would go and circle the masts, gazing up at the tightly wrapped sails, and daydream about how they'd look unfurled. Filled with wind.

He wasn't ready do to anything more than daydream. Not yet.

16

THE MOMENT CAME two days later.

Esme was standing at the stern when she saw Gabriel emerge from the hold with the Codex in his arms. He made a beeline toward the forward mast—the one with the two sails attached at the rigger. Without hesitating, he began to pull at the thick rope that held the sails securely against the massive wooden post. Esme shielded her eyes from the sun and stared in amazement, not quite believing what Gabriel was about to do.

The others gathered in a loose circle around him, watching as he circled the giant masts, testing the tautness of the lines, pulling on this one and that. The children had all spent long hours staring at the sails, countless sessions learning the proper names for their various parts. But no one had thought they were ready to sail the ship themselves.

"What are you doing?" Carlos said anxiously.

Gabriel replied without stopping.

"I'm going to raise the sails."

"Ha," Quincy snorted, flipping up the collar of his gold jacket. "I'll believe it when I see it."

"Then watch."

Rose crossed her arms and smirked skeptically. "You're going to break it."

"Enough," Gabriel snapped, breaking his flurry of motion to glare at Rose and Quincy. "Either help or get out of the way."

Rose slunk back in a huff just as Baron stepped forward.

"I'll help," he said.

"Me too," said Esme. "But—" she continued cautiously. "You really sure about this?"

"No," Gabriel said, and shook his head. "But I'm sick of sitting around and doing nothing. We can't just keep floating along." He looked away from the lines and directly at Esme. "We have to try."

Esme nodded solemnly. "Tell us what to do," she said.

Gabriel sucked in a deep breath, calculating the worst possible outcomes. Damaging the boat was possible. Capsizing? He didn't know. He handed Esme the line he'd been holding. Then, lifting the Codex from the ground, Gabriel placed the heavy tome into Baron's hands and opened it to where the crimson ribbon was holding his place. He pointed down at the page. The canvas of the mainsail was beginning to rustle in the breeze.

"Baron, follow the diagram here."

"What do you mean?"

"Just watch us, and look there to make sure we're following the steps right." He turned to Esme. "Es, stand over there by that far mast and wait for my instructions. Q?"

Surprised, Quincy tentatively touched his chest. "Me?"

"You climb into the crow's nest and tell us if bad weather is coming our way."

Quincy's eyes lit up. "I'm on it!" he called over his shoulder, already scrambling off toward the high perch.

"What should I do?" Carlos said eagerly.

"You help Esme over there with those lines." Gabriel replied. He glanced over at Rose beside him. "You too, Rosie. We need your help."

Rose muttered something inaudible, but grabbed Carlos by the elbow and dragged him over to where Esme was standing astern.

The wind was picking up now, the ship listing in the waves. From his place at the prow, Gabriel could see Quincy climbing into the wide bucket at the top of the main mast. When he'd settled in, the boy put up a hand to shield his eyes from the glare and gave Gabriel a hearty thumbs-up. Gabriel nodded back, then peered down into the choppy water below. He felt his stomach tighten as he remembered what the Codex had said about pointing the boat in the wrong direction during a high swell—how the hull might crash down perpendicular to the sea and snap the *Defiant* in two. Gabriel willed the thought from his mind. Then, just as Ventana had instructed, he began moving his head this way and that in the cool, soft wind.

For a moment, everything around him fell away. He was filled with a perfect stillness. He closed his eyes and faced the prow, letting the sun warm his eyelids, the tip of his nose. All at once, he felt the wind skirt the tips of both his ears at once, and his eyes shot open.

"Esme!" he called out. "Untie that thing from that other thing!"

"Huh?" Esme stared at him, baffled.

It was the moment Ventana had promised would come, when the wind was hitting the boat head-on. *You will feel her on each side of your face, upon each cheek.* It was the signal to raise the sails.

But now that the moment had arrived, all the terms that Gabriel had learned in the library had vanished. All he could think to do was awkwardly mime an untying motion while Esme struggled to understand.

"Hurry!" he hollered, the panic rising in his voice. "Before we lose the wind!"

Esme flailed about, trying to make sense of Gabriel's instructions. The thing from the thing? There were so many things! Then Baron's voice boomed out over the deck.

"The ties around the sails! Just in front of you there." Baron was peering down at the Codex in his hands. Esme looked back at the tangle of ropes. All at once, she saw what she needed to do. Quick as she could manage, Esme loosed the sail ties, freeing the sails from the mast. Gabriel, meanwhile, unlashed the halyard, the line he would use to raise the mainsail.

The gusts were coming on fiercely now, and the *Defiant*'s sails flapped wildly overhead. The harsh clapping terrified Gabriel. The ship rocked steeply back and forth, completely at the mercy of the wind. They were going to fail, he thought. Then he felt the wind move against his right cheek and, before he quite understood why, he began to pull the halyard. A stronger gust came at them then, and instantly he felt it: the kinetic

jolt, the exact moment when the wind caught the sail. He looked up and, sure enough, the mainsail was holding the wind like a large cupped hand.

All of a sudden the ship keeled hard to the left. Gabriel let the sail out in response, and slowly the vessel began to right itself. Once more the sails above him filled, ballooning with power, and in that instant Gabriel felt he understood everything Ventana had written about the wind as a living being, as a friend and companion. The *Defiant* herself seemed to come alive beneath him, to move as he moved, and almost to breathe. All the charts and maps—all the technicalities of the Codex and the old Greenly books—fell away. The ship became an extension of Gabriel's body. He could feel each tiny shift of it beneath him, could intuit if he should take in or let out the sail to keep propelling them forward. It took a moment to trust the power of the wind, but if you trusted it, you could harness it. It had worked. They were finally in command of the *Defiant*.

Late that night, once he was sure everyone was asleep, Gabriel lifted the Codex off the highest shelf, turned to the final page, and, below the others, inscribed his name:

Gabriel Torres.

17

AS THE SUN set on their third week at sea, five of the six the children sat together in the middle of the rough deck. They had eaten and then scrubbed their driftwood dishes using seawater they'd pulled up in an empty fizzy-water bottle. Now Rose was propped up against Esme's thick legs, Esme absently twisting a glossy strand of Rose's hair, Carlos leaning against her shoulder. Quincy sat cross-legged next to Carlos, chewing at the skin around his nails, and a few feet from Quincy, Baron polished and repolished his glasses and explained aloud to no one in particular how the continents had once all been connected as part of something called Pangaea.

Esme's eyes were closed as she half-listened to Baron's monologue. She felt a nudge on her shoulder, and turned to find Quincy holding a can of soda out toward her.

"Your turn," he said.

Esme took it and gave a nod of thanks. She put the can to her lips and tipped it back, letting the bubbles tickle her lips. Tipping it back a little more, Esme savored the sweet liquid popping and fizzing in her mouth for a moment before swallowing. It was the best part of the day, when dinner was over and they passed around the can, and she wanted to enjoy it for as long as she could. Not just because she knew she had to pass the can to the next person after one full sip (that was the rule she'd established), but because she knew they were about to run out of soda entirely.

This was beyond frightening to Esme. If their liquid rations ran out before they were rescued, all the fish in the world wouldn't save them. Esme watched Baron move toward the pole he'd secured against a large wooden barrel and bring up the line. It was empty.

What would they do if the fish stopped biting? Esme took the small yellow notebook from her back pocket and went over their reserves. Absently, she ran a finger across her birthmark, tracing its outline. She wished Gabriel was around to talk to about all this, but he was below deck, with the Codex. Another nudge at her shoulder pulled Esme from her troubled thoughts. It was Rose, reaching her casted arm out for the soda.

"Other hand," Esme instructed, not wanting to risk a spill.

Rose switched hands, and Esme handed the soda over. As she did, she caught a whiff of the rotting cast. She turned away. Propped back on her elbows, she tried to focus on the conversation going on around her.

"No one is looking for us," Baron said matter-of-factly. "I'm sure they think we're dead."

"Shut up, Fatty," Quincy snapped back. "No one asked you."

"Can I wear the gold jacket now?" Carlos asked hopefully.

"My gold jacket?" Quincy laughed. "No. You cannot."

"But Esme said everything belongs to—"

"This is my jacket. You want it? Come take it."

Carlos sat back and pouted. Esme, sensing trouble, tried to redirect them.

"You don't really believe that no one is looking, do you, Bar?"

"I don't mind not going back," Rose huffed. "I mean, I miss my parents, but definitely not working in their stupid store."

"You have to work?" Carlos asked in amazement.

"Chen's Magic Market." Rose laughed bitterly. "Every day after school. No pay. It's completely unfair."

"I know that place!" Baron leaned forward, excited. "They have that specialty candy aisle."

Quincy rolled his eyes. "'Course you'd know that."

"I miss candy," Carlos said dreamily.

Baron nodded in agreement. "If I were home right now, I'd be eating so much good stuff."

Quincy gave him a small shove. "You're an idiot."

"Well, what would *you* be doing?" Baron said, shoving him back.

Quincy sat a moment, thinking. "If I were home right now," he started, "I'd be playing ball. My brothers and me."

"My brothers and *I*," Baron corrected.

"I'd be at school!" Carlos cried.

Quincy laughed. "Now, that's *really* dumb."

"What?" Carlos said. "I liked Greenly. It was better than my old school."

An uncomfortable silence descended. Everyone had heard the story; it was legendary. But for some reason, it had always felt forbidden to discuss it. Baron, though, wasn't bothered by social graces.

"Why *did* you set the fire?" he asked.

Carlos looked at the other boy, speechless for the first time anyone could remember. Baron was just about to repeat the question when Carlos said, "It's hard to explain. I mean, I know *why*, but it's hard to say WHY, you know?"

The group shook their heads in unison, and leaned forward.

"My dad always said it was good to ask questions when you don't understand something. So I raised my hand a lot in class. But I never got called on. It was really frustrating. I think my teacher didn't like me. Anyways, I started doing little things to get his attention, like whistling or doing a wavy dance with my hand. But he still wouldn't call on me. Then one day we read about how the Native Americans used smoke signals to get attention, so I thought it'd be neat to—"

"Oh no," Esme whispered. Carlos nodded sadly.

"It got out of control."

"So they sent you to Greenly."

Carlos nodded again. "I just wanted someone to pay attention. To notice. You know?"

The other kids looked away. It was such a foolish, careless thing. Setting a fire! But somehow, to hear Carlos tell it, it made sense. Nobody knew what to say.

*　　*　　*

Gabriel had been below deck for some time now, mulling over a complicated thought. He'd spent the last few days turning over his memory of that moment when they'd raised the sail. They'd taken control of the boat, but more than that, they'd worked together. It hadn't taken all that much—just Gabriel taking charge, in that moment.

He climbed back to the deck, still not entirely sure what he intended to say. For a moment, he had the urge to sit down with the group, to join their easy cluster. But before it could settle, Gabriel shook the thought away. This was important. He would stand to address them. Five curious faces turned up toward him.

"I—I want to start by saying that I'm really proud of how we've come together," Gabriel began. "In just a few weeks, we've figured out how to fish—how to feed ourselves. We've learned how to raise the sails. We aren't just a bunch of kids anymore. We're a crew."

"A crew!" Carlos cried out, and the rest chimed in with claps and whistles. Bolstered, Gabriel waited until the cheers died down to go on.

"Someone will find us soon, but until that happens, we've got to keep on working together as a team. As a crew. And as a crew, I think we should have assigned roles. Esme?"

Esme tilted up her chin in his direction.

"I think it makes sense that you continue to keep track of rations. Making sure we have enough food and water and all that."

She gave a solemn nod of acceptance, hoping no one saw her cheeks reddening. Gabriel moved on.

"And Baron, I think it makes sense for you to act as our navigator.

You should always have a sense of what direction we're heading in, and record our progress, like Ventana did."

Baron straightened his shoulders. "I'll work on my maps every day."

"Good," Gabriel said happily, encouraged by the pride that lit Baron's round face. He turned to the smallest kids. "Rose and Carlos, you two work together as lookouts, okay?"

"What does that mean? What do we have to look out for?" Carlos asked eagerly.

"It means you climb up into the crow's nest." Gabriel pointed, and they all tipped back their heads to gaze at the large basket lashed to the top of the mast above them. "Best seat in the house for keeping watch. That's your job, every morning and at the end of each day. Climb up there and let us know what you see."

"How is Rose supposed to get up there with her bad arm?" said Esme.

"I'm a really good climber," Rose said with quiet pride. "I can do it."

"And I'm really good at spotting things!" Carlos cried, putting his hands to his spiky hair.

"That's why I picked you guys," Gabriel said evenly, trying to keep a straight face. "It's a really important job."

Sporting their most serious looks, Rose and Carlos shook hands and then immediately burst out laughing. Gabriel let himself laugh with them. And then a low, rasping voice broke in.

"What about me?"

Gabriel turned just as Quincy was lowering his eyes to the deck.

"You—" Gabriel stammered, buying time. The odd, prickling feeling—the very same one he'd felt the morning of the pink flash—had returned to his throat. This was going to be the trickiest moment, he knew. He put a hand to his neck and rubbed, watching Quincy's face crumple.

There was no turning back now. Gabriel pressed ahead. "First mate!"

Quincy looked up, narrowing his eyes at Gabriel. "First mate, huh?"

"That's right," Gabriel said quickly, trying to cover his uncertainty. "That means you check in on everyone and report on the overall status of the ship to the captain."

"Hm." Quincy nodded slowly. "But tell me this," he went on. "Who's the captain?"

Gabriel froze. He could feel the others waiting for him to speak. His throat pinched and prickled.

"I—I thought—" Gabriel faltered, embarrassed.

"Yeah, I know what you thought," Quincy spat. "But here's what I think. Who died and made you boss of everyone?" His face wrenched into a scowl, his mouth twisting cruelly. "Oh wait, I know. Your parents."

The searing spin in Gabriel's chest was furious and immediate. A white light streaked across his vision. When it cleared, he was surprised to find his face pressed inches from Quincy's. Somewhere far off, Rose and Carlos were crying. It was another moment before he registered that this was because he was screaming. But it felt so good that he kept shouting into Quincy's stunned face.

It was as if it was all happening to someone else entirely. Gabriel looked on calmly from outside himself, watching with curiosity as the skinny boy before him sank down low and drew back his arm.

And then Quincy was on the ground, howling in pain, that same arm twisted high behind his back in Esme's grasp. Though he kicked and thrashed, he was no match for the girl. Esme sat on his back as he struggled, holding his arm tight until she felt his body relax beneath her in defeat.

"Gabriel is the captain," Esme said, her voice firm as iron. Gabriel shot her a grateful look, but she did not meet it.

"He's the oldest," she went on. "He can read the Codex best. It was his idea to fish and to raise the sails. He saved us during the pink flash. Gabriel is captain," Esme repeated evenly. "Anyone disagree?"

No one spoke.

"Good," Esme said. "That's settled, then." She let go of Quincy and climbed off him. Quincy sprang to his feet, cradling his twisted arm. He glared at Gabriel, his face gleaming with contempt, and Gabriel knew he deserved it. He'd scared everyone with his anger, scared himself, even. He'd failed in his very first moments. All he wanted to do was go and hide in the hold, alone.

But he knew this would only compound his failure. And so, instead, ignoring every instinct, Gabriel straightened his back, walked over to Quincy, and extended his hand.

Quincy stared at the hand before him, then laughed a hard, mean laugh.

"Yeah, right," he grunted, batting the outstretched hand away.

Not again, Gabriel thought, setting his jaw tight. Pushing through the humiliation, he dropped his hand to his side.

"The titles don't even matter that much," he said, forcing his voice to stay steady. "Like I said before, someone is going to find us soon. Another week at the most. I'm sure of it."

18

A WEEK PASSED. Then another. Before long, the weeks had collected into a second month, and still the *Defiant* sailed on under a blood-red moon. They were clumsy sailors at best, but now that they could use the sails, they became more fluent in the rhythms of the sea, more comfortable with its odd patterns and short temper. The first time black clouds covered the sky and the sea began to churn, the crew huddled below deck, leaving the sails unprotected, convinced that they'd soon capsize and drown. But by now they'd learned to trust the keel, the weight under the ship, to provide the ballast they needed. It kept the ship afloat no matter how rough the wind or waves became.

The children grew accustomed to their stations. They weren't rigidly fixed: Esme and Gabriel would trade off standing at the helm, Esme taking the post while Gabriel studied the Codex, Gabriel relieving Esme when she wanted to run or go over the rations. Up in the crow's nest, sometimes together, sometimes not, Rose and Carlos kept the lookout. Rose had sifted through the box of party decorations Farn had stashed below deck, and retrieved a few silver streamers; these she tied to the basket, and everyone appreciated the glinting tinsel fluttering in the wind high above.

As first mate, Quincy made it his business to oversee everyone. This mostly meant pacing around the deck, barking orders no one paid much attention to, or doing push-ups and sit-ups by the prow of the ship.

They had other chores, too. The latrine jar had to be emptied, the shelf of the hold kept in order. On laundry day, they peeled off their filthy clothing and scrubbed it with seawater, hanging it on the gunwales to dry in the sunshine. The boys mostly went without shirts now, and everyone was happy to strip to their underthings in the hot afternoons. Their clothes had been bleached to muted fades by the sun, and always stank of mildew and sweat. The few things they still wore were ragged, weathered, and salt-eaten, and they carried the sun and the sea on their skin. Still, they made an effort to keep to the weekly wash. It felt important, somehow, to maintain the routine.

They now welcomed the storms they had once dreaded. The rainwater kept them alive. Rose quickly became sensitive to the electricity that crackled in the air before a shower, and at her signal, the crew would place their empty bottles out on the deck to collect the rain. When the bottles were full, they transferred the rainwater into the earthquake-kit water container they kept below. The soda and sparkling water were gone now, so the rain was all they had. Which meant that as much as they hated being tossed around and soaked through, everyone knew it would be far worse if the storms stopped.

* * *

The *Defiant* sailed on—south, Baron thought, past what he told everyone was Mexico, though they were never really quite sure where they were. The water around them turned from grey to topaz, until eventually it became so clear that the crew could see straight down to the pearly white-sand floor. Even though they all ached to feel the earth beneath their feet again—to get off the undulating ship—most days now, in these temperate climes, the *Defiant* kids were content. They had control of their course now, more often than not, and plenty of fish to keep their bellies full. Without anyone really noticing, a new sort of life had taken shape. After all, hadn't the rest of the world given up searching for them? Given up hope? What else did they have, besides each other?

Twice now, they had seen a distant splash of green peeking up from the water. But each time, after fighting the sea for hours, they could do nothing to make the wind carry them toward their target. The currents would not obey them, and the hints of land, if they were ever there at all, disappeared.

Gabriel waved away the crew's frustrations. "Next one," he'd say, hoping he sounded confident. "Next one is where we'll land." And the discouraged children pleaded and whined and grumbled and ultimately understood that there was nothing they could do.

The truth was, Gabriel was terrified to try to get to an island. Quincy's accident with the rowboat had firmly planted the seeds of doubt in him, and now that doubt had grown into fear. What if the rowboat flipped when they were trying to lower it, this time with all of them in it? What if a swell came and swept the rowboat away from the *Defiant*, stranding them all at sea? He could barely get the larger vessel to obey his commands, now; leaving it might mean surrendering that power altogether.

There was also the problem of the anchor. Farn's warning about the untested, ancient hunk of metal haunted Gabriel: every time he imagined trying to lower it, he'd picture it crashing through the hull and sending in a great flood of water, sinking the ship and all of them with it. He saw the panicked crew flailing in the waves, gasping and drowning. It made his stomach lurch, the prickle in his throat swell.

But he couldn't put off the other kids much longer. To do so would mean revealing how afraid he was, and since becoming captain, Gabriel had resolved to never show his fear. Fear was poison—to them and to him. And fear aside, how long could they survive on rainwater, fish, and good luck?

All these troubles were on Gabriel's mind one mild afternoon as he sat up on deck, eating lunch with the others. Lost in his thoughts, Gabriel took a bite of his cod, chewed it a bit, moved to swallow, and found that he couldn't. He spit his mouthful out on the deck and coughed. He coughed again, and tried massaging his throat. Nothing. Gabriel looked around to make sure no one had noticed. He didn't want to add to the worries of his crew; he hadn't told anyone that the strange prickle in his throat had lately been bothering him more than ever. He had figured it would go away on its own—sometimes he even forgot it was there. But if he couldn't swallow, he couldn't eat or drink, and if he couldn't eat or drink—Gabriel felt the panic start to swell.

Stay calm, Gabriel repeated to himself as he made his way toward

Esme and Baron. From the way their heads nearly touched, it seemed like they were in the midst of an important conversation.

"Hi!" Gabriel blurted out when he reached them, much louder than he'd meant to.

"Gabe!" Esme looked up from the deck, grinning. "Look what Baron's done."

Pushing his hair from his brow, Gabriel arched his long body forward and peered at the large square of paper resting between his crewmates.

He knew Baron had been working on a map, but he hadn't realized that the other boy was such an incredible artist. He could see that Baron had ripped pages from the notebooks and taped them together with white medical tape. And it was clear he had used the maps in the Codex for reference, although there wasn't much to depict beyond miles and miles of water. But it was the *way* he had captured the scale of the ocean around them, the detail of swirling current and wave—there was the burning rim of San Francisco, the two tiny islands they had seen, with shaded areas indicating other disputed sightings from the crow's nest. There was even a key at the bottom to indicate distance. Gabriel couldn't help but be impressed.

"I've never done cartographic work before," Baron said, "so I'm not sure how accurate this is."

"Who cares?" Esme thwacked him on the shoulder. "This is amazing!" Baron smiled and rearranged his glasses on his nose. He looked down, his face alight with pride.

Esme looked up at Gabriel eagerly. "Isn't it, Gabe?" she said. "Amazing?"

Gabriel did think it was amazing. But he couldn't seem to find his words. He was swaying slightly now, and pale. Something was off. Esme stood up.

"What's going on?" she said.

Gabriel didn't reply. He needed to get her alone—he didn't want Baron to see him panic—but he was so distracted by his throat that he was having trouble coming up with an excuse. Then, all at once, everything came spilling out of him.

He told them about the first time he'd ever felt the thing in his throat—the morning of the pink flash. How Angelica had tricked him, and Rodney had flown around their heads, and he'd run away. He kept going, recounting all the times the weird feeling in his throat had returned, until he arrived at this moment, today, and the new swallowing problem. When he finished, he looked at Esme and Baron, desperate for their thoughts. Esme sat there in silence, rubbing at the splotch on her neck.

"Well?" said Gabriel.

Esme looked back at him. "Well, what?"

"Well, what do you think it is?"

"I have no idea."

"Es!"

"What?"

"Come on!"

She turned to Baron, who raised his large shoulders in a shrug. Gabriel felt a familiar anger start to rise up within him. Why weren't they helping him? Didn't they get how serious this was? He tried to take a calming breath, but the air caught in his throat. His knees buckled.

He would have crashed to the deck if Esme hadn't swept in, caught him beneath one arm, and lowered him down.

As Gabriel lay there, blinking up at her, she was surprised to realize that the sparkly feeling she'd once had for him was gone. In its place, though, was something firmer: it was what she imagined having a brother must feel like. She turned to Baron.

"Help me lift him," she said.

The pair bent low and wrapped Gabriel's arms around their necks. Then, hoisting him to his feet, they dragged the lanky boy to the base of the forward mast.

"Where are we going?" Gabriel asked weakly.

"We need to get a better look," Esme replied.

When they saw Esme and Baron dragging Gabriel across the deck, the rest of the crew rushed over.

"What's wrong with Gabe?" Carlos asked.

"I don't know," Esme said, looking down at their captain. The grey pallor of his skin was frightening her. "But we're going to make it right."

"How?" Carlos pressed.

The sun was high overhead, shining directly down on Gabriel, who sat with his head drooped, slumped against the mast. Esme suddenly felt woozy herself. She needed help.

"Rose, come over here," Esme called.

Rose didn't move. "Why?"

Esme whipped her head toward the girl.

"Get over here *now*," she barked, pointing to the deck beside her.

Next, turning back to Gabriel, she said, "Tilt your head back and open your mouth." Gabriel obeyed at once.

"Okay. Now Rose, look down and tell me if you can see anything caught in his throat."

Cautiously, Rose took a step forward. Then, putting her good hand on Gabriel's shoulder and her casted arm against the mast for support, Rose leaned forward until she was peering directly into the older boy's open mouth.

"What's going on—" Quincy started.

"Quiet," said Esme, not taking her eyes off Rose. "Do you see anything?"

"I—I'm not sure." Rose lowered her face until one eye was almost touching Gabriel's upper lip. She looked back at Esme. "It's really dark down there."

"Move so you're not blocking the sun," Esme instructed.

Rose repositioned herself and stood farther back, letting the light shine down on Gabriel. She cocked her head this way, then that. Her eyes grew wide.

"I see something!" Rose cried.

"What?" Gabriel raised himself slightly. "What is it?"

"Stop talking and keep your mouth open," Esme commanded.

"It's really hard to see," Rose said, scrunching up her face. "Can you say *ah*, or cough, or something?"

Gabriel coughed.

"Do that again."

He coughed again, twice. Rose narrowed her eyes and peered in closer.

"It's a piece of food, maybe. It looks sort of long. And it's pink."

"Pink?" Esme's face grew puzzled.

"Yup. Pink."

"You're sure it's not a bump or something growing there? Something connected to him, I mean?"

"I don't think so. Not unless he's growing something pink," Rose said, and shrugged.

"Okay then." Esme nodded. "Good job, Rose. Carlos, you come over here now."

Carlos hopped over to where Esme was standing. She crouched down so her eyes were level with his.

"I need you to do something really important," she said. "I need you to reach your fingers into Gabriel's throat until you feel something. You have the smallest fingers, so you're the best person for this job, okay? When you feel it, pinch it with your fingers and—carefully—I want you to pull it out."

"What?" Gabriel cried. He tried to sit up, but Esme pushed him back down and turned again to Carlos.

"You're going to have to do it fast, because as soon as you touch his throat he's going to gag."

Carlos looked at Esme skeptically.

"Got it?" she said urgently.

"That sounds gross," Carlos said.

Placing both hands on his shoulders, Esme moved him until he was standing directly in front of Gabriel. The two boys looked warily at each other, like boxers waiting for the bell. Gabriel shot a glance at Esme, searching her face for any sign of doubt. But the girl's jaw was set, her gaze steady. Gabriel tipped his head back once again.

From below, a strange rhythmic pulsing moved up through him, as if the ship was beating in time with his own quickening heartbeat. He studied this feeling and tried to think about the rotations of the planets, the War of 1812, photosynthesis—anything at all but what was about to happen to him.

Hovering behind Carlos, Esme put her mouth right next to the boy's ear and spoke in a low voice that only he could hear.

"You know how Gabe always tries to make things better for us?"

Carlos nodded.

"Well, now he needs you to help make him better. Okay?"

Carlos was quiet a moment. Then he said, "Okay."

"You ready?" Esme asked.

He nodded. "Ready."

Esme stood and looked down at Gabriel.

"*You* ready?"

19

THE CREW HAD formed a horseshoe around Carlos, who was holding his right hand suspended over Gabriel's open jaw. Now the boy extended his tiny fingers, counted *one, two, three* in his head, and plunged his hand deep into Gabriel's throat.

The result was gruesome, just as Esme had predicted. The instant Carlos's squirming fingers touched the soft pink inside of Gabriel's mouth, the older boy convulsed in a violent spasm. His body shot forward, flinging Carlos hard into Quincy's legs. The boys fell back onto the deck, Gabriel on all fours, hacking and retching and gasping for air, as the rest of the crew stood frozen, unsure of what to do or who to help.

Esme snapped into action first. She plucked Carlos up into her arms and held the frantic boy tightly against her chest, keeping an eye fixed on Gabriel, who looked as if his spine might snap from the force of his coughing. "You're okay, it's okay," Esme murmured to Carlos. She was trying gauge whether he was just scared or had actually been hurt. She couldn't tell with him screaming like his skin was on fire.

After a minute, Esme felt the boy begin to relax against her body. His screams turned to sobs, then whimpers. Gabriel had stopped coughing and now lay limply on his back, eyes closed, a hand cradling his injured throat. It seemed like they'd both exhausted themselves. Still holding Carlos, Esme peeled the boy away from her shoulder and looked into his red, tear-stained face. His eyes were raw and puffy; his lips quivered. When she looked down, she noticed he was cradling his balled-up right fist in his left hand.

"You okay?" Esme asked gently.

"Gabriel bit me!" Carlos cried, burying his face in the crook of her neck.

"I didn't mean to!" Gabriel shouted back hoarsely. "He nearly choked me to death!"

"Okay, okay," Esme said, shooting Gabriel an exasperated look. She turned back to Carlos. "Can you can show me how bad it is?" She felt Carlos nod against her shoulder. As she let go of him, the rest of the crew gathered around to see what terrible injury Gabriel had inflicted on the boy. Carlos bravely lifted up his fists for inspection.

Slowly, Esme peeled away his left hand. Then, one by one, she uncurled the fingers of the afflicted fist until his right hand was splayed open, palm up.

The hand itself was fine. It was what the hand was holding that made Rose scream. It was pink, just like she'd said, and thin and long, though it had been bent in half by Carlos's fist. Now it formed a sort of V. It was slick with blood and thick yellow mucus. It took Carlos—who had

secretly been enjoying all the attention—a second longer than the rest of the kids to look down and realize what it was he held. But when he saw the dark, slimy thing on his palm, he reflexively whipped his hand down and flung it off. The thing hit the deck and stuck.

Gabriel was sitting up now, but his vantage point was obscured by the backs of his crewmates. What was going on? If he had bitten off Carlos's finger, there would have been chaos. Why were they so quiet? "How bad is he?" he asked.

Nobody answered, too engrossed by the alien thing that had slowly started to move. It continued to unfurl wetly, straightening itself, leaving a thin trail of slimy bile on the wooden plank beneath it. It kept uncurling until it rested in a perfect straight line. Then it stopped. Nobody spoke. Nobody moved.

"What is *that*?" Gabriel cried. He had crossed over to the group.

"I think it's a sea worm," whispered Quincy.

"It's an alien finger!" Carlos said, and giggled nervously, his dark eyes wide and shining.

Baron shook his head. "It's not a worm or an alien finger," he muttered. "But we don't know what it is."

"Okay. But where did it come from?" Gabriel pressed, not taking his eyes off the wet, dead-looking thing on the deck.

"I'm pretty sure it came out of your throat," Esme said.

Gabriel grew pale. Esme watched as he began to weave slightly on his feet. She didn't want to do it, she really, *really* didn't, but she knew it was her turn to step up. And so she gritted her teeth, leaned forward, and plucked the thing up with her index finger and thumb.

Esme lifted up the bottom of her shirt and wiped off the slime. When the thing was clean, she shook her head. It's amazing, she thought, how completely fear could blind you.

"What is it?" Carlos asked. He was hopping up and down.

With a dramatic flourish, Esme held the thing straight out in front of her. The crew stared in disbelief. A long pink feather was pinched between her fingers.

"I wonder how long it was in there?" Rose whispered.

Carlos giggled nervously. "How'd you get a feather stuck in your throat, Gabe?"

Without a word, Gabriel reached out and took the feather from Esme. He turned it over once, twice, then dropped his hand to his side.

"Rodney," he finally said. "That's where it came from."

"What's a Rodney?" Carlos breathed.

"You know," Gabriel muttered.

"You don't mean…" Quincy cackled. "Angelica's nasty bird?"

"That's… so… gross," Carlos said, amazed. "And it's been there this whole time? How'd it turn pink?"

Gabriel didn't answer. His face began to darken.

"Just—be calm a second while we figure this out," Esme said, glancing at Gabriel. He seemed to be folding further and further into himself.

"You probably just breathed it in while you were sleeping," Baron offered. "Back home, I mean. And the pigment…"

"Maybe," Gabriel replied softly, a muddy sadness flooding him. That his old life could still reach him, still hurt him, seemed like too much to bear.

At this last thought, it was as if a great gust of wind blew through him, clearing all the darkness out. It had only been a feather, after all. He hadn't been hurt. And he had a crew to captain.

"Rose, Carlos," he called out, beckoning them over. The two of them cautiously stepped toward him. Gabriel placed a heavy hand on each of their shoulders.

"Thanks for helping me. I know it wasn't easy. Carlos, you in particular. And I'm sorry I hurt you."

"It's okay!" Carlos replied, beaming. Even Rose let the corners of her mouth tug upward. Gabriel looked up over their heads toward Esme.

"Es?" he called out, his voice cracking with strain.

But Esme didn't get a chance to reply. Baron had rushed to the rail, and now he turned back to the group.

"Look!" he shouted, pointing across the water.

Far off, something red was marring the space where slate sky met black water. They watched as the red slash took the shape of a thin triangle. From the way it was moving, Gabriel realized that it could be only one thing.

A ship.

All around him, the others were cheering, hollering, jumping up and down, doing everything in their power to signal the other vessel. Only Gabriel stood stock still. He had imagined this moment as a great relief: knowing, at last, that they were not alone out here on the ocean. So why did he feel afraid? Gabriel reached up to rub his eyes, suddenly exhausted. When he lowered his hands and looked again across the water, the red-sailed ship was gone.

20

THEY SET OUT after it, of course, working the sails as best they could, hollering across the water; Gabriel's reservations were hardly enough to contain the crew's excitement over the sighting of another ship. But in the days that followed, as they cut across empty ocean, it was as if the ship had never existed. What they found instead was a dollop of green in the distance—a new island.

They had been circumnavigating it for three days now. "We're observing it first," Gabriel told the eager crew. "Just making sure we find the best angle to approach."

This was not exactly the whole truth. Gabriel still wasn't sure he could drop the anchor successfully. But after the disappointment of losing the red-sailed ship, he didn't want to let down his crew again.

As he surveyed the land in the distance, Esme at his shoulder, Gabriel's focus was trained so intensely on the shore that the small tug at the back of his shirt made him jolt upright. When he turned to find Rose blinking up at him, his words came out more harshly than he'd intended.

"What do you want?"

"*Sor-ry*," Rose drew out the word, scrunching up her face. "Didn't mean to interrupt your *privacy*."

"What is it, Rosie?" said Esme distractedly.

"Well." Rose crossed her arms. "IT is Carlos, and WHAT is really, really bad."

Esme turned to Rose. "What do you mean?"

"Carlos." Rose repeated. "He's getting worse."

Esme grabbed the girl's good arm. "Where is he?"

"Ow," Rose whined, shaking Esme off.

"Rose!" Esme barked.

"He's below deck!" Rose shot back, still rubbing her arm. "He's—" But before she could say anything more, Esme was running toward the stairs.

When Rose turned back to the rail, Gabriel was already staring out at the island again. Hadn't he heard what she'd said about Carlos? Rose felt a heavy scowl tugging her mouth low, and pulled the red windbreaker tight around her. She surveyed the deck, noting everyone's station. Baron was fishing, Quincy doing push-ups at the prow. Gabriel was not doing much of anything, she thought. They should be trying to land already! She had said as much three days ago.

They wouldn't even know about the island if not for her sharp eye. Perched high in the crow's nest, she had seen a tiny jade dot gleaming through the grey waters. Someone else might have missed it, but she'd reported it immediately to Gabriel, and been thrilled when he gave the order to point the *Defiant* in the exact direction she'd indicated. But now, just when they were so close, he'd told them they had to wait. It wasn't fair. Rose kicked at the deck, hard.

Gabriel jumped and looked up, surprised to find the small girl so close to him, her face so gnarled with anger.

"What?" he said. "What is it now?"

Rose glared back at him, unmoving. Gabriel sighed, trying not to let his exasperation show. Her unhappiness over the last few days had not escaped his attention, but he'd figured she was just homesick, or hungry, or any of the things the rest of them were all the time. But he was the captain, and as long as Rose was on the ship, she was his responsibility.

"What's going on, Rosie?" Gabriel said, taking a step toward her. As he drew closer, he was startled to find Rose no longer seemed like the tiny girl he remembered from Greenly. It was incredible. Somehow, without any of them really noticing, she had grown half an inch.

"What?" Rose said, flinching under Gabriel's stare.

"Sorry, nothing, I just—is there something wrong?"

Rose puckered her mouth. "It's not fair."

"What isn't?"

"You never listen to my opinion."

"What do you mean?" Gabriel sighed. "What opinion?"

"I've got ideas, too! Good ideas. But you guys never listen to me. "

"Well, tell me—"

"Just because I'm younger. Because I'm younger and because I'm a girl."

Gabriel raised his eyebrows. Rose immediately realized her misstep: he always listened to Esme.

"Anyway," Rose mumbled. "All I know is nobody listens to me around here, and it's not fair."

"Okay," Gabriel said. "I'm listening now. What do you want to say?"

"It's just—" Rose started, but she seemed unable to find her words. A flush crept up her neck and onto her cheeks, and she stooped down to pick at a bit of crud on her shoe. She opened her mouth, but nothing came out. Caving her shoulders, Rose turned her back to Gabriel.

"Just—just *make a decision*," she muttered, slowly walking away.

As she picked her way down into the shadows, Esme cursed herself for not paying closer attention. How had she let things get so bad? It had crept up on all of them so slowly that they'd failed to notice how serious it was. Carlos had started going to bed earlier and sleeping later, she knew—in the last few days, Quincy had needed to splash him with a cup of cold seawater just to wake him in the morning. Even then, Carlos struggled to get up. And when he was awake, he seemed to drag himself around only with great effort, as if his legs were shackled together. Instead of bursting with questions, as he had before, he had fallen mostly silent. And now, she saw, a strange green-yellow color had crept into his face.

He was on his side, his back to her, curled into a nook just big enough for the body of a small boy. Esme watched as his tiny chest swelled and fell back with short, shuddering gasps. Lowering herself to her knees, she put one hand on his shoulder and let the other settle lightly on his forehead. Instantly, she recoiled. It was hot—too hot—and wet with sickly sweat.

Keeping one hand on his shoulder, Esme turned the boy over until he was lying on his back. Carlos blinked once, his eyelids impossibly heavy. His gaze settled on Esme, but he didn't seem to register the girl bending over him. Esme swallowed hard, willing her voice not to shake.

"Hey there," she whispered.

Carlos blinked up blearily, gave a wan smile, and tried to set his chattering teeth. Scanning the room, Esme spotted Rose's grimy white parka on the shelf. And next to it, she saw the emergency kit.

"Hold on," she whispered, easing herself up from the floor. Moving to the shelf, she quickly popped open the small white box and retrieved two aspirin. It wasn't much, but it might help with the fever. Then, dipping a cupped hand into the water container, Esme carefully walked back to where Carlos lay on the ground.

He was able to raise his head just high enough to take the aspirin and let Esme tip the water into his mouth. When she was sure he'd swallowed, Esme tucked him into the puffy parka, pulled his arms through the sleeves, and zipped it up to his neck. He was burning up and shivering all at once. After a moment, she saw that he was struggling to move his cracked and bleeding lips. Esme placed his head in her lap again and bent down close. But just as it seemed he was about to speak, angry coughs racked his frail frame.

She placed a hand on his back to steady him and felt the arrows of his spine. When his coughing began to ease, she put her ear close to

Carlos's mouth once again. She waited. When his voice finally came, it was no more than the driest whisper.

"I don't like being on the boat anymore."

"We're going to get off soon, okay?" she said. "We're going to get you better. I promise." Esme didn't know if this was true, but it seemed like the best thing she could say just then.

"If you were home right now," she said, "what would you be doing?"

Carlos tried to speak, his voice barely a rasp. His head fell to the side with a soft thud. Then, slowly, a rumble came from his throat. Esme bent her head low.

"An orange?" Gabriel repeated. "He asked for an orange?"

"It's scurvy," a low voice rang out across the deck. Esme and Gabriel looked up, surprised to find Baron standing behind them.

"Scurvy?" Esme said.

"It's a vitamin C deficiency," Baron replied. "Sailors used to get it all the time because they didn't eat fresh fruit for months. That's how you get vitamin C. Fruit."

"The orange!" Esme cried.

Baron nodded. "I'd bet a million dollars that's what's wrong with Carlos. We have to find him fruit. Meaning, we have to get to that island. Fast."

"Which means we have to learn how to cast anchor," Esme said.

"And lower the rowboat."

"And row."

"But we can do it."

"Of course we can do it."

"We can do it because we have to do it. Or…"

And then they fell silent, their triumphant smiles fading as they remembered the little boy curled up in the nook down below.

21

EARLY THE NEXT morning, the crew stood above deck together, buzzing with impatience. They could see it clearly now, spread across the water in the near distance: a crescent shape, so densely green it seemed almost black, encircled by a bar of pale white sand. They were finally going to land.

The night before, Gabriel had given the order to bring the ship in as close as they could. They had made some progress overnight, and now a strong wind was blowing in from the west as he untied the docklines on the east side of the boat and looked up to the mainsail. The wind was changing; it could be dangerous if the heavy boom swung across the deck. He needed to lower the sails, so the wind wouldn't overwhelm the ship.

"Reef the sails!" Gabriel yelled, and the crew scrambled across the deck. But before they could lower them, the ship heeled sharply to port, then struggled to right herself. Gabriel looked to Esme. "Lash the reef line to the boom!" he called.

Esme wrapped the line tightly around the boom and secured it with a square knot. The rest of the crew was still scurrying around the deck, securing the other lines. Gabriel felt a surge of pride as he watched the sails come under control. How far they'd come! After more than two months on the water, they had an island dead ahead and a lucky wind by their side to help them along. Maybe salvation was in sight.

Of course, getting close to the island was going to be the easy part.

Gabriel had spent all night worrying about the anchor. It could still rip free and crash into the hull, sinking the ship; or, too rusted after centuries of disuse, it might not drop at all. In that case, they'd have an awful choice to make: the island or the ship. They could run the *Defiant* aground, or abandon the ship and make for land in the rowboat, or resign themselves to a life aboard the vessel until their water ran out or they capsized in a storm. The terrible possibilities cascaded through Gabriel's mind as he stepped down from the prow and walked toward the great metal mass of the anchor.

"Maybe we could just test it a little?" Baron offered.

Gabriel shook his head. "No. Once we start, we'll have to keep on lowering. We won't be able to stop it."

"Well, maybe some of us could stay aboard and man the ship, and some of us could row to the island?"

"No good, Bar," said Esme. "If we lose one more crew member, we wouldn't be able to control the ship anyway. And we've got to stay together. "

From where he lay propped against the mast, Carlos raised his head a bit and tried to summon his strongest-sounding voice.

"Hey, guys—I'm feeling better today. Really, I am! Maybe we should just keep going?"

For a moment, Gabriel clung to this idea. But when he looked again at Carlos, he couldn't ignore how hollow the boy's eyes were, how he shivered despite the sun's heat. They had to drop the anchor.

A few minutes later Gabriel emerged from the hold with the Codex Mare. He lugged the giant book over to the middle of the ship, where the rest of the crew anxiously awaited him, and placed it on the deck, turning the yellowed pages until he found the section dedicated to the anchor. He spent a moment running his eyes over the text, rehearsing Ventana's instructions; then, standing up straight, he told the crew to take their posts. A moment later, he began calling out orders.

"Esme! Free the anchor from any bonds that connect it to the roller."

"Check!" called Esme.

"Quincy! Make sure the bitter end is secured to the boat."

"What's the 'bitter end'?" Quincy shouted back.

"It's the tail end of the rode."

"What's the rode?"

"The anchor chain."

"Got it!" Quincy called. "And check!"

"Hey, Rose!" Gabriel shouted. The girl was high above him now, perched up in the silver-spangled crow's nest.

"Yeah?" she called down.

"Are we facing into the wind?"

"Yep!"

"Okay," Gabriel said. "Here we go!"

With that, Gabriel released the brake on the chain and let the anchor fall. There was a sharp jolt as it jerked down hard, and the ship lurched to the left. The crew held tight to whatever they could. Just below, the anchor swung past the delicate wood of the hull.

Gabriel tried not to be sick, tried to focus. There was no turning back now.

"Esme! Let out the rest of the rode!"

Esme bounded across the deck as Gabriel called out the final command.

"Q! Wrap the rode around the deck cleat!"

Esme released the last section of chain, whipping the rode over the side of the boat. The heavy iron plummeted toward the ocean floor. A loud twang vibrated in the air over the ship, and the crew looked to Gabriel, who shouted out reassurance from the Codex.

"That's it! 'When the anchor takes a bite, you'll hear the line ring like a plucked string'!"

A cheer rang out from the crew. They had heard it!

"We're not done yet, guys!" Gabriel called out, though he too was already laughing with relief. There was no giant hole in the side of their boat. Baron helped Quincy struggle with the tense rode while the others danced around, hollering and slapping each other on the back. Even Carlos was grinning now. The boys finished wrapping the rode around the cleat, securing it with a knot.

The crew stood together a minute, arms draped around each other's shoulders, marveling at their victory. Then Esme called, "Everyone into the rowboat!" There was an unknown island awaiting them.

22

AFTER QUINCY'S MISHAP, Gabriel had become obsessed with plotting how best to get the rowboat into the water without it flipping. He'd reconfigured the way the ropes were attached, looping them through the small gaps at the rowboat's tail and nose with sliding knots that gave them more purchase. Best of all, with the help of the Codex, he'd figured out how to control the rowboat's descent from within the rowboat itself.

Now, though, as the six of them sat in the boat, suspended over the side of the ship, the precariousness of their position seemed like insanity. If he'd gotten his knots wrong, the rowboat could easily flip in the air; if it did, his whole crew would be tossed into the water, and the wooden boat would come falling on top of their heads swiftly thereafter. Carlos was too weak to swim by himself, and there was no one waiting on the *Defiant* to haul them back in. The crew sat very still, trying not to disturb the balance.

"Ready?" Gabriel called out. They weren't, but they had no choice now. Gabriel gave the order, and the crew began to loosen the ropes.

Together they managed to work the lines well enough to slowly, haltingly lower themselves down. After a minute, the small boat hit the water with a satisfying smack. It wallowed for a second, and the crew clutched the gunwales for support. When it settled, stable, they allowed themselves one brief moment of celebration before freeing the rowboat from the ropes. Then Esme reached beneath her narrow seat and brought out the two wooden oars.

"Who wants to row?" she said.

"I will!" Rose cried, stretching out her good arm. Her cast was gone now; it had disintegrated off entirely, revealing a pale, withered, and slightly crooked arm.

Esme shook her head.

"We need our strongest rowers first."

"But that's not fair. I can do it."

"Rose…" Esme warned.

"Fine," Rose grumbled, scratching at her puckered arm. Esme turned to the others. She didn't need to say anything else; the strongest rowers knew who they were. Gabriel and Baron each took up a splintering oar, settled them into their locks, dipped them into the water, and began to pull.

They quickly fell into a rhythm. The *Defiant*, anchored firmly in the water, faded in their wake, and it was only a short while before Rose declared that she could see sand beneath the aqua waves. The island began cresting from the water ahead like the back of a giant turtle.

As Baron and Gabriel continued pulling them closer to shore, an awed silence fell over the small boat. They hadn't been this close to land since the day of the pink flash. Now the white sands before them shimmered golden in the sun; the island was stretching itself out with every oar stroke. When the belly of the boat finally scraped the sand, Baron dropped his oar and hopped out. The water lapped as high as his calves.

"It's warm!" he shouted.

The others (except for Carlos, who was still too weak to move on his own) quickly followed. As they pulled the rowboat through the bobbing waves, everyone felt a deep, bursting thrill. It had been so long since any of them had stood on solid land, and the feeling of the ground beneath their feet was overwhelming.

They dragged the wooden boat a good distance up onto the beach, where they hoped a high tide wouldn't claim it. When they felt it was at a safe remove from the waves, Gabriel scooped Carlos up and lay him down on the powdery sand. Beyond the shoreline, the *Defiant* now looked like a tiny bird bobbing on the distant waves.

The beach couldn't have been longer than two miles end to end. Hairy, coconut-laden palm trees ran along its rim; beyond the palms, a dark jungle curled. Gabriel squinted into the vegetation. Who knew what awaited them there?

Quincy was the first to move to the treeline. He reached down, picked up a small coconut, gave it a shake, then threw it hard at Baron.

"Hey!" Baron said, rubbing his wounded arm. Quincy rolled his eyes.

"Baby," he said.

"Enough," said Esme.

Quincy scowled at her. "I wasn't even—"

"I feel funny," Rose grumbled.

Quincy glanced at Rose, considered what she'd said, and nodded. "Yeah. Me too."

"That's because we're not moving," Baron said.

"Huh?"

"Remember how sick we all felt when we were first on the boat?"

"Not me," Quincy shot back.

"Okay, not you, but everyone else, basically. Well, have you noticed that no one really gets seasick anymore?"

Everyone nodded, realizing for the first time that this was true.

"It's because your brain and body adjust to the feeling of constant motion. It becomes your normal state. So now that your body isn't moving up and down anymore, your brain thinks something is off again. That's why you feel weird."

"I don't like it," Rose muttered.

Gabriel shook his head. Finally on land, and still not happy! He dropped down onto the powdery sand. "Just give it a minute," he said. "We can rest here for now. But we need to start looking for water soon." He closed his eyes. One by one, the rest of the crew plopped down around him. Before long, they were all dozing in the mild afternoon sun.

Gabriel dreamed of his sister. When he was awake, he didn't let himself think about Franny at all; he couldn't remember her toothy smile without also remembering the day she'd been yanked away by a grim-faced social worker. He couldn't picture her coppery curls without also picturing her twisted, screaming face, trying to get back to him, her small fists banging against the car window.

But in his dreams, they were together, he and Franny. He was his true age, but Franny was always three years old and chubby, always a little girl. In this dream on the beach, they were standing in a field of long silvery grass. Gabriel held a huge round wand, blowing bubbles big as watermelons. By his side, Franny leapt up to burst them, springing higher than seemed possible for such a tiny girl. But something was wrong, something hard to pinpoint. She was fading or blurring, becoming translucent; he could see the grass swaying through her. He reached out—if he could touch her, he thought, she couldn't fade away—but when his hand connected with her shoulder—*POP!* She burst like a bubble. He was alone, calling her name into the empty yellow sky, his body starting to shake—

"Gabe!"

Gabriel's eyes snapped open. Wincing against the harsh sunlight, he registered Esme's face hovering above him, peering into his, her hand still resting on his shoulder.

"What?" he snapped, brushing Esme's hand off a bit more roughly than he meant to.

"You looked liked I should wake you up," she said quietly.

Brushing the hair from his eyes, Gabriel scanned the beach. Except for Carlos, sleeping beneath the shade of a palm, the shore was empty. Gabriel scratched the sand from his neck.

"Where is everyone?"

"Gone to look for fruit."

"Why are you——?"

"Someone had to watch Carlos," Esme mumbled.

Suddenly, shouts in the distance broke through the quiet. Someone was running toward them. Esme and Gabriel shot to their feet, transfixed, squinting through the shimmering heat until the form began to clarify. Quincy! He was running at top speed, arms waving wildly above him. When he reached them, he fell to his knees in the sand and doubled over, trying to catch his breath.

"What is it?" Esme said, dropping down beside him. "What happened?"

Quincy took a deep gulp of air. "People!" he gasped.

23

ESME GRABBED QUINCY'S heaving shoulders and turned him toward her.

"Where?" she said sharply.

Quincy pointed up the beach, and Esme was on her feet and running. The boys stayed close on her heels. She spotted Rose and Baron ahead and tripled her speed.

"Esme, look!" Rose called out. "People!"

"Shhh," Esme hissed, putting her finger to her lips as she stumbled up to them.

"What?"

"Just be quiet, okay? We don't know anything about who these people are, or—"

"They look like other kids," Baron ventured.

Gabriel and Quincy had caught up to Esme, and now they all stood together, staring at the strangers. It was undeniably a group of girls and boys, just beyond a cluster of stocky palms.

"Definitely kids," Quincy agreed. "But what are they doing?"

From where the crew stood, they could count about thirty of them. They were sitting in a circle, not speaking. Esme rubbed the mark on her neck, a troubled look marring her face. But Gabriel was unafraid.

"Well, we aren't going to figure out anything from over here," he said. "Let's go."

"Wait!" Esme called, but Gabriel was already walking toward the circle, the rest of the crew close behind him. There was nothing Esme could do but follow.

They were thin, the island kids. Shockingly thin. Sinewy arms dangled limply at their sides, where their ribcages poked through. Their cheeks were a series of gaunt caves, purple crescents bruised beneath their eyes. Did they not have enough food here? Esme wondered. She could see the branches of the jungle trees on this part of the beach bowing down with fruit; it didn't make sense.

The *Defiant* crew stood awkwardly at the edge of the gathering, unsure exactly what to do now. They'd expected *some* sort of reaction to their approach. Weren't the thin kids excited to see them? But the thin kids stayed silent, their eyes tracking a strange object being passed from hand to hand. Was it a shell? A small bowl? Esme could see its pink surface winking in the sunlight. Then, all at once, the whole circle clapped three times, stood in unison, and turned to the puzzled crew. They didn't say a word.

The *Defiant* crew began rubbing the dirt from their faces, smoothing down their matted hair, and brushing off their filthy clothes. Finally, Gabriel stepped forward.

"I'm… I'm Gabriel, captain of the *Defiant*."

The island kids said nothing. Gabriel cleared his throat.

"Thank you for allowing us to land on your island. We respect your ways, and are willing to work in exchange for food and a protected place to sleep."

"That sounded pretty good, Cap!" Quincy whispered, digging an elbow into Gabriel's side.

Before he could elbow Quincy back, a tall, angular girl took a few paces toward the crew. There was something weird in her walk: her movements were both loose and jerky, like her skeleton wasn't assembled quite right. She wore a faded yellow dress that reached to her knees, and her hair was plaited in two corn-colored braids that hung in limp ropes down her back. When she spoke, her voice was low and clear as a clarinet.

"It has been decided by a group vote that I—Marie—will speak for our community at this time. Welcome to our island. We're sorry to have made you wait, but we have a rule here: every person gets a chance to speak at each meeting."

"We understand," Gabriel said, trying to match Marie's official-sounding tone. She gave a small nod and continued.

"We haven't had any visitors yet, so when we saw your sails we had to meet to discuss your arrival. We discuss all changes on the island as a group." Here, Marie held her hands out toward the crew, and Esme saw that she was holding the pink object. It was shaped like a star with rounded points, and its surface had a milky translucence. But Esme still couldn't quite tell what it was.

"We're so happy that you're here!" Marie went on, dropping her hands to her sides. "We didn't know if there would ever be others."

"Neither did we," Gabriel said, nodding solemnly. He swept the hair from his eyes, his hand lingering at his temple. "It's—it's pretty strange, actually."

"How long has it been?" asked Marie. "Since you were on land last, I mean."

"We've tried to keep track," Baron said. "We're pretty sure three months."

"Yes, that corresponds," Marie nodded.

"Sorry," Gabriel shook his head. "Corresponds to what?"

"To how long we've been here. We think it's October."

"That's what we've got, too," Rose said, a small, satisfied smile creeping up her face.

"There was this huge storm!" Quincy cut in excitedly. "All this pink lightning!"

Marie looked hard at Quincy, her narrow face serene, and gave a tight smile. "Yes, of course," she nodded. "We all saw it too."

"Then you know what happened?" Quincy asked. But Marie seemed not to register the question. She looked back to Gabriel.

"Now, can you tell me what's out there? What have you seen? Are there other ships?"

"We just saw another one!" Carlos cried.

"But we couldn't make it see us," Rose finished.

"That's true," said Gabriel. "But honestly, we've mostly just seen water."

"Just water," Marie repeated, a shadow falling over her face.

"I've seen land from the crow's nest a few other times," Rose said proudly. "That's my job. I'm the lookout. But our boat couldn't reach it."

"This is the first time we've been on land since the pink flash," Gabriel confirmed.

Marie knitted her brows, her face crinkled in concern. "I can't imagine. All that time at sea."

"We almost died in the storms a bunch of times," Quincy said.

"And we basically starved at first," Rose chimed in.

"We've done okay," said Baron. "Our fish keep us fed."

Esme, who had been listening anxiously, suddenly cut in. "Sorry, Marie, but we have a sick boy with us. Back under those trees." She pointed down the beach to the waving palms. "We need to find him some fruit."

Marie dipped her head, seeming to understand. "We'll wait here while you get him," she said. "And please don't worry. We have a store of mangos back at camp."

"I'll go, Es," Baron offered. Esme nodded, feeling the anchor in her chest give way at last. Carlos wouldn't die. They had saved him.

24

THE CREW TROMPED through a dripping jungle. All around them, the trees bowed to the ground, heavy with broad, thick foliage. It was still difficult to fully absorb that they were actually off the ship, on land at last. Every few minutes, one of them would break a flower off a tree, or pick a rock up off the ground, as if to confirm that it was real.

As they walked along, the thin kids asked the crewmembers all about themselves—where they'd come from, how they'd managed to live on the *Defiant*—and listened attentively to each reply. Quincy was telling two rapt islanders the story of how he'd almost lost the rowboat. Baron, who had the still-sleeping Carlos slung across his back, was telling an exceptionally tall boy about the peculiar shape of Madagascar. Rose talked by turns to whoever would listen.

Gabriel stayed silent. For the last hour, he had been intently watching the dark, delicate girl walking just ahead of him; there was something about her, something he couldn't quite name, that had captured his attention completely. She was small, elfin almost, her hair shiny and black as an arrowhead. She walked alone, chin up and hands shoved deep in her pockets. Gabriel had been trying to think of an excuse to speak to her, but his mind was cotton candy. Eventually, he gathered enough nerve to ask her to tell him her name.

"Cameron," she said. "But everyone calls me Cam."

"Gabriel," he replied, extending his hand. But Cam kept her hands in the pockets of her shorts and gave him a quick smile.

A few paces back, Rose was taking the opportunity to ask a few of the kids about their life on the island.

"It's completely great here," a ruddy-faced boy reported. "You always get a say in everything."

"Even about the really important things?" Rose asked cautiously.

"*Especially* the important things," the boy replied. "But everything, really."

"That sounds good," Rose said. She struggled to contain a grin but failed, and the ruddy boy noticed.

"It's great!" he exclaimed. "Did you see the talking star we have?"

"The what?"

"The big pink piece of sea glass shaped like a star. The one we were passing around?"

"Oh yeah, I saw that," Rose said, and nodded.

"Well," the boy said, pride alighting his face, "when you hold it, only *you* get to talk. And you can talk as long as you want. And no one is allowed to interrupt."

"Wow," Rose breathed. "How'd you come up with that?"

"It was Marie's idea. I think she read about it somewhere."

"So you're saying that everyone is just as powerful, just as in-charge as everyone else?" Baron asked skeptically. He had been listening in just behind them.

"One hundred percent," the boy replied.

Quincy poked Baron in the ribs. "Why don't *we* have stuff like that figured out, huh?"

"We have chore distribution," Baron said defensively. "And our stations on the ship."

"Yeah, but that's nothing," said Quincy. "These guys are miles ahead of us."

"We're still working some things out," a sunburned girl beside them said softly. "It's not all perfect."

"Marie was in student government or something," the ruddy-faced boy chimed in. "And fairness, rules, and systems—they were the most important things from day one."

"Interesting," said Baron. He shifted Carlos's limp body across his back. Though Carlos was light and Baron was strong, the extra weight and the jungle heat had quickly drenched the bigger boy in sweat. He was tired, but there was a question he'd been turning over in his head as they walked.

"So how did you guys all get here?" he asked.

"It was different for all of us," the thin kid behind him, a girl of about twelve, replied. "Twenty or so washed up from a cruise ship they were on. One girl floated here on a raft, all alone. Some just opened their eyes, and here they were."

"Are there any adults?"

The thin kids all shook their heads no.

"That's bizarre," Baron muttered. "So what do you guys think it was? The pink flash, I mean." Blinking through the steam that had settled on his glasses, Baron readjusted Carlos again, then took off his glasses and wiped them on his shirt. When he placed them back on his face, he was surprised to find the thin kids staring at him.

"What?" said Baron.

"We don't really talk about that anymore," a pale girl replied. "It's a rule."

"Why?"

To his left, a wiry boy answered, "We decided as a group that it was better to look forward to the future."

"But you can look to the future *and* try and figure out what happened in the past," Baron replied. He paused, trying to understand. "Can't you?"

The thin kids exchanged pointed looks. Then the pale girl fell in step just beside him, so close that Baron could feel her sharp shoulder. She lowered her voice as she spoke in a rush.

"We don't talk about it here. And we don't know much. But what we know is that some important thing got messed up with the flashes."

"What sort of *thing*?" Baron whispered back.

"Don't know exactly. Some sort of balance."

Then the pale girl lifted her head and said in a strong, bright voice, "Rules restore the order!"

The two girls just in front of them nodded in unison. They were around ten, it seemed to Baron, and precisely the same height and size, with identical rust-colored pigtails that bounced as they walked. They had been walking side by side the entire way, and now he realized that they weren't just similar—they were identical twins. He quickened his step to take a closer look, and realized something else: a thin, bright pink webbing of skin attached the girls to each other at their elbows.

A few feet in front of Baron, Esme was trying to eavesdrop on Rose, who had run up ahead of her. Marie had fallen into step beside the smaller girl, and there was something about their conspiratorial postures, about the way Marie was leaning in close and nodding, that Esme found suspicious. She watched Rose's hands flutter around her as if to emphasize some urgent point. What could she have to say that was so important? But just as Esme leaned in to listen, Marie stopped abruptly and turned to the group.

"Here we are!" she called, spreading her bony arms wide. "Welcome to our camp."

Before them was a vast circular clearing, a fortress of thick ropey trees surrounding its periphery. The camp itself was little more than a flat ring of hard-packed black soil dotted with identical square huts—twenty or so. In the center of the clearing, a strong fire burned. The smell of smoke made the crew's stomachs growl.

Marie moved to stand by the fire, her face tight with concentration as if she were puzzling out a difficult equation. Then her shoulders pulled back, and she looked up at the group.

"Emergency vote!" Marie called out, cupping her hands around her mouth.

The thin kids hurried to gather around her. Marie made no indication that the *Defiant* crew should join them, so they remained by the edge of the clearing, watching. When the last thin kid had settled into the group, Marie called out in a clear, loud voice once again.

"Move to suspend food distribution to lend necessary mangos to the sick boy. All those in favor?" Around her, every single hand shot high into the air. Marie looked over their heads and locked eyes with Esme.

"That's settled, then. Esme, you follow me."

An hour later, as Carlos sucked on the pit of his ninth mango, sticky juice running down his chin and a bit of color returning to his cheeks, Esme tried to let herself settle into the happy calm the other crewmembers seemed to feel. They were spread around the campground, talking with the thin kids. Baron had relayed what the pale girl had told him about discussions of the past, and the Defiant crew was trying their best not to accidentally mention the pink flash. Esme, feeling increasingly shy, just listened to the snippets of chatter that hopped and bounced around the fire.

"Of course we ate the eyeballs. We were starving!"

"You just know not to look. You can tell."

"The feather was, like, four feet long probably!"

"That was the worst one. After that, we knew…"

"You get used to the smell, after a while."

"She was there on deck one minute, and then..."

"I don't get the gold jacket that much. Only if he's sleeping. But the red one's okay."

"Under the sand? Really?"

"And then Gabe said, 'Reef the sails!' which means..."

"They all barfed, but not me."

"In a wooden barrel that was already on board. We just cup our hands, like this."

"It had sails like ours, only red, not white."

The excitement of having discovered new companions had made everyone burst with questions and stories. Esme wanted to join in, but she couldn't make herself relax. Her eyes darted from kid to kid until they settled on Marie, sitting with Rose by the dying fire. Once again, they seemed lost in some private discussion, one that Esme hesitated to interrupt. But curiosity and her rumbling stomach soon urged her onto her feet and over to the fire pit.

"Marie?" Esme called out timidly.

The girls stopped talking, and Rose looked away at the fire. Esme tried to ignore the guilty look on Rose's face as she pressed on.

"Do you think I can get the rest of my crew fed? Sorry, it's just that we've been short on rations these past few days, and I know we could all use something to eat."

A warm smile spread across Marie's long face. "Of course! Yes, you'll be well fed. I completely forgot to tell you! At our meeting earlier we decided to have a celebration meal tomorrow to honor your arrival. A feast! The food committee is already working on menus and seating charts. It's going to be spectacular, really something."

"Tomorrow?" Esme said weakly.

Marie's smile turned bemused as she tilted her head to one side. "Is that a problem?"

"Well, actually—" Esme began, but was startled silent when Gabriel grabbed her arm.

"Esme," he said, giving her a stern look. He turned to Marie. "Tomorrow is great, of course."

Then, with great ceremony, Gabriel thanked Marie and the rest of the kids for their *exceedingly* generous hospitality, and apologized for anything his crew might have said to cause offense. It was an opportunity to draw Cam's attention to him, and he took it, making sure his eyes rested on hers a beat longer than necessary. The rest of the crew stole sly glances at Esme, who was looking down, her face burning. She had just been trying to take care of them. But she knew she'd made some error—embarrassed Gabriel somehow. Why was he acting so strange?

It wasn't until later, as she lay inside the dark hut the thin kids had cleared out for the crew, that Esme remembered how Gabriel had looked at that small, dark-haired girl, and felt a pang vibrate through her. She shook it away. Ridiculous! Gabriel was her friend, her crewmate, and he could like any girl he wanted. Esme turned onto her side and tried to think about all the good things that were happening. They'd made it to an island—one that seemed to have plenty of fresh drinking water and fruit. They'd discovered other kids still alive. Carlos wasn't going to die. As she drifted off to sleep, her final thought was of all the delicious food she'd get to eat in just a few hours' time.

25

BRIGHT FINGERS OF sunlight poked them awake at dawn. As the sleepy crew picked their way out of their hut and into the camp, they were surprised to find that all the thin kids were already up. It was impossible not to feel a tense buzzing in the air.

"Something's wrong," Esme whispered to Gabriel. He nodded in agreement. From the way the thin kids stood in tight clumps, whispering furiously, it didn't seem that they were eager to share the news.

Just then, Gabriel spotted Cam. She was crossing the camp alone, head down and both hands shoved deep into the pockets of her dress.

"I'll be right back," Gabriel said. He made a beeline for the dark-haired girl. When she noticed him approaching, her eyes widened, and she turned to go the other way.

"Please, wait!" Gabriel called out, jogging up alongside her. Cam stopped, but kept her eyes to the ground. She didn't move, wouldn't look at him, and suddenly Gabriel found himself unable to speak. He'd had so many questions, but now he couldn't remember any of them. Then Cam bit her lower lip, and his heart cleaved.

"We—we have a rule not to talk about group matters individually," she said. "It's not fair to—"

"It doesn't seem like the rest of your group is following that rule," Gabriel interrupted, gesturing to the clusters of thin kids nearby. "Please, Cam—you have to tell us what's going on here."

At the sound of her name, Cam looked up at Gabriel's face. Whatever she found there made her go on.

"There—there was a robbery. Something was taken." Cam's dark eyes darted around the camp. People were watching them talk, whispering. "I have to go."

With that, Cam stepped around him and hurried off toward the beach.

Gabriel struggled to understand what she'd told him. A robbery? What was there to take around here that could be such a big deal? The thief would have to be pretty stupid to steal from the group that he lived with, moreover—where would he hide what he took? Where would he go?

Then, all at once, he understood. The thin kids thought it was one of *them*.

This was not good. He had to tell Esme right away. But before Gabriel could reach her, he was stopped by the sight of Marie coming toward him. The gangly girl's odd frame made her halt and jerk. She looked older than she had before—her expression, Gabriel realized, was the look of a disappointed adult. When she stopped in front of him and spoke, her tone was icy.

"We're meeting now," she said.

"I think there's been some mistake," Gabriel said, trying to explain. But Marie raised a knobby hand, silencing him.

"Please. Save it for the meeting."

It began with the circle. In Gabriel's mind, it was a good circle. He could see everyone, everyone could see him. What else did they need? But apparently it wasn't perfect, wasn't circle-y enough. The thin kids inched forward, then inched back a bit. They scooted left, then right. They measured to make sure the amount of space between each person was uniform. That took about ten minutes. Then they measured the distance from each person's chest to the talking star resting directly in the center. That took maybe twenty more minutes. By the time everyone was satisfied, nearly an hour had passed. Gabriel thought it was the dumbest display he'd ever witnessed.

Truthfully, though, he didn't mind the wasted time so much. He was sitting next to Cam.

But he was finding it difficult to ignore his empty stomach. He looked around for any evidence of the feast they'd been promised, and came away disappointed. The rest of his crew must be starving, he thought. They needed to eat.

Only Carlos felt no desperate hunger. And that was why everyone was here.

A boy stood. He walked to the center of the circle, picked up the talking star, and stolidly returned to his spot. There was some sort of rash across his shoulder, which he now scratched thoughtfully as he spoke.

"Open meeting!" he shouted.

In unison, the thin kids gave a single clap. The rashy boy continued.

"We are here today to talk about the Banana Incident: what happened, and what the consequences should be. First, does anyone have a point of clarification?"

Two hands went up: a freckled girl and a boy with a large forehead. The speaker called on Freckles: "Naomi has the circle."

Naomi walked over to the speaker, took the talking star from him, and returned to her spot. She cleared her throat. "Point of clarification: I sort of have a problem with calling what happened the Banana *Incident*. I mean, he robbed us. We should call it the Banana Robbery."

Seven hands shot up. Four people thought any reference to robbery started the conversation off with an unfair bias—a bias that should not be introduced until all parties had been heard. The remaining three suggested an amendment to the wording. There was a vote. The circle decided to stick with "The Banana Incident" after all.

The boy with the large forehead was still waiting with his point of clarification. He stood, walked to the girl who now held the talking star, took it from her hands, and walked back to his spot. He sat.

"Point of clarification," he said. "What happened?" A few people snickered, and his forehead reddened. "Sorry, I overslept."

Marie stood and made her jerking way over to the speaker. She picked up the talking star, walked back to her spot, and said: "When we first saw the ship, we were so excited to finally, *finally* have visitors. We were so excited that before we even met them, we decided that there should be a feast thrown in their honor. As head of the Food Committee, I can say that everyone has been working very hard to make this feast something really memorable. It's going to be a really special feast." Here, Marie stopped to make sure everyone had enough time to think about how great the feast was going to be. Then she continued.

"We didn't ask much of our new guests. Next to nothing was asked, really. Only that they wait to eat until the feast. So that it would be special, right?" Everyone nodded. "This morning, I went to find some fruit— some fruit for this great feast—and I see this." From her pocket, Marie produced the offending item. It was a single bruised banana peel. "It was lying next to that boy there. He was just sleeping away like nothing had happened." Here, she pointed a long finger at Carlos. "He took it from the stock house. I know because I went and counted. Sure enough, one banana was missing."

Tongues clicked. Someone booed.

"So that's what happened," Marie said. "Now we need to decide what to do about it."

26

THE TALKING STAR went around the fire counterclockwise. There were rules for how to disagree with a point someone made, and rules for how to speak if you had just spoken one turn back. There was lots of tabling and amending. Out of the corner of his eye, Baron noticed a girl recording every word spoken using a piece of charcoal and a stack of banana leaves. Eventually the talking star dropped into Carlos's tiny hands.

He placed it in his lap, started to speak, then hesitated. He looked up. All eyes were focused on him. It was clear that all he wanted was to disappear.

"You have the star," Marie said, her clear voice ringing across the circle. "Please, speak."

Puffing up his chest, Carlos swallowed once and stood up. He looked around the circle. Then he made his case.

"I was…" he said, and paused. "I was really, really hungry."

Low, angry murmurs rumbled all around. Esme watched the tears gather and spill down Carlos's cheeks. This is ridiculous, she thought. She didn't care what the rules were, or even if they got to stay on this island anymore. She'd had enough.

"Come on!" Esme called out. "He's just a little boy. And we were starving."

Gasps let forth from the circle. Immediately, Esme realized what she'd done—in her frustration, she'd spoken without the talking star. She glanced at Gabriel, and was relieved to see him taking the pink star from Carlos's hands. He would defend her—her and Carlos both.

Defending them was just what Gabriel intended to do. But as he opened his mouth, he glimpsed Cam shifting her weight beside him. A moment later he was surprised to find himself apologizing.

"We—we're new here, and still learning," he stammered. "But I think once we've all had something to eat—"

And then, before he knew what was happening, Gabriel felt spindly arms reaching around from behind him and lifting the talking star from his hands.

"I would like to table the discussion for a moment to bring up another topical item," said Marie, elbowing her way back into the circle, the talking star clutched to her chest. "In light of the Banana Incident, the group has voted to postpone today's feast."

Gabriel stole a look at Esme, who was glaring back at him, arms crossed. "When—when did you vote?" he managed to sputter.

"Your crew was still asleep. I'm explaining this because I know you may be wondering why we have decided to postpone the meal." Marie paused thoughtfully, then continued. "And I think the decision can best be explained by talking about the dinner situation. You see, we used to eat dinner whenever we wanted. There were no rules at all." Here, a few of the thin kids laughed, and Marie stopped to smile herself. "But then one day Ali said, 'Maybe it would be nice if we all ate dinner together.' And so we met, and everyone agreed that, yes, it would be really nice if we all ate dinner together. But then of course we had to decide on the proper *time* to eat dinner. This is when things got tricky.

"There were some of us—like Carla and Lucy and Walter—who really like an early dinner. They'd eat at five and just be done with it. But then we have, for example, myself and Penelope and Sean—we'd all rather wait until eight or so. And, of course, we have a bunch of people in between. It ends up splitting the vote."

"So what happens?" Carlos asked timidly. "You just don't eat?"

The thin kids all let out a good-humored chuckle.

"That's ridiculous," Marie said, and laughed warmly. "How would we live?"

Carlos looked around at the thin kids in the circle. He didn't think the answer to that question was so obvious.

"We just don't eat *dinner*," Marie continued. "Not yet, anyway. But I'm sure it'll all be resolved soon."

"How long have you been deliberating on this dinner question?" Quincy grumbled, narrowing his eyes.

Marie remained cool, her voice light. "Oh, probably about a month now. Anyway, the greater point is that it seemed like we were on the verge of running into a similar problem with the feast. Some people thought it should be an afternoon sort of thing, while others felt more like making it a dinner. But let's put that aside for a moment and return to the issue at hand. We need to vote on what to do about the robbery. "

At the mention of his crime, Carlos shrank a bit.

"A vote!" Marie trilled, raising her arm high above her head. "All those who think the boy should be punished, hands up."

Bony hands shot into the air. It seemed most of the thin kids were in favor of the idea.

"Okay, hands down," Marie called out. "All those opposed?"

The crew of the *Defiant* raised their hands high, along with a few of the thin kids—including, Gabriel was grateful to see, Cam. But it hardly mattered. The vote was a landslide.

"All right, then," Marie said. "The group has voted for punishment." The firelight flickered in her eyes as she uttered the last word. She turned to Carlos, whose head was now completely buried beneath Baron's arm. "Carlos, on this island, in situations like this, everyone receives the same punishment. So far, we've only had one other person undergo it. So I think, and I'm sure the group agrees, it's only fair that she administer your punishment, as I administered hers."

The thin kids all stared at Marie, bobbing their heads up and down. Marie smiled back, and took her time gazing around the circle before addressing the only islander who had kept her eyes to the ground.

"Cam?"

Cam didn't look up. She didn't move. Though the smile didn't leave Marie's face, Gabriel could see the muscles of her jaw tightening as she called the girl's name again.

"Cameron, come over here."

With her head still bowed, Cam stood, hunched her shoulders, and stepped toward Marie, hands buried deep into her pockets. After a moment, Gabriel caught a glimpse of her face. The terror there was clear.

"Hey!" he shouted, springing to his feet. The thin kids whipped their heads toward him and glared. "Before this goes any further—what's this punishment you're talking about?"

For a second, Marie looked unsure of what to do. Then she lunged forward, grabbed hold of one of Cam's arms, and yanked up hard. Cam struggled to thrust her hand back into her pocket, but Marie was far stronger, and she held Cam's hand up high for the crew to see.

Something was not right. The hand was too pink, too smooth, almost blurry. Then, all at once, Gabriel realized what he was seeing.

"You *burned* her!" he said.

Marie let go of the girl's wrist and shrugged.

"She stole, too."

27

"WITHOUT FAIRNESS, THERE is chaos. You need rules to enforce that fairness. Sometimes those rules are harsh, yes. But if you can't live by them, you can't live here with us."

Marie's gaunt face had turned stony. Her voice was low.

"You think we're going to let you burn Carlos?" Esme laughed, disbelieving. "Are you insane?"

"We're leaving," Gabriel said. "Now."

"What about her?" Carlos whispered, pointing at Cam. She was still standing by Marie, eyes cast down.

"Cam?" Gabriel called. At the sound of her name, the girl looked up, fear glistening in her eyes.

"You could come with us," Gabriel said, reaching out a hand. "You *should* come with us."

Cam seemed to shrink into herself. She shook her head once. Then she took a small step back, and another and another, until she was hidden behind the circle of thin kids.

Gabriel watched her retreat, stunned. She couldn't stay here! But there was no time to argue. He had to get the others to safety.

"We're leaving," he repeated.

"That's your decision," Marie said flatly. Then a sneer snaked up her face, and she looked directly at the small girl beside her.

"Say goodbye to your friends, Rose."

"What?" Esme turned to Rose, who was digging intensely at the sand with her foot. Gabriel took a step toward Marie. "What are you talking about?"

"We discussed it," Marie said evenly. "Rose wants to stay."

"No, she doesn't," Esme scoffed.

"Ask her," Marie said.

Esme moved beside Rose. She placed a light hand atop Rose's glossy head. "Come on, Rosie," she said softly. "We're leaving."

Rose stopped digging but didn't reply. Esme crouched down so her face was even with the small girl's.

"I said we're leaving. Get up."

Rose didn't move.

"I'm staying," she whispered.

"No. You are not."

"Yes I am!" Rose cried, leaping to her feet. "They *listen* to me here. They don't just boss me around all the time. I'm staying and there's nothing you can do to stop me!"

Esme took a step back and looked hard at Rose's face. She took in the raised chin, the firmly set jaw. It was an expression she'd come to know well. She felt a hard knot tighten in her belly. She could tell Baron to just pick Rose up and carry her back to the boat, but were they really going to take her against her will? Esme turned back to the rest of the crew.

"Say goodbye to Rose, everyone."

"What?" Carlos cried.

"She wants to stay."

"You can't be serious," Baron said.

"She's made up her mind." Esme said. Without another glance back, she started walking toward the trail to the beach. The crew stared on in disbelief.

"Rose," Gabriel said slowly. "We won't force you. But please. Think about this. This is forever."

Not meeting his eye, Rose shook her head fiercely. "I'm staying," she repeated.

Carlos tried searching his friend's face. Then he threw himself onto Rose and clung to her tight until Gabriel stepped forward and gently pulled him away. Burying his face in his hands, the smaller boy turned and ran down the path after Esme.

This is good, Rose thought. I've decided to stay. I'm staying. I've decided. As the last of her crewmates disappeared down the trail, a bony hand gripped her shoulder.

"Come on," Marie said, turning Rose away from the path. "We need to finish the meeting."

"About what?" Rose said.

"About you, of course."

"What about me?"

"Oh, there are a million things to decide now," Marie trilled.

Rose frowned, confused. "Like what?"

"Well, what micro-group you'll be in, for starters. That will determine what chores you have, and what time you'll go to bed and get up each morning. And then we have to vote on your name—"

"My name?"

"Oh, yes. We already have another Rose here, so we have to vote on if we want two, or if we should change yours to something else. And then there's—"

Rose had stopped listening. Her stomach grumbled. When was the last time she had eaten? She tried to remember, but Marie's fingers had encircled her arm, dragging her back to where the thin kids were just beginning to reform the meeting circle. Rose watched as they shuffled their frail bodies back and forth. For the first time, she saw that they looked like dead things, like zombies. She looked at Marie: her cheeks were jagged. The bones of her skull showed just underneath her thin grey skin. A gargoyle, Rose thought. When she looked down at the fingers gripping her arm, all she saw was a claw.

Down at the beach, a few yards out into the water, the *Defiant* crew had already climbed into the rowboat. They were about to dip the oars when a shriek pierced the air. They turned back to see Rose sprinting toward them across the sand. Carlos cheered as she crashed into the waves.

She didn't stop her thrashing until she reached the rowboat. It was

Esme who scooped the dripping girl out of the sea. Quincy wrapped his gold jacket around her shoulders.

"I'm here," Rose sputtered, once she'd caught her breath. "I'm sorry, I'm here, I'm sorry, I'm here, I'm here, I'm here."

"It's okay," Esme said, smoothing the wet hair back from Rose's eyes.

"That wasn't—" Rose gasped. "It wasn't me who wanted to stay. It wasn't really me!"

"No," Esme said, and smiled. "But it was you who came back."

28

LATER THAT WEEK, on a night when the winds were warm and the stars scattered above them like a broken chandelier, Esme and Gabriel stood at the prow together, enjoying the calm that always settled over the ship after the crew had eaten the day's last meal. It had become a sort of ritual of theirs, this quiet hour, but tonight, there was something that Gabriel wanted to say, something he'd been meaning to say.

Standing in the quiet dark, Gabriel considered the past few days— how life aboard the ship somehow felt more bearable than ever. The encounter with the thin kids had forced them all to recognize the advantages of being aboard the *Defiant*, of being in control. And though the crew had fallen back into their regular routines, there had been a small change, a slight shift in the pattern of daily life: now, whenever there was a real decision to be made, Gabriel would bring it to the crew so they could decide together. They didn't always agree, and they didn't confer over every little thing, but they trusted each other. Just the thought of those bony arms and endless meetings made them all slightly queasy, now.

Gone, too, was the immediate fear of scurvy. After they were safely back on their ship, Baron had produced a backpack full of golden mangos. He had stolen them during their retreat to the beach—not *stolen*, he said; foraged—and now they had not only relieved the crew's fear of getting sick, but also made for a great improvement to mealtimes.

And yet, though the crew was content, Gabriel felt certain that he should be building a new plan to get them off the *Defiant*. Those mangos were going to last only so long, he knew. They had to find another place to stop—it was far too dangerous at sea. But where could they possibly go? They hadn't passed a single other island since fleeing the thin kids; and San Francisco, far behind them, had been swallowed by fire.

Every night, images of Franny crept into Gabriel's mind—Franny, alone and hurt and afraid. He just couldn't shake the feeling that they should try to find their way back home. The others would balk if he raised the idea—they didn't think there was anything to go back to. Even mentioning it would make them doubt him as their captain.

All at once, Gabriel remembered the girl standing quietly beside him, and the thing he'd been preparing himself to say.

"Es?" he started.

"Mhm?" she replied dreamily, looking out across the purple water. Gabriel swallowed, cleared his throat once, and swallowed again. He felt dizzy. Just say it, he thought. Just go!

"Well," he started, "there's something I've been wanting to tell you—"

In the darkness, Esme felt the blood rush to her ears. These past weeks, she'd made a real effort not to stare at Gabriel the way she had back at school. They were in a serious situation now, members of a crew who depended on each other for survival, and there wasn't room anymore for that kind of stuff. And of course it was impossible that he would see her that way anyhow. She was short and, well, just plain. So why was he stammering so badly?

"It's not a big thing, but I just wanted to say, um—"

Gabriel kept struggling for the words. Why was this so hard? All he wanted to say was that he was sorry. He was sorry he'd done such an awful job of protecting them, of guiding them somewhere safe. He'd made himself their captain and he'd failed them. Esme should've been in charge all along. He should have at least made her first mate.

But just as he got all this in the right order, his thoughts were broken by a disturbance in the water.

If it had been a ship like the *Defiant*, Gabriel might not have been able to see it from so far off. But there was no chance of missing this vessel's blood-red sails. They were fully raised now, slicing across the cloudy grey sky. There was something else, too—thick black smoke was rising in great plumes from the other ship's deck. Were they on fire? Gabriel realized with a cold dread that the question would be answered soon enough—the red-sailed ship was heading straight for them.

"Who's on that boat?" Carlos whispered, walking up behind them. The rest of the crew had all gathered around Gabriel and Esme at the helm.

"We don't know," Baron said. "It could be—"

Quincy cut him off. "I don't like this," he muttered.

"Don't worry," Gabriel said, trying to gather his nerve. He was the captain, responsible for his crew, and he had to be brave for them now. Maybe this was a rescue ship? Or a band of friendly sailors from a nearby port? It could even be a group of islanders who would lead them back to land. Gabriel tried to reassure himself, but as the red-sailed ship drew closer and the sharp smell of smoke singed his nose, he felt his courage drain away. A thin drizzle was beginning to fall.

"Are they going to hurt us?" Carlos whimpered.

"Of course not," Esme said quickly. "They're probably just looking for a safe place to go. Just like us."

Rose leaned forward, squinted, and looked up at Esme. "They don't look like us to me."

Peering through the misty dark, the crew strained to see what Rose meant. They could see ten, maybe twelve individuals on board the other vessel, standing spread in a row along the stern rail. Then, with a start, Gabriel realized that he was looking at another group of kids.

They were both boys and girls, all different heights and shapes. They didn't seem to be chattering to each other; these weren't the island kids come to find them, Gabriel thought. They barely moved at all. And they shared one bizarre, glaring similarity: their hair was completely white. Not pale blond or sun-bleached, and not the dull white of the old, but some other hue entirely. Through the mist, the tops of their heads seemed to glow with an unnatural, otherworldly light.

The *Defiant* crew was so transfixed that, in their astonishment, they momentarily forgot their terror. More kids, like them, out on the sea! How was it possible? As Esme stared across the water, she noted something else: though their clothes were as ragged as her crew's, she could still see that they all wore the same thing. The white-haired kids all had the same light-colored button-down shirt, with a sort of dark marking at the breast pocket. Something began to rise at the back of her brain, some distant understanding.

"It's the kids from the dock," Rose whispered. "The sailing team."

The voice, when the call came, seemed too loud to be human. It cut through the eerie stillness, vibrating down the spines of the crew. Carlos covered his ears as the rest of them struggled to locate its origin. None of the white-haired kids appeared to be speaking. They stood rigidly at the rail, staring across the dark waters. Gabriel was standing perfectly straight himself, eyes closed, head cocked slightly toward the red-sailed ship. He barely breathed as he struggled to place exactly what he was hearing.

"Give it to me!"

That voice—he *knew* that voice, and yet he couldn't figure out whose it was. Something pricked at the back of his throat. The realization hit him so hard he had to grab hold of the rail to keep from falling backward.

"What do you want?" Gabriel bellowed across the water.

For a moment, everything was still. Then, slowly, the white-haired kids started to shift, spreading apart evenly, clearing a wide space. As if materializing from the mist itself, a small girl appeared before them. Her

hair glowed white, too; it was gathered on top of her head in a huge twisted knot. In one hand she held a large black conch. On her shoulder sat an enormous bird, its feathers bleached white as bone. The girl glared as she raised the black conch back to her lips.

"So it *is* you!" Angelica shrieked, the conch amplifying her cries.

Gabriel nodded. Angelica shook her head and let a shrill laugh escape. Clutching her shoulder, Rodney beat his wings and squawked, his caws filling the air around them. The crew was stunned. They had all seen Angelica swallowed up by the sea. She couldn't have survived that storm! Yet here she was, bringing the black shell to her frothing lips once again.

"You have the Codex," she cried into the shell. "I know you do. Give it to me!"

Gabriel shook his head. What did she want with it? Lewis Farn's words flashed in his mind—the old battles fought for that book, the idea that the knowledge it held was all a captain needed to survive at sea. This was what Angelica wanted, he realized: she wanted the power. And she wanted them to lose it.

"We could share it with them," Carlos said. His eyes grew wide as he spoke. "I mean, they could just come look at it over here, right?"

Gabriel moved to argue, but stopped. It wasn't a bad idea, really. What was he so scared of? It was just Angelica! He leaned forward to shout across the gap again.

"Come aboard the *Defiant*. You can learn from the Codex Mare, and share whatever else we have."

Through the darkness, Gabriel could just make out Angelica's mouth as it twisted into a crazed grin.

"Share?" she cackled into the shell. "I don't *share*. I don't need *you*."
She took a step forward. "I don't need anyone."

From the deck of the *Defiant*, the crew watched as Angelica raised
her right hand until it hovered just behind the back of the boy to her
left. Then she gave a small push, and the boy flipped over the side of
the ship and plummeted into the black water below.

"No!" Esme screamed. She flung herself against the side of the ship,
frantically searching the empty waters.

"What did you do?" Gabriel cried. But Angelica did not answer, her
face a blank mask as she took one giant step back. In another moment
she had disappeared completely from view.

The storm was upon them now. Sheets of cold rain poured down
as the ships rocked steeply together and apart. For a moment, the only
sound the *Defiant* crew heard was the dull strum of the torrent on the
wooden boards beneath them. Then Quincy began to scream.

29

QUINCY WAS ON the ground, clutching his leg to his chest, writhing on the deck. Esme dropped down beside him, wrenching his hands away. She could feel something hot and wet, too slippery to be blood, and ripped open the cloth of his pantleg to get a better look. There, just beginning to bubble up above his ankle, was an angry cluster of huge yellow blisters.

What had they done to him? And how? A smell unlike anything Esme had ever known seeped up around her. It was chemical, acrid, but also had a distinct edge of burning meat. Panicked, she scanned the deck until she saw it, just a few feet away. Steaming in the rain was a hollow silver shell slick with hot oil.

WHOOSH WHOOSH.

The sound made Esme's bones go cold. *WHOOSH. WHOOSH. WHOOSH.*

It was right above her head. When she looked up she saw the white wings beating through the rain, hovering high above the deck. With a sickening jolt, she understood: Angelica's bird had dropped a shell filled with burning oil down onto them. But the realization hit her too late. A few feet away, Rose fell to the ground and began to scream.

"Esme!"

Gabriel was calling to her. He leapt forward and swept Rose off the ground with one arm. But Esme couldn't move. Rooted to the spot, she watched as Gabriel scooped up Carlos, as well, and called Baron over to him. They were running toward the stairs leading below deck. Struggling to make himself heard over Rose's shrieks, Gabriel called to her again.

"I'll get everyone else below. But you have to get Quincy!"

Esme blinked, nodding dumbly.

"Get Quincy!" he cried again. Before she could answer, Gabriel was running down the stairs after Baron, a small body dangling under each arm.

Quincy was still writhing on the ground. Still screaming.

He's hurt. Quincy's hurt.

It all snapped together, bolts of electricity shooting through Esme's muscles as she lifted the boy off the ground and began to run. The rain stung her eyes, blinding her, but it didn't matter—she knew the way— and she was almost to the top of the stairs when she heard it again. *WHOOSH. WHOOSH. WHOOSH.*

She looked up and saw a white blur in the black sky just over her head, another silver shell clutched in its gnarled talons. Quincy was heavy in her arms but she did not drop him, did not move, just stood frozen

as the bird released its grip. There was a dull roaring in her ears. The last thing she heard before the blackness came was the deep, pounding thunder rolling across the water.

When Esme blinked her eyes open again she saw nothing. Her mind felt heavy, full of fog. She peered through the darkness, trying to place exactly where she was. There was silence all around, and a singed, musty smell, like burned leather or dried leaves. Esme moved to sit up, but was stopped by a searing pain. It began at the base of her neck and sliced clear down to her ankles. She lay back again and waited as her eyes adjusted to the darkness.

She was below deck. Then, all at once, everything came rushing back.

"Quincy!" she cried.

She tried to sit up again, but a firm hand gently pushed her back down.

"Quincy's fine," Gabriel whispered in the darkness.

He had been sitting on the floor beside her bunk. Now he rose to his knees and bent his long body over her. Esme blinked up at him.

"But how——?"

"You threw him down the stairs," he said, and smiled. "You saved him."

"I don't remember," Esme whispered. She ran her fingers over her head, her arms, her stomach, wincing as sharp pain flickered up the backs of her legs. She looked at Gabriel, afraid.

"You got burned pretty bad. You'll be okay."

Esme nodded, trying to take it all in. She let her head drop down onto her arm.

"I miss my dad," she whispered.

"Try to go back to sleep," Gabriel said, straightening up. Esme nodded again and closed her eyes, but a sudden black thought made them burst back open.

"Gabe!" she called into the darkness, and he was beside her again. "What happened to the red-sailed ship?"

"The storm," he said softly. "We got lucky. It separated us after you fell."

Esme was quiet a moment. When she spoke again, her voice cracked with fear.

"But what will we do if it comes back?"

"I have a plan," Gabriel replied. "Don't worry about that now. Just rest."

Esme searched his face a moment, looking for signs of doubt. Then she closed her eyes.

Gabriel remained nearby, tucked in the shadows, until Esme's breathing evened out. Then he made his way back up the stairs. Up on the deck, standing in the cool, starless night, he tipped back his head and took deep gulps of air, trying to still his racing heart. He hoped he'd looked brave for Esme just then—like a captain should look. He needed to convince himself that she was safe, that they were all more or less okay now, despite the fact that, at that moment, he had absolutely no idea what they'd do if the red-sailed ship came back.

30

THE LONG DAYS that followed were some of the darkest aboard the *Defiant*. Beaten and worn, the crew hardly dared close their eyes at night for fear the red-sailed ship would return. Esme and Quincy were both burned so badly that they were forced to stay below deck to keep their blisters away from the sun. Rose's injuries were less brutal, but she had welts along her back and calves that made it painful to move or lie down. The rest of them, besides some cuts and bruises, were mostly unharmed. But not since the pink flash had such a heavy feeling of doom wrapped around the crew.

Each night after the attack, Gabriel would stand post at the helm, scanning the black waters for any sign of disturbance. He still had no plan for their defense, but if Angelica's ship was near, he wanted to know it. What could he do, though, really? They needed to get off the water. They needed to find land.

On the third night, his eyes to the seas, Gabriel startled slightly when a dull creaking sound cut through the inky silence. Carlos, wrapped in a dirty wool blanket, was making his way across the deck.

"What are you doing?" the small boy asked, yawning.

"Nothing," Gabriel replied. "Go back to bed."

"Can't," Carlos replied matter-of-factly. "Nightmares." He took a few steps forward to stand beside Gabriel. Together they looked out across the water.

"You looking for the evil ship?"

Gabriel glanced down at the boy. Carlos was scratching at the peeling sunburn on his forehead and squinting at the ocean, and Gabriel was moved by a desire to protect him. What harm would it do to tell Carlos that he was just looking for land? But the boy was part of the crew. He deserved the truth.

"I am, yes."

"Those were the kids from the dock? The sailing team?"

"I think so. They must have climbed onto that ship in the big storm. There were other ships at the dock near the *Defiant*, remember?"

"And that was really Angelica? With the white hair?"

Gabriel nodded. "Yes, it was."

"I thought she drowned," Carlos said.

"I thought so, too."

Carlos nodded, taking this all in.

"And that bird," he continued carefully. "That was Rodney? Even though it was white?"

"Yes," Gabriel replied. "That white bird was Rodney."

Carlos considered this a moment, rubbing his spiky hair. Then a troubled look crossed his face.

"But how did they turn white? Was it the flash? Are they magic now? Rose said the ghost kids are magic. Bad magic."

Gabriel put up his hands in surrender. "Listen, Carlos—I don't know any more than you. But no, I don't think they're magic." He put a hand on the small boy's back and guided him back to the stairs. "Come on. Let's try not to think about it any more tonight."

As their wounds continued to heal, the black cloud of dread hanging over the *Defiant* began to lift. The crew still kept a watchful eye on the waters, but the day-to-day problems of life at sea soon stole their attentions away. Baron's fish hauls had been particularly small lately. One of the plastic water jugs had developed a tiny crack. It leaked only a drop every hour, but that was a drop they could not spare. And someone needed to talk to Quincy.

The severity of his burns had kept him cooped up below deck for more than a week now—far too long for a boy with so much roiling around inside him. He'd tried to leave the hold several times already, but Gabriel had demanded he stay below and recover. When he finally emerged one day after sunset, he was spilling over with a strange, manic energy. The fight with Baron was inevitable.

At first, before the attack, the playful wrestling matches he'd been getting into with Baron had been funny. They would start over something small: Quincy would accidentally bump Baron's shoulder, or Baron would correct Quincy's grammar, and before you knew it the two boys were tumbling across the deck, trying to pin each other down, while the crew cheered them on. It was ridiculous: skinny, clumsy Quincy and giant, gentle Baron, rolling and puffing around the mast. But Quincy had a scrappy intensity that made him take things too far. A pinch would bruise; an arm would wrap around Baron's throat.

"Let Baron take care of himself," Gabriel had told Esme. The boy was huge, after all, much bigger than Quincy. "Just leave it be."

But Esme couldn't. Whenever Quincy pounced, she would remember the time she'd seen him walking home from school with his two big brothers. They weren't just older; they were enormous, far bigger than Quincy could ever hope to be. Esme had watched as they shoved Quincy between them, back and forth, tripping him as he walked. When Quincy tried to push back, the brothers had chuckled in deep baritones.

"I think I hear a fly buzzing around, but I'm not sure," one said. "You hear a fly?"

"Nope, you must be mistaken. I don't hear any fly," said the other.

It was just a game to them, but it was clear that getting tossed around and teased like that wasn't much fun for Quincy. And now, after all those days below deck, his frustration had boiled over.

The fight lasted only a few minutes before Esme pulled the boys apart. It may have started as another wrestling match, but it was quickly tipping into something else. The look of rage in Quincy's eyes was very different than the playful aggression he'd shown before their run-in with the red-sailed ship. And for the first time, Baron seemed actually afraid.

If Quincy kept up like this, the bigger boy was going to get hurt. After dinner that night, Esme insisted they call a meeting.

"So what's the problem?" Quincy muttered. They were back below deck, he and Gabriel and Esme sitting in a circle, old boards creaking beneath them. Esme glanced at Gabriel, who made no move to speak.

"Well," she began, "we wanted to talk to you about the fighting with Baron."

"We're just playing."

"I don't think he really likes it."

Quincy eyes narrowed. "He say something to you about it?"

"He didn't have to," Esme replied evenly.

"If Baron has a problem, he can talk to me directly." Quincy looked poised to say more, but instead he sprang to his feet and glared down at Esme. "I don't need you to bring me down here and scold me like a little kid," he snapped.

Gabriel stood and met Quincy eye-to-eye. "What's going on with you?" he said.

"I just don't see what the big deal is. So we mess around. It's something to do. No one ever *does* anything on this stupid boat."

Gabriel reached for Quincy's shoulder, but he pulled away sharply.

"Come on," Gabriel said. "We all get restless out here. But you gotta find better ways—"

"Better ways like you, *Captain Gabriel*?" Quincy sneered. "Ways like letting that ship attack us?"

"Gabriel did what he could—" Esme said quickly. She touched the burn at the back of her neck. "He did try—"

Quincy cut her off. "What exactly is the plan here? You want to sail us all the way back to our mommies, Gabe? Because as *first mate*, I think we should—"

"We're getting off this ship as soon as possible," Gabriel said, trying to make himself sound certain. "We're going to land at the next island we see. That is the plan."

Quincy's face opened in surprise, but quickly curled inward. "I don't need you to tell me how to act," he said, turning back to Esme. "You're not my mom. You're not even one of my stupid brothers." And with that, he bolted up the stairs to the deck.

Esme moved to follow, but Gabriel put out a hand. "Let him go," he said.

Esme shook her head. "Things can't go on like this."

"I know. But just leave him for now."

"Leaving people alone isn't always the answer, you know."

Gabriel thought a moment before speaking. "You remember how Quincy was always getting into fights at Greenly?" he said.

"Of course."

"Well, I saw him once down in Leibowitz's office after he'd really gotten into it. He was sitting in that grey chair. And I remember his face—how he didn't look mad or hurt." Gabriel let out a breath. "Just scared."

"So?"

"So he's scared now. And he should be, because he's smart."

"We're all scared!" Esme shot back. "That's no excuse."

"Maybe not," Gabriel said. "But try convincing Quincy of that."

Above deck, Baron was sitting alone, head bent over a diagram he'd been working on, when he was interrupted by a hard thwack to his shoulder. He looked up to find Quincy glaring down.

"Really, Quincy?" Baron sighed, rubbing his stinging shoulder. "What's your problem?"

"You're my problem," Quincy snapped back. "Why'd you have to go cry to Gabe and get me in trouble?"

Baron stood slowly, raising himself to full height. Staring directly into the other boy's eyes, he said calmly, "I have no idea what you're talking about."

The tension in Quincy's body seemed to give. His shoulders drooped slightly.

"You didn't say anything to them about me?"

Baron shook his head. "No. I didn't."

"Oh," Quincy mumbled, dropping his gaze to the ground. "Sorry about that."

Baron studied the other boy a moment, confused by his defeated state. He was just about to tell him it was fine, that it didn't matter, when Quincy sprang up straight.

"Well, then they have no business saying anything to me about it!" he cried, giving the deck a swift, angry kick.

"Saying what?" Baron asked, more confused than ever now. "What happened?"

Quincy looked up at him, cat eyes flashing. "Doesn't matter. Point is, it's become pretty clear to me that Gabe's not really up to the job anymore."

"What?" Baron stammered. "Why?"

"Well, he obviously can't defend us. And Esme makes the decisions, mostly. So what exactly is he doing that makes him great enough to be the captain?"

"I think Gabe's a good captain," Baron said slowly. There was something dark in the other boy's voice he didn't like.

"Ha," Quincy scoffed in disgust. "Of course you do. You've got no spine."

"I just think—"

"Who cares what you think?" Quincy spat back.

"Come on now," Baron said, holding up his hands. He took a step toward the other boy, but his crewmate sprang past him, knocking a shoulder into Baron's side. It didn't hurt so much as surprise him, but it took a moment for Baron to collect himself. When he looked back up, Quincy was already halfway across the deck, stomping away, shoulders high, hands clenched in tight fists by his sides.

31

"WHAT'RE YOU DOIN' down there?"

Gabriel's eyes snapped open to find Carlos leaning over him, a quizzical look on his face. Gabriel blinked, his cheek still pressed against the smooth pages of the Codex. He'd meant just to rest his head there for a minute, but as he pulled himself up onto his elbows and pushed the hair away from his eyes, he realized he'd slept through the night. Yawning, he stretched his long arms up, his muscles aching from their hours spent on the hard boards.

"You missed breakfast!" Carlos chirped. "You never miss breakfast. Why are you still sleeping? You sick?"

Gabriel bolted up. "What time is it?"

"Almost noon! You sick or what?"

"No, no, I'm not sick. I—"

"Good. Because we found another island!" Carlos cried, and dashed back up the stairs.

Springing to his feet, Gabriel bounded after him. He winced as the high sun hit his eyes. Esme was at the helm, her face set in concentration. A huge swath of green lay across the waters directly ahead.

Gabriel inhaled deeply, tasting sunshine on the briny air. The rest of the crew was pressed against the gunwales, staring eagerly at the island off the prow.

"We're getting off!" Carlos kept shouting. "Off the ship!"

Quincy bobbed on his toes. "I'm going to eat a hundred mangos," he said, rubbing his hands together.

"Will there be people there?" Rose asked softly.

"I hope so!" Baron cried.

"What if they try to hurt us?" she whispered. "Like Marie?"

As small as she was, Baron had never picked Rose up before. She was just so contained. So tough! But now he swooped the girl up off the deck and held her tightly to his chest. Rose gasped, hiccupped once, then relaxed against him.

"No one is going to hurt you," said Baron. "I won't let them."

Nestled in the tiny rowboat, the crew struggled against the sea, beating their oars against the rough white-capped waves. The shore looked close enough, but they knew the distance didn't matter so long as they kept getting pushed back out. It was punishing work, and nobody spoke much as they fought against the currents. Just as Baron opened his mouth to offer an explanation of the tidal forces working against them, something on the approaching island caught his eye. Half-standing, careful not to tip the boat, he peered through the spray, trying to get a better look.

"What is it? What do you see?" Carlos asked eagerly, his eyes shining.

"Huh," Baron said. "It looks almost like…" he trailed off, lost in his own confusion.

"What?" Carlos yelped. "What is it?"

On the shore of the island was a group of kids. There were about fifty of them, spread out in loose formation. As the crew watched, one of them let out a shout, and then they all broke into a run. Baron shook his head in amazement.

"It almost looks like—"

"Football!" Quincy shouted, and before anyone could stop him, he leapt from the rowboat into the shallow water, nearly capsizing them. The rest of the crew held tight as the boat tipped.

"Hey!" Rose cried, but Quincy was already thrashing his way to shore, leaving them with the job of dragging the boat up the beach.

By the time the crew reached the game, Quincy had already joined in. He wasn't a particularly good player, but what he lacked in skill he made up for in energy— bursting through the packs of kids, laughing wildly and slapping his new friends on the back. None of them seemed to notice the rest of the crew standing there—or if they did, they didn't see them as any reason to stop the game.

It was definitely some version of football, with full-body tackles and a coconut in place of a pigskin. The kids played for another hour, running at top speed along the beach, crashing into each other without so much as a time-out, until a high whistle trilled and the game broke apart. Then the teams trotted over to where the *Defiant*'s crew had gathered in the shade of a cluster of knotty palms.

Gabriel stepped forward, ready to offer an official greeting. But Quincy, grinning broadly, had already started the introductions.

"—and this is my crew. Guys, this is Sam and Ali and Mikah and Javier and JT and—what's your name again?"

"Anthony," said Anthony.

"Right! Anthony." He turned back to his boatmates. "You can all introduce yourselves, I guess. These guys are the greatest."

The crew all mumbled shy hellos, trying not to stare at the kids beside Quincy, who were standing with arms flung easily around each other. They were all different ages, sizes, colors, and just as caked with dirt and grime as the *Defiant* kids. But something made them seem not so much dirty as rugged. Their teeth seemed whiter than normal, their hair shinier, and their sweat made their skin shimmer and glow. Their clothes were sparse and torn, like the crew's, but somehow this made them seem more vibrant. Even the smallest ones seemed to ripple with strength and good health.

Gabriel looked around for any sign of an adult, someone older than fifteen, sixteen. But there was no one. The ballplayers stood grinning, taking the new arrivals in. Gabriel felt it was time for him to ask who was in charge.

A large boy stepped forward from the group. He was tall and broad shouldered, with a square jaw and powerful arms; a thick black rope of hair hung down past his shoulder blades, and a jagged white scar slashed his collarbone. His eyes were narrow and ice-blue. Gabriel, extending a hand, couldn't help but think that this was the most impressive-looking kid he'd ever seen.

"I'm Gabriel," he said. "Captain of the *Defiant*."

The boy took his hand in a firm clasp and shook.

"Carrick. Welcome." The boy had a serious face—the muscles in it barely moved as he spoke—but he did not look unkind. "I'm sorry we didn't come to meet you earlier. We saw your ship approaching, but we were in the middle of practice."

"We respect your ways," Gabriel replied. "Thank you for letting us onto your island. I can see by how easily you've accepted Quincy that we're among friends."

Carrick glanced at Quincy, who was standing just to his right, and placed a hand on the other boy's back.

"He's not the most elegant player," Carrick said, and smiled. "But he's a warrior, no doubt." Quincy looked down at his feet, the pride in his face unmistakable. Carrick turned back to Gabriel.

"How long have you been at sea?"

"Four months," Gabriel replied.

"And have you seen any others?"

"We landed once before. On another island. There was a group there, but..." Gabriel paused, unsure how to explain.

"We didn't believe in their systems," Esme finished for him.

Carrick, looking appraisingly at Esme, nodded as if he understood.

"And the ghost kids!" Quincy said excitedly. "We got attacked by a ship with a girl from our school and a crazy white bird and—"

"There will be plenty of time to share battle stories," Carrick said, removing his hand from Quincy's shoulder. "We have a few ourselves."

Carlos had been hanging back a few feet from the rest, awed and a bit afraid. But now curiosity overtook his fear.

"Hey—who are you guys? How did you get here?"

Instead of acknowledging Carlos, Carrick turned to Gabriel once again. "We were on a plane when the war started," he said. "Our team was heading to a national swimming competition."

"What war?" Esme asked.

Carrick laughed, though there was no joy in the sound. "The Greatest War. The Final War. The War of a Thousand Lights."

"The pink flash," Baron said, and nodded. "You think it was a war?"

"I don't *think*," Carrick replied. "It *was* a war. The last battle between all the world's civilizations."

Baron frowned, about to counter this, but Esme grabbed his arm.

"And you crashed on this island?" she asked.

Carrick nodded.

"Did you have a coach? A chaperone?"

"We did, yes. But we never found him."

"What about the guy flying the plane? The pilot? Or the other passengers?"

Carrick shook his head. "We never found them either."

Esme shook her head in amazement. It was too uncanny—it felt like

213

they'd crossed half the ocean, and the only people they'd encountered had been other kids. What had happened to all the adults? Could the pink flash have really taken them all? How could that be?

Carrick had his eyes closed now. So too, she realized, did the other ballplayers. Esme glanced at Gabriel. He jutted his chin out toward Carrick, who was standing perfectly still, barely breathing, head tilted toward the water. Gabriel took a small step toward the boy and lowered his voice.

"Sorry, but what is it? What are you hearing?"

Carrick did not open his eyes. "Circles," he replied, his voice a low growl.

"Sorry?" Gabriel whispered back, confused.

"They're circling the island," Carrick murmured. "Swimming in circles around us. Coming closer with each lap."

"Who?"

Carrick opened his eyes. "Seals."

32

IT WAS AS if the word itself unfroze them. Instantly, the ballplayers burst across the beach and began ripping branches off the nearby trees, their faces set in concentration. Gabriel looked to Carrick, who had not left his post.

"What's happening?"

Carrick kept his gaze on the water, but Gabriel saw a shadow pass over his face. "Seals," he said again.

"Right, seals," Gabriel repeated. "But—"

"We've got to get them before they get to the island." Carrick's pale eyes flickered across the beach, then settled firmly on Gabriel. "Ready your crew," he said. "We're going out."

With that, Carrick walked briskly down the beach, toward a fleet of canoes lining the shore. Gabriel turned to Esme.

"This feels wrong," he whispered. "Don't you think?"

"I'm not sure," Esme whispered back. "Maybe we should trust him?"

"Based on what?"

"I don't know. He just seems like he knows what to do."

Gabriel shook his head. "Maybe we should—"

"You should follow Carrick."

The voice had rung out from behind him. Gabriel turned to find a slight olive-skinned boy standing there.

"Trust me," the boy said. He took a step closer and raised a hand in greeting. "I'm Mikah."

"You caught my long pass!" Quincy said excitedly.

"You've got a good arm," Mikah said, and smiled, a deep dimple stitching one cheek. Dark curls coiled around his face, which, like the other ballplayers', seemed somehow lit from within.

"Sorry, but what exactly are we following Carrick into?" Gabriel asked warily.

Mikah's golden eyes passed over the crew. "Don't worry," he said, turning toward the water. "Just come with me."

The crew could hear them now, the eerie cries of the seals echoing through the air, seeming to come from everywhere and nowhere at once. Esme felt the hair on her arms stand up as the barks shattered the cool afternoon.

"I think they're going to eat us," Carlos whispered. Esme had never actually heard of seals eating people, but then she remembered the way the sea had boiled the day this all began. She had no idea what that had done to the animals in the water.

"Seals eat fish," she said. "You know that." She tried to sound calm, but the tremble in her voice betrayed her.

"I've seen seals," Baron said skeptically. "At the wharf. I grew up hearing seals. Those don't sound like seals."

"Of course they're seals, stupid," Quincy said, rolling his eyes.

"But that doesn't mean they aren't dangerous," Baron said.

Carlos let out a small whimper, and Gabriel shot Baron a pointed look. This discussion wasn't helping. Gabriel was nervous, too, but he needed to prove to them that things were going to be okay. If hunting seals was the way to do that, then that's what he was going to do.

"Ten per canoe!" Carrick shouted. "*Defiant*, disperse yourselves evenly among us. Gabriel and Rose, Canoe One. Baron and Carlos, Canoe Two. Esme and Quincy, come with me."

Carrick gave a sharp whistle, and the kids around him dragged their canoes into the freezing water. Mist curled around them as they hoisted themselves into the long, rugged boats. On Carrick's second whistle, the canoes paddled out, splintering oars slicing through the waves.

The sea had turned grey and choppy, and the bones of Gabriel's arms quickly began to feel molten. He looked around and was surprised to find that he was the only boy in his boat. Was Carrick making a point? Before he could consider what it might mean, a tiny girl with a short shock of blonde hair raised herself to a crouch and began barking commands. "Oy! Left!" she called, and the girls all pulled left, issuing a low grunt in response.

Gabriel felt a surge of relief. Obeying orders, rather than having to give them, was a welcome change.

"Double-oar!" the girl cried, and the rowers started paddling with a speed Gabriel had trouble matching. Rose had given up several strokes ago. Through the spray, Gabriel could make out Carrick's boat leading the formation, Esme by his side.

"You see them out there?" Carrick shouted to make himself heard over the pounding oars.

Esme couldn't see them. But she heard them. Wails of pain, a weeping chorus, were rattling through her skull. All at once, huge jagged rocks jutted out from the water about thirty yards away, and Esme saw the rubbery black bodies. There were hundreds of them.

Esme kicked at the backpack at her feet, wishing she'd left it behind on the beach. What was the plan here? What if the gauze and tape she'd brought were getting wet? They'd need medical supplies if they kept on toward the rocks at this pace. She looked to Carrick, who was glaring at the lounging seals. It was a struggle not to grab the boy and shake him.

"Plotting their next move against us, you can be sure of that," he muttered.

Esme squinted. How Carrick knew the seals were plotting was beyond her, but she was fairly sure that ramming a wooden canoe into the crags was a terrible idea. And yet, that was exactly the course they were on.

If it were Gabriel leading the charge, Esme wouldn't have hesitated to make her opinion known. But there was something about Carrick that gave her pause. If he's not afraid, Esme thought, I won't be either.

On they paddled. They were so close she could see the ragged pink insides of the seals' open mouths. And then, just before they reached the rocks, something curious started to happen. One by one, the seals began

rolling their blubbery bodies into the water. They hit the waves and lolled over lazily, barking as they fell, bobbing and twisting in the surf.

"There they go!" cried Carrick. "Double-oar!" And the canoes turned, racing after the creatures, who were swimming in a massive, frothing pack back toward the island.

Esme was so relieved to be paddling away from the rocks that she found new strength in her arms. It had been months since she'd tested the limits of her body, and she put herself back into her old track-star mindset, focused only on the finish line. It felt incredible to be racing again. She looked over at Carrick, pulling roughly at the waves. She felt powerful.

"You see that there?" Carrick called to Quincy over the crash of the oars. The thick pack of seals ahead had begun to separate and swim in opposite directions. Over his shoulder, Carrick called out, "What are they up to, Mikah?"

"They're trying to divide us!" Mikah called back.

"Exactly." Letting go of his oar, Carrick raised his branch high and brought it crashing down onto the water, sending a spray over the canoe. "It's a standard trick of theirs, but we're prepared."

Quincy nodded, eager to show that he understood completely.

The canoes gave chase for another hour, always dragging just behind the pack of thrashing seals. There were many moments when it seemed they might overtake them, and when they drew close, the kids all raised their clubs high above their heads, ready to bring them down on the enemy below. But the seals were dark bullets in the water, and the kids never got quite close enough to club them.

Eventually, as the sun dipped down, the seals started circling back to the rocks. By the time the canoes caught up with them, the seals had already dragged their bloated bodies out of the water and resumed their taunting barks.

Carrick raised his left arm in the air. Buoyed on the waves like ducks, the rowers glared at the seals just ahead, just out of their reach. The seals barked, and the rowers let forth a guttural cry, something between a gargle and a scream. Back and forth they went, the sky darkening far above, the first stars winking in the dusky blue twilight.

It had been another hour by the time Carrick, apparently satisfied with the day's chase, gave two short whistles. The rowers dipped their oars. The canoes began to pull through the black water, making their way back toward the island that, they all hoped, would be safe from the seals for one more night.

33

THE *DEFIANT* CREW ate well that night. After dragging the heavy canoes up the beach and walking a long three miles through dark jungle, they were all so weary that they could do little beyond collapse around the camp's enormous fire. But the exhaustion wasn't unwelcome; there was purpose in the ache of their arms and the blisters on their hands. The chase had been hard, but it was thrilling all the same. They had succeeded in protecting the island. They were protectors now, too.

The camp was large, an open square bordered on all sides by high scraggly trees. On one side, embers smoldered in another small fire pit, this one used just for cooking. All around were small huts, uncomplicated structures: just pieces of driftwood with a few palm fronds thrown on top for cover. As Gabriel gazed at one, a boy placed half a coconut shell in his hand. Gabriel stared down in amazement. Inside the shell was a hunk of sizzling, greasy meat. The smell was so deliciously fragrant that, for a moment, Gabriel couldn't speak.

"What is this?" Gabriel finally managed to ask.

"Boar," the boy replied. "They run wild all over the island."

It was the first meat Gabriel had seen in months. As he tore a fatty piece off and popped it into his mouth, he found himself thinking that this was the sort of place where he could happily stay a while.

The fire crackled as the crew finished what felt like the best meal they'd ever had. Her hunger sated, Esme looked around the camp, happy to see how well everyone was getting along. Quincy had long since abandoned his dinner and was playing some sort of taglike game with a few of Carrick's boys. Across the fire, Gabriel sat with Carrick himself, their heads inclined in what looked to be serious talk. Even Rose, usually so standoffish, was sitting with Carlos among a cluster of Carrick's kids, listening to story after story of seal chases past. Only Baron seemed a bit lost.

Esme stood and walked over to where her friend was sitting by himself, tossing sticks and bits of dried leaves into the fire. She sat down beside him and, from the corner of her eye, snuck a look at Baron's face. His eyes were lowered, his mouth turned down slightly at the edges. Nearby, Quincy let out a loud whoop, and they both looked up to see Mikah hoisting the other boy onto his shoulders.

"Why don't you go over there?" Esme said gently.

"Nah," Baron sighed. "I don't really like all that stuff. Quincy doesn't want me to, anyway."

"I don't think—"

Baron stood, cutting her off. "I'm gonna go walk a little."

"Don't go too far," Esme called, but Baron had already disappeared into the night.

On the other side of the fire pit, Carrick wiped grease from his mouth and stared into the dying embers. Beside him, Gabriel sat unmoving, listening closely.

"The most important thing," Carrick was saying, "is to be prepared. You should have started stockpiling your defenses the minute the last battle ended."

"But we don't even know if we'll see them again."

Carrick gave a short, harsh laugh. "If you go back out there, you'll see them again. The enemy is like the ocean. Turn your back for one second, and BAM!" He crashed his hands together. "That's when they overtake you. You said the sails were red?"

Gabriel nodded.

"Well, like I said, it's not a question of *if* they'll be back. It's a matter of when." Reaching into his belt, Carrick shifted slightly and slid out a long white dagger. He held it up to the fire a minute, the light dancing across its gleaming edge.

"What is that?" Gabriel murmured, staring at the blade.

"I carved it from a walrus tusk," Carrick replied, handing it to the other boy. Gabriel turned it over in his hands, impressed by its weight.

"It's yours," Carrick said. "Keep it as a reminder."

Gabriel looked up in surprise. "Of what?"

"To be ready."

"Thank you," Gabriel stammered. A strange calm was washing through him. Maybe a reminder was all he needed. Maybe this was a place they could stay until the real danger had passed.

He was about to thank Carrick again when the massive boy stood up and gave a single sharp clap. Instantly, everyone fell silent.

"What's going on?" Carlos whispered to no one in particular.

"It's time to tell the story of the chase," a small girl whispered back, leaning toward him. Before Carlos could ask exactly what that meant, Carrick's low voice swept over the circle.

"Who are we?" Carrick called out.

"We are the people!" the other kids called back in unison.

"What makes the people?" Carrick cried.

"The people are connected!" the group called back.

"Can the connection be broken?"

"It will never be broken!"

"Why do we chase the seals?" Carrick boomed.

"For Sarah!" the group called back.

"And who will tell the story of Sarah? Who will remind us why we chase the seals?"

Now a short, round girl stood. Her skin glowed deep bronze in the dying fire, the whites of her eyes alight.

"I will tell the story of Sarah." The girl's voice was rich and complex, like burnt honey. It was clear why she had become the storyteller.

"When the people first came to this island, the people would go out swimming in the water," the girl said. "Sarah was a strong swimmer, a strong fisherwoman, powerful in the waves. She was our sister."

That last word struck Gabriel in the chest. Despite his attempt to stop it, an image of his own sister flashed across his vision. He shook it off, forcing himself to focus on the storyteller's voice.

"One day, Sarah swam out farther than she had ever gone before, out toward the great rocks. The people had never had problems with the seals of the rocks, then. They had never disrupted our way of life, and we did not disrupt theirs. But this day, a seal was also swimming in the waters. And this seal struck Sarah on the head with its tail. She became dizzy and weak, too weak to swim back to shore, and when her drowned body washed up on the beach, the people knew it had been a seal that killed her."

At this, the others wailed.

"And so now we fight the seals. We fight the seals for the memory of Sarah, and so that the seals will never hurt another member of the people. And we tell the story to remember why we must never, ever stop chasing the seals."

The storyteller dropped her head, signaling that she was done, and lowered herself to the ground. The rest of the kids sat silently, staring at the dying fire. Then, slowly, a deep keening moan began to rise from the group. They clasped each other tight as their cries grew louder, voices rising together in mourning for the friend they had lost. The crew of the *Defiant* joined in, swept up by the swell of sorrow. Whatever exhaustion they had felt seemed lifted by the invisible strength of that collective cry.

It was a kind of electricity, flowing from one body to the next. As their voices continued to rise, a glowing light seemed to gather from the belly of the fire and envelop the circle, binding them. Their cry cut through the night, louder and louder, until it seemed certain that something inside them all would burst. Then Carrick stood, and the keening ceased.

He was still for a moment, looking around the circle, nodding. The fire smoldered and flared as, one by one, the hunter kids rose and stepped back from the circle, into the darkness, back toward the huts, until only the *Defiant* crew remained.

Esme tried to make sense of what she'd just felt. They had been so sad, Carrick's kids, but the feeling she was left with now was not sadness. It was power, an energy she couldn't describe but knew existed thanks to the pink light that still seemed to dance across her skin. She felt like her whole body sparkled with it. Esme looked over at Gabriel and was surprised by the heavy, drawn expression she found on his face. Did he not feel what she did? Had something happened? She had thought it strange, the way he and Carrick had been talking for so long; it hadn't seemed that Gabriel had liked Carrick all that much when they'd first arrived. She had been happy to see them becoming friends—they'd have to learn to get along if the crew was going to stay on this island, after all. But now Gabriel's face showed plainly that something was troubling him.

"You okay?" Esme said, moving toward him.

Startled, Gabriel looked up. "Oh, yeah. Just thinking," he said quickly, slipping the tusk knife in his pocket.

"You think it's good here?" Esme said carefully. "I mean, like we could be happy here, maybe? They're sort of like us, right?"

"Sure," said Gabriel. "Sort of." He gazed into the fire a few seconds longer, then glanced up at Esme. "Hey, give me a minute, okay?"

"Okay," Esme said, and sighed. "I'm going to take the crew to one of the huts."

Gabriel nodded, already turning back to the fire, lost again to his thoughts. Esme gave him a weary look. He was so secretive! But she didn't have the energy to pry—her eyelids felt twelve pounds heavier as she dragged herself around the camp, gathering up the crew, and ushered them into a hut, and to sleep.

34

HOURS LATER, AT the blackest time of night, the roof caved in.

The crew was ripped from their dreams, at first, by a loud cracking noise. Their eyes shot open just in time to shut tight against the crumbling branches above them. A moment later, stunned and groggy, brushing the dirt and leaves from their faces, they stumbled out of the hut and into the frigid night air.

Gabriel picked up one of the palm fronds, held it up to the moonlight, and was surprised to find it rotted through. Why had Carrick's kids not replaced it? Gabriel handed the rotted piece of roof to Esme, who turned it over in her hand. Just as she was holding it up to take a closer look herself, Carrick stepped out of the darkness, Mikah by his side.

"Good, you're all up."

"Our roof fell in," Gabriel muttered.

Carrick seemed not to hear him. "The seals are back. We need to go out."

As he said this, Carrick turned his head, cocking it toward the distant ocean, as though he could still hear the animals. There was an absent look in his pale eyes, one that Gabriel didn't like.

"My crew needs to rest," Gabriel said firmly.

Carrick whipped back around. "This is not a discussion. Your crew needs to help us fight. If the seals come onto the island, it'll be worse than some missed hours of sleep."

"I'm ready!" Quincy bellowed.

"I knew you would be," Carrick said, flashing Quincy a rare smile. He turned to the boy beside him. "Mikah, you make sure the rest are ready, too."

"Of course," Mikah replied, and then they all watched Carrick walking off toward the water, leaving the tired crew huddled in the darkness.

"He can seem rough, I know," Mikah said quietly. "But all he ever thinks about is the safety of the people. He wants to protect us, and he knows best how to do it. Believe me." Mikah turned to Esme, fixing his golden gaze on her face. "Will you help us?"

They were all exhausted, Esme especially. She wanted nothing more than to lie down where she stood. But they had been asked to go out, and Esme knew she had to lead by example. She turned to the crew.

"Come on, guys," she said. "Let's go help."

"What exactly are we helping, Es?" Gabriel asked wearily.

Esme clenched her jaw. "Carrick says the seals are a threat."

"I don't think Carrick knows—"

"Carrick knows more about his island than you do, Gabriel, and he's worried. And I for one am happy not to be the only one around here who worries about anything."

"What?" Gabriel was incredulous. "I worry—"

"Oh yeah, I know the sort of thing you worry about," Esme shot back hotly. "We all saw how you *worried* after that girl on the last island." She blushed fiercely and turned on her heel, marching in the direction of the beach. Mikah followed close behind.

Gabriel watched her go, mouth agape. Esme never got mad at him. What had he done besides speak his mind? He looked around at the rest of the crew, who stood waiting to see what he'd do next. Through the darkness, he noticed a smirk creeping up Quincy's face.

"What, Quincy?" he snapped.

"Oh, nothing." Quincy shrugged, holding out flat palms. "Just wondering what you want to do, *Captain.*"

Gabriel looked away, not wanting to feed the gathering heat he felt in his chest. It didn't seem like there was much choice, at this point. They would have to go out in the canoes again. Though maybe there was still one way out.

"Okay," Gabriel said. "We're going to vote on this. All those who want to go out?"

Instantly, Quincy's hand was up. There was a lull. Then, slowly, Rose raised hers, too. Carlos looked at Baron, who stood with his arms crossed tight across his chest. He looked over at Quincy, next, and when he saw those cat eyes glaring at him, Carlos's small arm shot straight up, as well.

"Opposed?" Gabriel said, though the count was already clear. Baron and Gabriel raised their hands anyway, then quickly let them fall.

"Come on, then," Gabriel sighed. "Let's go."

The chase that morning followed the same rhythms as the one the day before. The kids broke off new clubs from the jungle's trees and dragged their canoes into the water. They paddled and paddled until, just as dawn broke, they came upon the ring of rock where the seals lay splayed out across the crags. When they drew close, the seals rolled into the water and started their swim toward the island. The crew gave chase for a few hours, nearly reaching the seals at times but never getting quite close enough to club them. And when they had fully circled the island and the rocks had come back into view, the seals bolted ahead of the boats, giving themselves plenty of time to wriggle their fat, slick bodies back up onto the perch they'd started from.

It was only afterward that things seemed different. As they walked back toward camp, Carlos decided to test out an idea he had on Rose.

"When we chased the seals yesterday, it was really scary, right?"

"Yeah, I guess so," Rose said, and shrugged.

"But today," he continued cautiously, "the seals just seemed sort of goofy to me."

Rose glanced at him. "What do you mean?"

"I don't know," Carlos replied. "It's just that, it never really seemed like the seals were trying to hurt us, you know?"

Rose was staring at Carlos now, and he quickly added, "I don't know. It's not like I know a lot about seals or anything." He hoped this would close the topic, but then Rose stopped walking and said exactly the thing Carlos had been trying his hardest not to think about.

"Do you ever wonder if Esme and Gabriel know what they're doing?"

"What do you mean? Like how?"

"I don't know," Rose said, and shrugged. "We always just go along with what they tell us to do because they're older. But sometimes I think they don't know any more than we do."

"Doesn't matter now." Quincy had been eavesdropping on their conversation, and now he strolled over to join them. "Carrick's in charge. And he definitely knows what he's doing."

"Maybe not," Baron said. He had slowed alongside them. "We don't really know."

"Yeah, like you know anything," Quincy sneered. He gave Baron a shove, not a hard one, but enough to make him stumble.

"I'm not saying I do," said Baron. "I'm simply introducing the idea that Carrick might not—"

"Shut up, Lard," Quincy shot back. "Nobody asked you."

They were at the edge of the clearing now, rounding the scruffy trees that bordered the camp. Esme had jogged ahead of the group, eager to rest in a hut for a while. And because she was ahead, she was the first to spot the devastation.

35

"NO," ESME WHISPERED. "Oh, no."

The others quickly gathered around her, staring at the disaster before them. Long fingers of dried seal jerky were strewn everywhere, mashed into the mucky dirt. Heaps of trampled bananas littered the camp, their peels splayed like broken limbs. The food hut had been dashed to splinters, the rations devastated.

"Who did this?" Esme whispered.

There was a silence as the hunters looked back and forth at each other. Finally, his voice shaking with rage, Carrick spoke one word.

"Seals."

Gabriel almost laughed, but stifled it.

"Seals? How?" he said. "They couldn't possibly have come this far inland."

Carrick gritted his teeth. "Technically, it was the boars. They won't come into camp when people are here, but—"

"Nobody was here," Gabriel finished for him.

"Because of the seals." Carrick kicked a banana peel. "They planned this."

The other hunters continued to trickle into camp. Nobody spoke; they only stared in shocked silence at the ruined food hut. Carrick stood apart, a fiery flush creeping up his neck. Eventually he clapped his hands together.

"Let this be a lesson to us! Seals don't just attack us in water."

"The seals are everywhere!" a small girl cried.

"We can't ever let our guard down!" another boy yelled, shaking a branch in the air.

Carrick nodded, his flinty eyes alight. "Everyone prepare. We'll meet here in one hour and get back out there." Carrick gave a whistle and the hunters scattered, darting back to their huts and down toward the beach, readying themselves for another chase.

"Hey!" Esme cried after them. "We should probably start cleaning this up, right? Try and salvage what we can?"

But no one was interested in cleaning up. They had seals to chase, and soon.

"I don't want to go chase the stupid seals," Rose mumbled.

"Yeah, me either," whined Carlos.

"You all are babies," Quincy scoffed, and stomped off toward a group of hunters who had clustered around the fire, away from the rest of the crew.

"This is ridiculous," Baron said, sighing. "Gabe?"

Gabriel agreed with him. But he had no intention of starting a fight with Esme again.

"We're going out there to help them," he said. "Right, Es?"

"What?" Esme said. Her face was drawn in thought. "Oh. Yeah, yes. Hey, I'm going down to the beach to wait. I'll see you all at the canoes."

Without another word, she turned toward the water and began to run.

Standing alone at the shore, Esme ran a hand across her neck and looked out toward the ring of rocks. The seals were arranged just as they'd been earlier, despite the many hours spent chasing them off. Their barks echoed across the water. A few of them were swimming again, close enough for Esme to see their oily black bodies somersaulting in the waves, but no closer than they'd been before.

Esme shook her head. She wanted to like it here. Carrick's kids all seemed so strong, so unified. They had good food, and their camp seemed secure, if maybe a little spare.

But now she had to acknowledge all the things she'd willfully ignored. How neglected everything was! It wasn't just their hut. *All* the huts had termite-chewed walls, roofs that needed repairing. The clothes Carrick's kids wore were in tatters. Their latrine was uncovered, and no one seemed to be concerned with making sure the food hut was protected. She had missed what was right in front of her, amid all their energy and emotion. She had been distracted by the seals, by those endless chases around and around and—

The realization hit Esme so hard it knocked the wind from her lungs. She thought of the circling, the gleeful taunting barks. How had she failed to see it?

She had to tell Carrick.

36

ESME KEPT CLOSE to the water's edge as she ran, sticking to where the sand was firmer. The hunters were gathered in a tight pack around the long canoes, and she doubled her speed until she arrived, gasping for air, in front of Carrick. He stood holding a gnarled branch in one hand, Quincy and Mikah flanking him. Their leader looked down at Esme, the edge of his lip curling in the approximation of a smile.

"Eagerness will help your hunt," he said approvingly.

"No," Esme panted. "I need to tell you something." She stood up straight and took in a long draw of air, trying to slow her racing heart. "The seals. They're—they're just—"

"Just what?" Carrick snapped impatiently.

"*Playing*," Esme coughed out. "They aren't trying to hurt us. They aren't dangerous."

The boys were silent, the only sounds the crash of the waves and the distant echoing barks. Then Quincy stepped forward with a nervous chuckle.

"She's kidding! It's just a joke, you guys!"

Along the beach, the hunters all exploded with laughter, and Carrick's eyes flashed as he joined in.

"Good," he said. "A little humor can be good before the chase. Too much tension can—"

"No!" Esme cried. "I'm serious. It makes sense that the seals—"

"It makes *NO SENSE*," Carrick bellowed, silencing her. A darkness had come over his face. "Were they just *playing* with Sarah?" he scoffed. "Hey, Mikah, when your sister's body washed up on shore, did you think it was a *game?*"

Mikah's eyes grew wide. He bit his lip hard and shook his head no.

Carrick turned to the other kids.

"Prepare the canoes," Carrick barked, and the hunters leapt up and began to lift the long boats. Carrick glanced back at Esme. When she saw the hard mask his face had become, a shudder ran through her. But she had already resolved to say it, and so she clenched her fists and summoned her surest voice.

"Our crew isn't going."

Carrick didn't reply. Instead, without uttering a word, he reached out, grabbed Esme by the back of the neck, and began dragging her toward a canoe. Thrashing and kicking, Esme struggled to free herself, but Carrick's grip was a vice, clamping her to him as he yanked her across the grainy wet sand. She thought to scream, but didn't want to give Carrick the satisfaction.

"Stop!" a voice behind them cried.

Still locked in Carrick's grip, Esme couldn't turn her head. But she knew that voice. It was Quincy.

"Stop," Quincy repeated, his voice trembling with rage or fear or both.

Carrick, looking back, issued a low growl. "Lower your club," he said.

"Put her down first," Quincy shot back.

A moment later Esme felt herself flying through the air, flung like a doll. She hit the sand with a thud, and raised her head just in time to see Quincy face-to-face with Carrick, his branch held high above his head.

"Quincy!" Mikah cried out. "Don't!"

"No, Quincy," Carrick countered, his voice low. "*Do.*"

Panic in his eyes, Quincy held the branch in one shaking hand and looked back and forth between the two boys.

"Come on, then," Carrick urged. "Do it. Defend your friend. Hit me."

"I—I don't," Quincy stammered. "I don't want to!"

He staggered back, dropping the branch onto the sand.

"Weak," Carrick spat, shaking his head. He glared at Esme, disgust pouring from him. "All of you. *Weak.*"

"We just—" Quincy said.

"*NO MORE TALKING,*" Carrick roared, pale eyes darting wildly over the stunned group. Quincy moved to Esme and grabbed her hand. They watched as Carrick's face became a blank mask once again. When he spoke, his voice was even.

"There is no room for weakness here. When the rest of your crew arrives, you will go back to your ship. You will leave. The rest of you," Carrick said, turning back to his hunters, "get ready. We're going out."

The sky blushed crimson as the crew rowed back toward the *Defiant*. Despite Carrick's dictate, they had lingered on the island for the rest of the day, cleaning up the hunters' storehouse and making what small repairs they could to the huts. Afterward, satisfied that they had helped, they agreed it was probably okay to take a few things with them. A bunch of bananas, a half-eaten jar of peanut butter, and a sealed liter of water had gone into the black backpack. When the sun began to set, they'd pushed their rowboat into the waves.

No one spoke as they rowed, all eyes settled on the tiny dots in the distance—Carrick's canoes, spread out in formation, positioned against the seals.

Esme watched Gabriel's long arms pull his oar through the gentle chop. She moved to touch his shoulder, but stayed her hand in midair. She knew she should wait until they were back on the ship and could speak in private, but she'd been turning over a speech in her head for the better part of an hour. If she didn't say something now, she'd burst with the effort of keeping it in. Timidly, she gave his shoulder a small tap.

Gabriel turned halfway back toward her, and Esme lowered her voice to a whisper.

"I just wanted to say sorry for yelling at you this morning."

"It's okay," Gabriel said softly. "I was just trying to watch out for our crew. You were, too."

"I know, but—it's not okay," Esme said. "I had no right to say those things. I know you worry, too. And the thing I said about Cam…" Esme faltered, trying to remember the details of her speech. "You can like anyone you want. It's not my business. I mean, I don't care what you do. I mean, it's not that I don't *care*, what I mean is—"

"I know what you mean," Gabriel cut in. "And you're right, it's not your business. You're also right that I put my own feelings ahead of everyone else's when it came to Cam. But you were wrong about why." Gabriel stopped rowing. Esme had to hold herself back from pressing him to go on.

"I did like Cam," Gabriel finally said. "But it wasn't that I *liked* her. It was just that she reminded me of someone."

"Who?"

"My sister. Franny."

And with that, Gabriel faced forward, dipped his oar into the water, and resumed his rowing.

The crew rowed another quiet hour, easy waves lapping at their boat, the sky above fading from lavender to a deep, rich blue. As they neared the great ship, the first stars were just piercing the sky overhead, and Quincy took a moment to admire them. The vast starry sky made him feel huge—huge and unimportant. It was an overwhelming sensation.

"Hey, Baron?" he called softly.

Baron didn't look back. "Yeah?"

"What's that bunch of stars right there?" Quincy asked, pointing up toward the sky.

Baron put down his oar and turned, followed Quincy's finger. "Which one?"

"Those. The blinking ones."

Baron searched the sky until he saw the spiral cluster Quincy meant. "Those ones?" he said, pointing high above their heads. "To the east?"

Quincy nodded in the darkness. "Yeah, those."

"That's a constellation," Baron replied. "Andromeda." He looked back at Quincy and smiled. "Let me tell you her story."

37

THINGS WERE BEGINNING to unravel aboard the *Defiant*. For two weeks straight, having sailed on from Carrick's island, the crew had been forced below deck by a ceaseless, pounding rain. Dark thunderheads crashed above as the ship swayed in the churning waters, the crew crammed tightly together in the hold, trying and failing not to be sick.

They were weary of being tossed around by the endless string of storms, of being trapped together for hours on end—but most of all, they were hungry. The rains had restocked their water reserves, but the swirling seas made it impossible to fish. They had been reduced to gnawing on tough, bland fish jerky for every meal. Fear fed on fear and grew, blocking out everything else. The tension below deck could be plucked like a string.

Then, one slate-colored dawn, the sun broke through the dark clouds. Gabriel gathered everyone on deck. He knew they needed to have a real meeting—to come together consciously, rather than being crammed together by default. After their loss of yet another home and the terrible weeks amid the storm, they had to rebuild themselves as a crew.

"I just thought," Gabriel started, "before we get back to our routines, that we could take a minute to talk about anything that might be on our minds. Maybe we'll begin by—"

"Baron's always trying to boss everyone around!" Rose cried.

"False!" Baron hollered.

"It's true," Rose huffed. "Yesterday you made me scrub the plates when Carlos wasn't doing anything."

"It was your turn!" Baron shot back. Rose glowered at him, then turned to Gabriel.

"It's not fair."

"Yeah," Quincy agreed. "Gabe made *me* first mate. Right, Gabe?"

Gabriel tried to think of a fair response, but Baron was already starting in.

"Actually, I've never understood exactly why Quincy is first mate. Technically, first mate is the person who helps navigate. So that would be me, right?"

"You?" Quincy laughed. "Yeah, right."

"I could do ten times the job—"

"Hey!" Carlos cried out. "I don't want to share a blanket with Rose anymore. Why can't she share with Esme?"

"Because you're the two smallest and it makes the most sense," Esme said hotly.

"But she drools," Carlos whined.

"Do not!" Rose shouted.

"Do too!" Carlos shouted back.

"ENOUGH!"

Everyone looked at Gabriel. He felt the burning spinning in his chest and shut his eyes tight against it. He would not be another Carrick, he told himself. But he couldn't seem to stop the anger from gathering speed. After everything, he thought bitterly, after all the terrible things we've been through together, they still—

The thought came to Gabriel like ice water poured over his head. In that moment, he finally understood why Cam had refused to leave her comrades, despite the hideous things they'd done to her. In the end, right or wrong, they were her family. Gabriel felt his body curl over into itself. For nearly a minute, he didn't speak. Finally, he straightened up, relaxed his fists, and lifted his eyes to the faces of his crewmates.

"We have been sailing together for four whole months now."

"Five, in two days," Rose whispered.

"And a lot of things have happened in those months, both good and bad."

Esme nodded.

"We've always gotten through them together," Gabriel went on. "But we aren't just a crew—we're all we have right now. We don't have anyone else." He shook his head sadly. "After everything, I can't believe you're still tearing each other apart like this."

Five heads nodded in unison. They knew he was right, and they were ashamed.

"Sorry, Captain," a low voice murmured.

Everyone looked over in amazement at Quincy. His face was calm. The others didn't even try to hide their surprise as he continued in a tone of careful respect.

"We didn't act right. We're better than this." Quincy made a sweeping motion across the crew. "But, the thing is, we gotta know what we're trying to do. It's just too much to keep sailing without a plan. It makes us all crazy, I think."

"Yeah," Carlos said, nodding vigorously. "We gotta have a plan!"

"They're right," said Esme. "Our water is okay, with all the storms, but our food rations are running low."

"Well, I think we should probably be—" Baron stopped mid-sentence as Quincy held up a hand.

"Stop," he said firmly. "Please." Quincy turned to Gabriel and cocked his head to the left. "Captain? Is there a plan?"

Early the next morning, Baron struggled up the ladder and nestled into the crow's nest.

He stayed there for an hour, his head bent over the wide sheet of taped-together pages. He'd added the two big islands they'd stopped at, along with a few other hesitant blips of green. In one corner, he'd drawn a dragon.

Baron found reassurance in his own small record. It helped him feel like he had the tiniest inkling of where in the world they might be. And his favorite place to study his map was in the high, perfect solitude of the crow's nest.

The morning was thick with fog—only sporadic sheaths of sunlight slashed the heavy, low-hanging clouds—and after a few minutes of scanning the horizon, Baron resigned himself to not spotting much that day. He was ready to call it quits when a flash of light caught his eye. A beam of sunlight was reflecting off of something in the distance.

Baron reasoned that it had to be something metal to cause that sort of sharp glint. He leaned forward, squinting into the grey morning, but the sea haze blocked any hope of a clear view. So Baron waited. He waited and waited until another beam of sunlight sliced the foggy curtain surrounding the crow's nest. That's when he saw it clearly, rocking in the waters ahead.

Hurling himself down the ladder, Baron dropped onto the deck with a tremendous thud and lumbered into the hold below, as fast as he could. The rest of the crew was still sleeping.

"Everyone on deck!" Baron cried. He spun around and bounded back up the stairs, hollering over his shoulder. "It's a ship!"

Gabriel's stomach lurched. "No," he whispered. "Not yet." The red-sailed ship. They weren't ready.

But when he stumbled outside and looked across the water, Gabriel was astonished to find it wasn't Angelica's ship at all. It was a modern ship, a metal ship—a ship for carrying cargo, or so it appeared from the huge rectangular crates scattered along the vessel's flat deck. Rust was beginning to creep up its flanks, but all in all it seemed to be in pretty good shape. Maybe it even still ran? And who knew what might be in those crates?

Esme was already one step ahead of him. "We've got to get aboard," she said.

"I don't know, Es," Gabriel said, a warning tone in his voice.

"Why not?" Esme turned to him, puzzled. "There could be *food* over there."

"There could be *anything* over there," Gabriel said. "Including something bad."

"Like what?"

"I just don't have a good feeling," Gabriel said, trying again.

"Fine," Esme said stubbornly. "I'll take the rowboat."

"You can't man the rowboat alone," Gabriel countered.

"I'll go, Es." Baron stepped forward and ducked his head shyly. "I mean, if you want me to."

"Perfect!" Esme cried, her green eyes sparkling with excitement. She turned to Gabriel. "You stay with the rest of the crew," she said, and laughed, hopping a little ways into the air. "Baron and I are going to explore!"

Gabriel watched as she crossed the deck and began filling the black backpack with her yellow notebook and a few other supplies. Baron was already fastening the ropes to the rowboat, preparing to lower it down to the water. Instinctively, Gabriel reached into his pocket and felt for the tusk knife Carrick had given him. It had reassured him, in their first few days back at sea—it had made him feel in charge. He held the knife now, waiting for that feeling to return. But it wouldn't come.

"Es!" Gabriel cried, rushing over to her. Esme and Baron looked up in surprise, and Gabriel, suddenly awkward, shifted on his feet. "Uh," he started, struggling for something to say. "Just be sure to triple-tie the boat when you dock, okay?"

"I know," Esme said, slinging her pack over one shoulder. "Is that it?"

He couldn't think of anything else to delay them. He could only stand there as Baron and Esme climbed into the rowboat, lowered themselves down along the side of the *Defiant*, and took off in the direction of the metal vessel.

The sea was still, the only sound the clean shush of the oars as Esme and Baron pulled the rowboat through the silvery water. Dropping her heavy oar, Esme took a moment to pick at an itchy patch of flaking skin on her arm, scorched pink by the brutal sun. She glanced over at Baron, who was taking off his blue button-down and laying it beside him on the seat. Esme took in the plummy brown of his arms and wondered if he was as bothered by the sun as she was. She wanted to ask him, but felt like it might offend him, or make her sound dumb.

Esme noticed something else about the boy. Those arms, which had always been big, were now thickly muscled. For the first time, she saw how much her friend had changed in the time they'd been at sea.

Esme had known Baron a few years now, and if she were honest, she had to admit he'd gotten pretty fat a year or so ago. At Greenly she had rarely seen him without a candy bar or a bag of chips. And back then he was always alone.

"Hey, Baron," she called out. "What would you be doing if you were home right now?"

"Fishing with my dad," Baron replied without hesitation. "Or maybe in Ms. Inez's room, on the computer."

"Can I ask you something?"

"Sure," Baron replied.

"Why did you always eat lunch in her room? I mean, why didn't you hang out with the other guys?"

Baron sighed. "I guess I just didn't like doing what they did. I didn't get why the only thing they ever wanted to do was play some dumb sport. Like, what's wrong with a board game or something?" He laughed. "Anyway, it's not like they really liked me much, if you didn't notice."

Esme smiled. "Well, you can sometimes be a little..."

"I know," Baron said quickly. "I don't mean to be rude. It just sort of pops out." He gave a small shrug, then mumbled, "I guess I don't really know how to act with people."

"We're all like that. Sometimes."

Baron nodded thoughtfully. "I suppose that's right. But it's not really the same." He paused, weighing whether or not to explain. "I used to get these attacks," he went on slowly. "When I was around new people. Or even groups of people I knew. I'd get really hot and feel like I couldn't breathe. Anyway, I figured out how to deal with it. But my dad says that the way I am, the way I can be with other people, it's to keep them away. To keep them away so I don't feel like that again."

Esme nodded. "That makes sense, I guess."

"Really?" he asked softly. "It does? Because I thought... Well, I thought I might be broken."

As Esme watched his large, owlish face brim with hope, she realized that Baron had just told her why he'd been sent to Greenly. She had always wondered why he was there. He was so smart! He had a good dad! She'd probably been too young to notice anything really wrong with him when he'd first arrived, and by the time she would have noticed, he'd grown out of it.

He was waiting for her to say something. She began shaking her head.

"Broken?" Esme laughed, brushing the idea away. "Not a chance! I think you're doing okay. And you've gotten so strong. The crew's lucky to have you."

Baron still didn't meet her eye, but he stopped rowing. "Can I tell you something, Es? Something you can't tell the crew?"

"Of course," Esme replied. "What is it?"

"I'm happier out here than I ever was back home."

The great metal ship was no more than a quarter mile away now. It didn't take them long to come up alongside it and tie up their boat, just clear of the heavy metal chain that dropped from the ship down into the water, securing it to what must have been an enormous anchor. Once the row-boat was secure, they began to ascend a narrow metal ladder that shot up the ship's hull.

Up they climbed, higher and higher, Esme scaling a few feet above Baron. When she reached the top, he watched as she expertly threw her leg over the railing and disappeared. He hesitated, willing himself not to look down. They were nearly fifty feet up—there was no way he'd survive the fall. Clinging tightly to the uppermost rung, Baron hoisted his thick leg over the rail and leaned all his weight

over, tumbling down onto the metal deck where Esme was already standing, hands on hips.

Baron staggered to his feet, brushed himself off, and tried to hide the immensity of his relief. He felt a trickle at his arm and when he looked, he was surprised to find a two-inch tear in his blue shirt. "Dang," he muttered, sticking a finger through the hole and touching warm blood. It wasn't the injury to his body as much as the one to his shirt that bothered him. He always tried to be careful.

Mist swirled across the deck. The metal ship was silent as death. It didn't creak and moan like the *Defiant* did, just rocked silently around its anchor. It was eerie, this hollow quiet. To break the silence, Esme called out in a booming voice.

"Foggy today, isn't it!"

"Yeah!" Baron hollered back. "But it looks like the sun might break through again!"

Their voices rang across the deck and bounced back at them. Esme turned to survey their discovery. The silence was odd enough, but it was the far end of the deck that took her breath away.

"Would you look at that?" said Esme.

Scattered before them, piled in huge heaps, were thousands and thousands of machine parts. Wires, gears, lights, glass tubes, computer chips, and countless other gadgets littered great swaths of the shiny chrome deck. There were also TVs, microwaves, stereos, and computers—some intact and some in various states of disrepair. It looked like a mad scientist and an auto mechanic had opened up shop together. And from the trails they saw cutting through the piles, it was clear that the stuff hadn't simply been abandoned. Someone intended to come back.

Esme moved toward the debris and picked up a brass gear. Turning it in her hand, she looked at Baron. "What do you think the ship is for?" she breathed.

Baron was about to offer a guess when a voice called out from behind them.

"It's my work ship!"

38

ESME LET OUT a yelp. Absorbed by all the gadgets, neither she nor Baron had noticed the boy walk up. He seemed to be about Gabriel's age, maybe a bit younger. His chin, nose, and eyes were all angles, his sandy hair shorn close. Both his shirt and pants were cut from crisp white material, something like linen, and perfectly clean. From his left ear, a blue light blinked on and off.

"Who—" Baron stammered. "Who are you?"

"Who are *you*?" the boy countered. "You're on my work ship."

"Oh, I—" Baron faltered, nervous and distracted by the blinking blue light. Esme stepped in.

"He's Baron. I'm Esme. We're crewmembers on the *Defiant*. We have a whole crew there who knows we're here, so—"

"Hey, hey," the boy interrupted, showing his palms in mock surrender. "I'm not going to *do* anything to you. Calm down."

"We're calm." Esme crossed her arms defensively. "So who are you? And what is all this?"

"I'm Devon. Master Engineer of our island. And this is our work ship. We come here to get the parts we need, when we need them. Which is often."

Baron pointed toward Devon. "What's that thing in your ear?"

"We call it a 3-tak. It's like a phone, or maybe more like a radio? Everyone on our island wears one."

Baron was impressed. He loved new technology. Or he had loved it, before the world exploded. "You mean you can talk to anyone at any time through that little thing?" he asked.

"Yep."

"Can I try?" Esme reached out a hand, but Devon shook his head, sighing.

"Mine's actually on the fritz. That's part of the reason I'm here. But I'll make you a deal. If you want to help me find seven X7L2 microchips, I'll give you directions to our island. Then you can really see the things we've come up with. I think you'll be impressed."

They didn't have to be asked twice. Esme and Baron rooted around in the piles of wires and lights for the next hour, Devon guiding them this way and that.

It wasn't easy—there were mountains of machines to dig through—but it gave them time to tell Devon all about their months at sea. And it was fun, too, like a treasure hunt; Baron was thrilled with the possibilities all the different components suggested. Eventually it was Esme who found the seventh X7L2. She handed it to Devon, who placed it next to the other chips he'd collected in a small metal box, then reached into his pocket and withdrew a piece of white cloth and a pen.

"It's winter now, so the sun's down real early. But you should reach land in two hours, give or take." Devon uncapped his pen. "Depending on the wind."

Lowering his head, he began to draw them a map.

The *Defiant* sailed west, a weak wind behind them. They had expected a two-hour sail, as promised, but two hours turned into four, and four into six, and darkness had long since set in by the time Rose spotted the black crescent of land ahead.

Ordinarily they wouldn't have considered dropping anchor and rowing in without any daylight to guide them, but after hearing Esme and Baron describe their hours on the work ship, the crew wanted to get to the new island as soon as they could. Could it really be? Lights? Machines? It didn't seem possible—not here, in the middle of the ocean. But as the crew rowed toward land, they could clearly see them: tiny blue lights hovering a few feet above the ground.

"What are they?" Carlos whispered.

"3-taks," Baron replied confidently.

"Huh?" Carlos half-stood in excitement, rocking the small boat. "What's a—what's that?"

Esme grabbed his shirt and pulled him back down. "It's a sort of talking device," she explained. "They wear them in their ears."

"I want one!" Carlos cried as the crew of eager rowers doubled their speed.

Dawn was breaking by the time the crew dragged the rowboat up the beach toward the blue-light kids lined up along the shore. They stayed close to their rowboat, mesmerized by the small winking blue lights, until the fair-haired boy from the work ship stepped forward.

"Esme, Baron," Devon said. "I was worried my map led you off course."

"It wasn't perfect," Baron agreed.

"It was great," Esme said, shooting Baron a look. "This is the rest of our crew: Rose, Quincy, Carlos, and Gabriel, our captain."

Gabriel extended a hand to Devon.

"Thank you for inviting us to your island. We've already heard impressive things, and we can see that they were all true," Gabriel said, nodding at the blue light in Devon's ear. "We're all eager to see more."

"There'll be plenty of time for all that," Devon replied. "But you must be exhausted. We'll take you to our camp to rest."

The weary crew followed the pack of blue-light kids up and over a dune and along a winding pathway into the woods beyond the beach, vaguely aware that the path was illuminated on all sides. A warm amber glow was emitting from curious bell-shaped lights at their feet. As much as they wanted to stop and examine them, the *Defiant* crew was thoroughly worn out—nearly asleep on their feet. So they let themselves be led until they reached a camp, and an empty hut, and sleep.

39

IT WAS LATE afternoon when Devon finally woke them. "Didn't think you'd want to miss the whole day!" he said brightly.

The *Defiant* crew rubbed their faces sleepily and began to rise. Esme blinked hard, trying to perk up. She would have traded anything for more sleep. Looking around, she saw what the darkness had hidden last night: the roof of their hut came to a point at the top, and when she crawled out she confirmed that it was in fact some type of teepee. Branches were splayed at the bottom and bound at the top, the whole structure covered in palm fronds. There were dozens more such structures lining the camp in neat rows.

"You ready to start the day?" Devon called.

As Esme looked at Devon, standing there well-kempt in his clean white smock, a shamed flush started to creep up her neck. All at once, she saw herself and the rest of her crew with fresh eyes. They were coated with a thin layer of brownish-green grime, and she was sure they smelled terrible, though honestly she could no longer tell. Rose's incredible growth spurt had made her purple corduroys split at the ankles, and now they hit her at the calf. She was wearing one of the boys' T-shirts, and her withered arm peeked from a gaping sleeve, still strangely bent. Quincy's hair had long since come unbraided and now sprang high above his head in a matted dome. Gabriel's hair hung halfway down his back in a series of tangled ropes. Carlos was particularly filthy—shirtless, his nose red and crusted, his teeth green with film. Baron had managed to keep himself the cleanest, but his lips were horribly chapped, his glasses rusting and smudged. As for Esme, her skin had become a strange canvas for the sun, layered with bright pinks and weathered whites. Her hair, lashes, and brows were bleached flaxen, and when she looked down at her dirty feet, she noticed the nails of three toes were black and falling off. It was grotesque and mesmerizing all at once, and Esme probably could have stared at her toes for a good long while if Devon hadn't asked the crew what they wanted to see first.

Esme started to ask him for a bucket of clean water, but the rest of the crew drowned her out, their voices raised in shared purpose. Everyone wanted to go see those extraordinary amber lights.

As the crew followed Devon back toward the beach, along the same path they had walked late the night before, they were surprised by what the darkness had hidden from them: the sand of the island was a pale, shimmering pink. Esme scooped up a handful and let it trickle through her fingers. Devon noticed her interest, and slowed.

"We don't know what makes it pink," he said. "Yet."

"Yet?"

"We're conducting some experiments. Back at camp. I'll show you all that later." They continued walking until they reached the bell lights. Devon reached down and plucked a glass orb from the sand, and the crew stopped just behind him, eager for explanation. The glass was a dull brown now, but they all remembered the honey-colored light it had given off. Lights! In the sand! How did they work?

"Solar power," Devon explained. "They gather energy in the sun all day and then use what they've stored at night. It's pretty basic, actually. These are one of the first things we developed after we discovered the work ship." Devon smiled, the blue light winking in his ear like a precious stone.

Baron picked up one of the glass bells and turned it over in his thick hand. "Incredible," he marveled, recalling their magic glow.

"You think that's something," Devon said, and grinned, "wait until you see what we've got back at camp!"

They headed back up the path, each crewmember tingling with anticipation. Devon looked over his shoulder at them as they approached the camp's perimeter.

"Ready?" he called, and the crew nodded excitedly. They could already see the dozens of metal workbenches lined up in neat rows beyond the huts, alongside an open courtyard. In front of each bench, sitting on metal stools, kids appeared to be working. They were sparking wires and welding and melting glass, and seemed to be conducting any number of experiments. Like Devon, they all sported plain, clean clothes and short-cropped hair. They were so absorbed in their work that they barely raised their heads to acknowledge the six strangers walking through their camp.

"…and then the filtration system kicks in through this mechanism, and voilà!" Devon was saying. He had taken Baron over to the closest station, where he'd broken down the workings of a long oblong box. The boys stood back to let Esme get a better look.

"So you always have, you never have to worry about…" Esme petered out, overwhelmed.

"Clean drinking water," Devon finished for her. "Not a concern around here."

"Wow." Quincy touched the shiny machine. "What else you got?"

"Yeah, what else?" Carlos echoed.

"Well, come look at this." Devon turned toward a workbench where a pudgy girl sat, stooped over what looked like a giant metal crab. She was screwing in a metal plate on its underbelly, chewing on her cheek in concentration. Devon touched the blue light in his ear.

"Vanessa," he said in a clear, firm voice. Without raising her head, the girl touched her ear, as well.

"Vanessa here."

"Devon. Can we come to your bench and maybe you can show off what you're working on for our guests?"

Now the girl looked up and over at them. "Of course!" She waved, smiling. "Come on over."

"Incredible," Baron murmured as he and the crew walked over. Crowded around, they watched raptly as Vanessa lifted up the machine for them to see.

"We call this a VitaSea," she explained. "When we first got here, we were literally starving. This island doesn't have banana trees, which are a major food source for most island communities, as you probably know. But what we do have is a ton of seaweed. It's something about the configuration of the coral beds surrounding us. Anyway, seaweed is a major source of essential nutrients, and it's basically what we survive on. So after we found the work ship, we were able to piece this together."

Here, Vanessa ran her hand down the length of the machine.

"What it does is collect seaweed all night at high tide, and then crawl onto shore and bake in the sun all day. The seaweed dries, then gets pulverized internally and condensed into a seaweed pill."

At this, Vanessa opened her fist with a flourish. On her palm sat three huge pea-green balls. She let the crew examine the pills for a moment before casually popping them into her mouth. Then, with what looked like great effort, she swallowed.

"So when it's ready, we won't ever have to collect or chew our seaweed!" Devon cheered, and Vanessa humbly bowed her head. Carlos inched forward.

"Can I have one?" he asked Vanessa, bug-eyed. She smiled down at him, then fished around in her pocket and produced another peanut-size green pill.

"Here you go," she said, handing it to Carlos. He popped it into his mouth as Vanessa had done, but promptly spat it out on the ground.

"It was too big," he said, and smiled sheepishly.

Esme gave him a withering look, and turned to Vanessa.

"How come it doesn't work yet?"

"Well," Vanessa said, "after we built the first one, we realized we needed to find some way to fuel it. We're experimenting with coconut oil and some other things, but so far nothing's quite worked. So that's the next step. But once we figure out the fuel, we'll have five operational VitaSea machines."

"Astonishing," said Baron. Just then there was a faint beep, and the crew saw Devon put his hand to his ear.

"Hold," he said, and turned to Vanessa. "I have an Outlier on tak here."

"No problem," Vanessa said, and nodded. "Take it." Devon stepped a few feet away, touched the blue light in his ear, and began to speak intensely.

"What's an Outlier?" Carlos whispered, pulling at Baron's sleeve. Baron shrugged at Vanessa, who had clearly heard the question.

"They're just kids," she said. "They used to live with us. When we first got here—"

"How *did* you get here?" Baron interrupted.

"Science at Sea. It was a trip our group was on. We conducted experiments based on... Well, you probably wouldn't understand."

"Baron would *definitely* understand," Quincy said hotly. He narrowed his eyes at Vanessa, who looked back, slightly shocked.

"Oh," she stammered, "I didn't mean to—"

"Never mind," said Baron, barely concealing a smile. "So. You were saying. Science at Sea?"

"Yeah, we all won this science competition. The prize was to go on a sailing trip. It was national. So each of us had the top entry at our schools. We'd been at sea about a week when the sky burst happened—we barely knew each other."

"The pink flash," Rose and Baron said together.

"You saw it too, then?" Vanessa leaned in eagerly. "Where were you?"

"In San Francisco," said Gabriel. "You?"

"Our boat left from Acapulco."

"That's Mexico," Carlos whispered to Rose.

Vanessa nodded. "But I don't know where we were when the burst happened, or where it landed us when it was through. We were just on the boat, floating. That was a very bad time." Vanessa's face blanched. She shook her head once, hard, as if trying to shake off the memory.

"We almost starved," Esme said gently. "At the beginning, after the flash. Then Baron figured out how to fish."

Vanessa looked at Esme blankly, and then seemed to remember herself. "Oh, yes. Fish. That's very good. And so tell me then, how did you get on this ship of yours?"

Carlos stepped closer to Vanessa. "We were on a field trip to see it. It wasn't our ship then—just *a* ship. It's called the *Defiant*. Now it's ours. We're the crew."

"And you knew how to sail?" asked Vanessa.

"Not at first," Baron replied.

"Our captain," Quincy said, gesturing toward Gabriel. "He figured it out."

"Very impressive," said Vanessa. She turned to Gabriel. "And you've been at sea all these months, then?"

"We've stopped twice," he said. "Both islands had groups of kids on them."

"Just kids?" Vanessa furrowed her brow. "No adults at all?"

"We haven't seen any adults since the flash," Baron said. "What happened to the ones on your ship?"

"I don't know," Vanessa said, her voice low and heavy. "It was all chaos. We figured they drowned. They must have drowned." Lost in thought, Vanessa's face seemed to draw into itself. Then, all at once, she looked up, eyes flashing.

"But you didn't want to stay," she said quickly. "On the other islands."

"No way!" cried Carlos. "The thin kids tried to burn me, and then they wanted to kidnap Rose."

"It was more complicated than that," Esme said quickly. "But they did have customs that didn't exactly work for us."

"I see," Vanessa said. "And the second island?"

"They had good food, but they just wanted to chase seals around all day," said Rose.

Vanessa shook her head. "I don't understand. Why seals?"

"They thought they were a threat," said Baron.

"Okay, but still," Vanessa went on, "you couldn't put up with some seal-chasing?"

"There was a boy who bossed everyone around," said Rose. "He almost hurt Esme."

Vanessa looked at Esme, who nodded in confirmation.

"How long ago was this?" Vanessa asked intently.

"About two weeks since the last island," Esme replied, wanting to change the subject. "So... how did you all get here? After the sky burst?"

Vanessa's face fell. "After about a week, a very bad week, our boat finally ran aground. We could see an island in the distance. This island. We knew we had to swim for it. It was the only choice. But it looked so much closer than it was." She paused. "About half didn't make it. It's just twenty-four of us here now."

"I'm sorry," said Esme.

Vanessa gave a shrug, then suddenly perked up. "Oh! And the three Outliers. That makes us twenty-seven. But they live out there." She gestured toward the dense green tangle in the distance. "They still talk to us on the 3-tak. But they choose to live alone."

"Why?" Esme asked. She couldn't imagine choosing to live like that.

Vanessa seemed about to reply when a clear voice behind them called out, "Okay then!" The crew turned to find that Devon had finished his call and was walking briskly back toward them, grinning. He came up alongside Vanessa and gave her a hearty clap on the back. "Thank you, Vanessa. We won't take up any more of your time. Keep up the good work."

"Will do," Vanessa said, already turning away to hunch over the silver crab.

The tour continued. Devon moved the crew from workstation to workstation, each mechanic explaining what he or she was working on. There was a pole that killed fish with electrical currents, and a laser that zapped sand off your feet. A pressurized gadget that cracked coconuts and a metal disk that warmed water for bathing. The *Defiant* kids could not have been any more impressed. And then Devon took them to his own workstation.

At first glance, it seemed pretty basic. Unlike the other tables, Devon's wasn't cluttered with gears and lights and wires. The only thing on it was a metal rod connected to a battery pack, and a long glass tube filled with pale pink sand. But what he showed them next was beyond anything they'd seen yet.

"Quincy," Devon said, handing him the glass tube. "Will you hold this, please?"

Quincy took the tube and held it out in front of his chest. Devon, in turn, flicked a switch on the battery pack and picked up the metal rod. There was a low buzz. Then, gradually, Devon began to draw the rod toward the tube.

At first, nothing seemed to be happening. But soon, almost imperceptibly, the sand resting at the bottom of the tube began to move. As Devon moved the rod closer, the sand started to whirl and bounce, as if it was trying to escape. Sparks flew, and the crew took a step back as a bolt of electricity shot out from the top of the tube. Startled, Quincy dropped it from his hands, and it fell to the ground with a clink.

"Sorry!" he yelped.

Devon laughed and scooped up the tube. "Don't worry. Everyone drops it the first time."

Quincy leaned forward. "So what was that?" he asked, staring at the tube in Devon's hand.

"We don't quite know yet," Devon answered. "We do know it's some new form of electricity. But look." Devon held the tube high. Most of the pink sand had spilled out when Quincy dropped it. The grains that were left had fused together, creating a peculiar smooth mass. Stranger still, the sand was now bright white.

40

THE NEXT MORNING, Esme woke to find herself alone in the *Defiant* kids' teepee. She sat up, surprised to be the last one awake. It was a nice change to have a moment alone, and she did her morning stretches slowly, uncoiling each muscle until she felt her whole body relax. Calm and unhurried, Esme dressed, then padded out to the camp to join the others.

Outside, though, Esme was again surprised not to see any members of her crew. Behind every workbench was one of Devon's kids, just like yesterday, eyes locked in concentration on their respective machines. But where was her crew?

Esme scanned the camp until she spotted Devon, leaning over the shoulder of a small red-haired boy who sat rigidly at his workbench. She made a beeline for him, but as she drew closer, she stopped, unsure of the protocol. She didn't want to barge in, and she didn't have a blue ear-light with which to signal her approach. Esme stood there for a minute, shifting her weight from foot to foot, until she decided it was sort of silly not to just walk up. So that's what she did, coming to a stop before the workbench. The boys did not look up. After a few awkward minutes, Esme cleared her throat.

"Yes?" Devon said, not taking his eyes off the machine on the table in front of him. Esme recognized it as a VitaSea.

"Um, sorry to interrupt—"

"Yes," the red-haired boy confirmed.

Esme blinked, taken aback. "I was just wondering if you maybe knew where my crew was."

"I sent them to the work ship." Devon's voice was distracted, far off. Clearly she was bothering him, but she had to figure out what was going on. So she gathered her nerve and pressed on.

"Why?"

Now Devon looked up at her, and Esme could see that, for the first time, his normal flat coolness was gone. Something was twitching across his face, something like fear, and when he spoke, there was a new tension in his tone.

"Listen, we're having a bit of a crisis here. I needed them to go get parts. It wasn't all of them. The skinny one stayed. I think he's walking around somewhere. And the little girl. She's with him."

"Quincy and Rose, " Esme replied, more to herself than to Devon. She knew he wanted her gone, but she still needed more information. "Sorry, but what exactly is the crisis?"

Devon let out a hard laugh. "Oh, nothing except our water filtration system blew a fuse, so we don't have any clean drinking water. You know. Just catastrophe."

Esme tried to think of something helpful to say, but she was stunned. Didn't these kids have everything figured out? It had seemed that way yesterday. How could they have no water reserves? How long could this many kids last without them? How long would it take to row back to the *Defiant*? Absorbed by her calculations, Esme noticed Rose only when she felt a yank on her shirtsleeve.

Quincy was standing just behind the younger girl, both of them glistening with sweat. Bits of leaves and dirt were stuck to their damp clothing. Something about their faces spoke of urgency and information. What was going on? Esme looked back at Devon, but he had clearly already forgotten she was there. She didn't bother with goodbyes.

"Come on," Esme said, grabbing each of her friends by an elbow and pulling them toward the beach.

They made their way through the camp and down the sandy path without speaking, the amber lights at their feet dead in the daylight. They walked for another twenty minutes once they reached the shore, making their way far down the beach. When they felt they had gone far enough to avoid a chance encounter, the three kids plopped down on the pink sand and sat cross-legged in a triangle, so close their knees touched.

"Okay," Esme said. "Where were you?"

Quincy looked at Rose, then started. "When we got up this morning, everyone was all panicked about the water situation and everything."

"And then I said I was going to get you," Rose jumped in, "but Gabriel said no, you were tired, and to let you rest. That he'd handle it."

Quincy nodded. "So Gabe volunteered our crew to go get the stuff they needed to fix the water machine."

"Right," Rose confirmed. "But then Gabe pulled Devon aside and said something I couldn't hear. And then Devon started waving his arms around, and Gabe started waving *his* arms around." Rose swept her own arm through the air to illustrate.

"Oh, no," Esme groaned, running her thumb across the purple mark on her neck.

"No, no," Quincy shook his head. "Gabe didn't explode at him. But right after that, he told me to stay behind with Rose so you wouldn't be worried when you got up."

Rose nodded. Then she looked over her shoulder, leaned forward, and whispered furiously. "And that's when we went into the jungle to explore. And found the metal huts. And saw *them*."

Esme stopped rubbing her neck. "Who?"

Rose opened her mouth, but Quincy cut in.

"The blue-light kids were running around all crazy, so Rose and I figured we'd better stay outta the way. There wasn't anything to do around camp, so we went into the jungle. Not far or anything. We just wanted to do a little exploring. We'd walked for maybe about forty minutes when we started to see—well, I don't know." Here, Quincy paused, his eyebrows joined in concentration. "They sort of looked like metal teepees, but with one side open."

"And there were kids inside!" Rose kept her voice low, but her eyes popped as she relayed this last discovery. "One in each teepee."

"What were they doing there?"

"Don't know," Quincy said, and shrugged. "We didn't go any closer. We wanted to come find you."

A queasiness bloomed in Esme's stomach. What had Vanessa called the kids living in the jungle? The name was right there, but worry was coating Esme's brain like mud, slowing her thoughts. Half her crew was out there attempting to make their way from one boat to another—what if something happened to them? To Gabriel? What would she do? It was all too much. She just wanted to curl up right there in the warm sand. Esme closed her eyes, but all at once she felt a small hand pulling her up to her feet. Rose and Quincy were tugging her back toward the camp.

Esme shook her head. "It's my fault. I—I'm just so sorry. I brought you here. To another bad island. I'm sorry, I just—"

"Esme," Rose said sternly. "Stop it." She shook Esme once, hard. "I mean it. Stop." Then Rose's voice softened. "There's nothing to be sorry for. We're here, and we'll figure out what to do. Together." Rose glanced back over her shoulder. "Right, Quince?"

"Right," Quincy replied. "Together."

Esme gave a few shaky nods.

"Okay, then," Rose said. "Let's hurry."

*   *   *

The afternoon passed uneasily. Esme avoided Devon and the rest of the blue-light kids, who seemed to be absorbed in their own work anyway. Instead she stayed close to the crew's designated teepee with Quincy and Rose, talking quietly, waiting for their friends to return. The hours passed, day turned to night, and eventually the two smaller kids nodded off. But Esme couldn't sleep. Sitting at the teepee's door, she kept a steady watch through the long dark hours. Finally, just as the first grey light of dawn arrived, Gabriel, Baron, and Carlos appeared at the edge of the camp. They had made it. The fog in Esme's mind instantly cleared. She felt her muscles warm and twitch, and before she realized it she was running at top speed. "Gabe!" she cried, skidding to a stop before him. "How could you leave without telling—"

He looked up and smiled, but there was something off in his expression.

"Not now, Es," he said quickly.

Esme looked at him, confused. "What is it?"

"Not now," Gabriel repeated. He glanced around the camp, then leaned in close. "I'll tell you everything tonight."

41

THAT NIGHT, AFTER the other kids had gone to bed, Gabriel confirmed everything Quincy had said earlier. Devon's kids had been panicked about the water filtration, and Gabriel had volunteered to lead a trip to the work ship. The journey had been uneventful (though they had seen a pretty incredible school of dolphins). Once on the work ship, it hadn't taken them more than an hour to find the parts Devon had described. Then they'd made their way back.

"But what happened with Devon?" Esme said, moving in closer and lowering her voice. "Rose said you were arguing."

"Well, maybe I shouldn't have said it. I didn't think he'd get so mad."

"What?"

"I just pointed out that there really wasn't any need to panic right away about the filtration machine being broken—they could just drink coconut water until they fixed it."

"I didn't even think of that," Esme murmured, shaking her head. "So then why the panic about the machine?"

Gabriel smiled. "That's what I thought, too."

"So why volunteer our crew?"

Gabriel looked down. "Well, I know you weren't so happy with me when I didn't want to help Carrick chase the seals. And when I didn't want you to explore the work ship with Baron. I just didn't want you to think..." Gabriel's voice trailed off.

Esme felt her face grow red, not with anger or embarrassment, but with shame.

"Let's leave," Esme said suddenly. Gabriel looked up at her, his eyes wide with surprise.

"But what about finding the perfect island?" he said. "It may not be perfect here, but this seems like a pretty good place, don't you think?"

"No, listen—it just doesn't feel—"

Esme froze. Devon was coming toward them through the darkness.

"Don't mean to interrupt," the boy said when he'd reached them. "I just wanted to say thanks. You really saved the day, Gabe."

"Of course," Gabriel replied.

"And hey, Esme—I also wanted to apologize if I was rude yesterday. We were pretty scared, you know?"

"It's okay." Esme was surprised he even remembered their talk.

"Anyway," Devon went on, "you'll be happy to hear we fixed the filtration machine. So there's water to drink now, if you're thirsty."

"Okay," Esme nodded. "Thanks."

"Well," Devon said. "Goodnight, then." He turned, and Esme

watched as he retreated back into the shadows. Then all at once, she remembered something, and before she could stop herself, she cried out.

"Wait!"

Devon turned. Esme felt hesitant—nervous without quite knowing why. But there was nothing to do but say it now.

"One of my crew said he thought he saw some other kids yesterday. Out in the jungle."

Devon smiled, his white teeth flashing in the dark. "Sure. Those are the Outliers."

Outliers! That was the word Vanessa had used. Esme pressed on.

"Why are they living out there? Away from the rest of you, I mean?"

"They're there because they want to be. They have this theory that the best inventions come through isolated connection."

"What does that mean?" Esme asked.

"It's what they call their philosophy: IC. It's complicated."

"Try us," said Gabriel.

Devon nodded, amused. "Okay, then. But first, let me ask you: in all your time at sea, have you seen any adults?"

"We haven't," Gabriel replied.

"Vanessa told me you had seen groups of kids on other islands. But no adults there, either?"

"No," said Esme. "No adults."

Devon nodded. "And of course, there are none here. After the burst, there were none left on our boat. Lots of people fell overboard, so we didn't think it was particularly strange. But then we were able to restore the radio. We've heard chatter, here and there, but no adult voices. Just other kids."

"What does it mean?" Esme's voice shook.

"I couldn't say for certain. But the Outliers have a theory. They say that people—adults—they got too… far apart. Then they came up with all these things to make them feel close again, but they weren't the right things. They created the wrong energy."

"Wrong energy?" Gabriel said, and shook his head. "I don't understand."

"Honestly," Devon chuckled, "I didn't either. But the first of us left to become an Outlier about three months ago. There are three of them now, and we think they're on to something. Maybe we'll all be like that one day. Who knows?"

"Can we go see them?" Esme asked.

It was hard to tell in the darkness, but Esme thought she saw some unease flicker over Devon's face. But when he spoke, his tone was wry.

"I don't think you'll find them very good company."

Esme wanted to tell him that wasn't the point, but instead she remained silent while Devon said goodnight again and left. Something was telling her to go and find those kids.

42

ESME DIDN'T SLEEP that night. Instead, long after Gabriel had grown tired and shut his eyes, she spent the remaining dark hours turning a plan over in her mind. She wouldn't tell Gabriel, she decided. She simply refused to put any more weight on his shoulders. She would be back before he even noticed she'd left.

As the first pale light threaded through the walls of their hut, Esme crept over to where Baron lay snoring and prodded him awake. When he opened his eyes, Esme put a finger to her lips and signaled for him to follow her outside. It was a grey day, but warm, the sun casting hazy rays through wisping clouds as Baron joined Esme and warily looked around the camp.

"What's going on?" he asked, still struggling to wake up. Esme didn't answer right away, but when Baron noticed her rubbing the ruddy mark on her neck, he knew something big was gnawing at her.

"I need your help," she finally whispered.

"Sure," he said. "Just tell me what's wrong."

"I can't stop thinking about those kids—the Outliers."

It took Baron a moment to place the word. Then he remembered Vanessa's speech. "The ones who live alone in the jungle?"

Esme nodded. "There's something wrong about it. I don't know. I just have a weird feeling."

"Okay," Baron said, and waited for Esme to continue. When she didn't, he spoke up again.

"Hey, I have a thought. I think the reason it seems so weird is that you and me, we've only *heard* about the Outliers. I mean, we haven't seen them for ourselves. So there's all this room to fill in the blanks. Maybe if we just saw them, we'd have a better sense of what's going on? Quincy told me where they were, more or less. I bet we can find them."

Esme grabbed Baron's arm. "That's exactly what I was thinking!" she whispered excitedly. "We could go now and be back before the others even get up." Esme's eyes glittered as she searched his face. Something about the way she stared at him made Baron uneasy. He looked up and noticed that the rising sun had disappeared behind some darkening clouds.

"Looks like it might rain, though," he said. Esme dropped her hand from his arm and turned away, frowning. Baron sighed.

"All right," he said. "I guess I don't have any other standing appointments today." He chuckled, and gave a shrug. "Let's go."

*   *   *

An hour later, Esme and Baron were deep in the jungle. They had snuck through the camp unnoticed, creeping past the huts where Devon's kids still slept. As they'd made their way past the workbenches, Esme had spotted a long length of filed metal. Not breaking stride, she'd snatched it up and passed it back to Baron.

"What's this for?" he'd whispered, but Esme had hushed him and kept walking. Now, as they made their way through the dense foliage, Baron took great satisfaction in raising the metal rod over his head and bringing it down with a *THWAP*, slicing through the thick ropey vines that blocked their way. He felt like a true explorer.

While Baron hacked the path ahead, Esme tried to ignore her rumbling stomach. They'd left so quickly there'd been no time to eat. We'll be back in time for lunch, she tried to assure herself. But hunger always triggered panic in her. Esme had never told anyone about the times Aunt Stevie had left her alone—the times she'd gone hungry. She thought about her aunt now, surprised by how little she'd missed her since the pink flash. Today she ached for her. Would she ever see her again? Was she even alive?

Baron had stopped chopping. He was standing stock still, a few yards ahead, staring into the jungle. When Esme stopped beside him, Baron lifted the metal rod, directing her sights straight ahead. A stream of sunlight was glinting off something metal, white light beaming through the dark. They took a few cautious steps closer. When the structure came into view, they both knew what they were looking at.

"That's probably one of them, huh?" Esme whispered.

"Has to be," Baron whispered back.

Esme felt her stomach tighten. Why was she so nervous? This was what she'd come for, wasn't it? She took another step forward. There was only a small thicket of vines separating them from the structure; a low hum was emanating from it, as if a swarm of bees had awakened inside.

"Well, we better go over there and say hi," Esme said.

"Okay," Baron answered, but made no move to follow. Esme looked back at him and shrugged.

"They're just kids, right?"

"Right." Baron nodded slowly. "Right!" He shook his head once, fast, as if clearing out the dust. "Right behind you."

43

THE GIRL INSIDE the hut couldn't have been more than ten years old. She was small, incredibly pale, and dressed in a shapeless navy shift. In her ear, a blue light blinked—the same 3-tak that all the other kids on the island wore. But unlike them, her head was completely shaved. Though her skin was bone white, across its surface were scattered even paler freckles, small pinpricks that seemed to glow in the darkness. A large square blue screen rested on her lap, sprinkled with shifting red dots.

The girl kept one hand nimbly on the screen, now and then glancing down at the little dots beneath her fingers. Her other hand rested on a keypad raised to chest-level. She was typing at an incredible rate, eyes rooted to a monitor just in front of her. There was no sound.

Esme counted seven different screens inside the teepee, beyond the one on the girl's lap. Dark blue text filled the main monitor; when the girl typed back, her words glowed red. Esme reasoned that the screen must be used for communicating with the kids back at the camp. The next monitor over displayed live running footage of the workstations— or so Esme assumed, after seeing Carlos race across the shot. The three screens beyond that were devoted to different movies; Esme was thrilled when she recognized *The Little Mermaid* playing on one of them. It had been her favorite when she was little, but she hadn't seen it for ages. It was bizarre to find it here, in the middle of a jungle on an island in the middle of the ocean. But it was comforting, too—the scene was one she'd watched so many times, back when she was home.

"This is creepy," Baron whispered. "Maybe we should go?"

Esme didn't respond. She just stood there, mesmerized by the swirling colors.

"Es?" he urged, touching her arm this time. Esme tore her eyes from the screens and looked up at Baron, who was staring down at her worriedly.

"No," she said, shaking her head. "Not yet."

Forcing her attention back, Esme focused on the remaining two screens. She tried to glean some information from them, but a snow-storm of static swirled across their faces. What was the girl seeing there that she wasn't? It was frightening, all the sprays of tangled wires connecting the blinking monitors filling practically every inch of the small, silent metal room. But she wasn't leaving without talking to the girl.

First, Esme tried clearing her throat. The girl just sat there in profile, tapping and blinking. Baron tried to get her attention next.

"Uh, hello," he started. "My name's Baron. This is Esme. We—"

No sooner had he spoken than the girl raised a finger and began

furiously stabbing at the blue light in her ear. Startled, Esme and Baron took a step back. Was that thing hurting her? Should they help? But then, just as abruptly as she'd started, the girl stopped. She put her hand back on the screen in her lap and resumed her typing. *Tap, tap-tap, tap.*

Baron took a step forward and cleared his throat. "We don't want to bother you, but we're friends of Devon's, and he said—"

The girl tapped at her earpiece again, exaggerating the motion even more. Suddenly, Esme understood.

"She wants us to talk to her through one of those things."

"But we don't have one of those things."

"I know."

"We don't have one of those things," Baron called out, louder this time. The girl stopped typing. Then she let out a long sigh, and touched her finger to the blue light in her ear.

"Devon? You there?" The girl's voice creaked, like an engine warming up in the cold. There was a beat of silence. Then Esme and Baron heard the buzz of another voice coming through the 3-tak.

"It's Ruth," the girl went on. "Yeah, I know, a while. Oh, fine, I guess. You know you'd be the first to hear if I'd found anything. Listen, there are some people at my door—yes, that's right. Well, it's really going to disrupt my IC to chat with strangers who can't even bother to use a 3-tak, so if—oh, yes, that would be great if they could leave me alone. Immediately. Thanks, Devon. Chat soon."

The girl's fingers resumed their tapping at the glowing square on her lap, the sound like raindrops pattering on the sea.

44

THEY MADE THEIR way back to camp slowly, Esme dragging her feet. Baron alternated between chopping a path through the vines and trying to console his friend.

"It's not like they're forced to be there," he offered.

"I know," Esme replied.

"So what is it, then?"

"She just seemed so… I don't know. So alone."

"You heard her. She wanted to be alone."

"I guess. It's just that—"

"What?"

"I just can't believe anyone would want to be *that* alone."

Baron shrugged. "I think it's sort of nice. Not having to be around people all the time. And she does talk to people—I mean, she can if she wants to."

Esme didn't answer, and though he did his best, Baron couldn't seem to lift the gloom that had fallen over her. After a while he focused on the business of defeating vines with his machete, whistling to himself as he went. He was sure they would be breaking through the jungle any minute when he heard Esme suck in a sharp breath.

Just off their path, half hidden behind a tree, stood the tallest boy Baron and Esme had ever seen. He had to duck a bit to fit beneath the leafy branches overhead, his head bowed to the ground. He wore a long shapeless smock, navy blue, like the Outlier they'd visited, but his stopped just short of his elbows and barely reached his knees. They couldn't see his face, just a short span of the palest blonde fuzz surrounding his head like a halo. In his ear, a blue light blinked. Baron stared, transfixed. Esme stepped forward eagerly.

"Hi!" she said brightly, her voice echoing through the jungle. Instantly the boy jerked his body farther back; he would have completely disappeared if not for the edges of his tunic peeking out from behind the black-barked tree. Baron shook his head at Esme, but she was already walking forward.

"Are you an Outlier?" she said.

The boy did not respond.

"It's okay if you are!" she tried again. "We met your friend already. The girl. And we know Devon. We're your friends!"

The boy didn't answer, but he didn't run away, either. The three of them stood there in silence, Esme seeming content to wait all day. Baron, though, was already growing impatient. These kids clearly wanted nothing to do with them; forcing them to talk didn't make sense. He was tired of waiting for Esme to understand that. He had taken a few steps back toward the camp, whistling absently as he went, when a low voice reverberated through the jungle.

"Stop."

Baron froze. He turned back to find the boy standing in full view, just beside the black-barked tree.

"Stop," the boy repeated, keeping his head tucked down low.

"Huh?"

"Whistle."

"Oh, I—"

"Whistle, Baron!" Esme cried.

Baron struggled to recall what exactly he'd been whistling. He hadn't even realized he was doing it! Then it came back to him, the silly song he'd had stuck in his head all morning: "Octopus's Garden." He shook his head once at the ridiculousness of it all, and began again. The other boy stared at the ground while Esme's eyes darted back and forth between the two of them. When he'd finished the song, Baron looked at Esme, unsure what to do next. But her full attention was on the tall boy.

"What's your name?" she asked. At the sound of her voice, the boy snapped back behind the tree. Esme looked pleadingly at Baron.

"Keep whistling," she whispered fiercely.

Baron didn't know if he should pick a new song, but the other one had worked before; he started it over from the beginning. This time the boy came out a little farther from behind his tree, and Esme couldn't help trying again.

"I'm Esme. That's Baron. What's your name?"

The boy hesitated and looked behind him. It seemed like he was calculating the best way to run. Esme held her breath. She stood perfectly still, willing him to stay with every inch of her being. Slowly, keeping his eyes lowered, the boy turned back toward them.

"Ren."

"Ren." Esme tried out the new name. "I'm Esme, and this is Baron. We're visiting your island. From the *Defiant*. We met Devon and the others, and they said we could come see you. I hope that's okay."

Ren made no gesture either way. Another long silence followed, so long even Esme was ready to give up. Then Ren spoke again.

"I know that song. The one he whistled. From back home. I haven't thought about that in a long time," he said. "Now would you please leave me alone?"

The smile dropped from Esme's face. "Why?"

"I need to reinstate Isolated Connection."

"But why?"

When Ren spoke again, his voice was empty, as if he were reading an instruction manual.

"We believe that the purest connection can only be achieved through IC. Connection with ideas, connection with others."

"But we're connecting right now," Baron countered.

"But it's not pure. It's interrupted by so many things."

"What things?" asked Esme.

"Your face. The expressions on the human face are highly vague. You can look one way but feel and say something entirely different. It's unclear. And the words you choose when you speak are loaded with double meanings, or the wrong meanings altogether. It's confusing. IC strives for the truest connection by eliminating these factors."

"Fascinating," Baron breathed.

Esme looked back and forth between the boys in disbelief.

"And talking through 3-taks is pure?"

"No." Ren shook his head. "It's not. But we're trying to find a new way, a better way. That's why we're here."

Esme shook her head. "I don't get it."

"Think about every bad thing that people do to each other. Lying, stealing. All the hurt. These things are born from not truly understanding the other person—from a gap in total communication. If you really understood someone completely, on every level, you would never do those things."

"I think I understand that," Baron said, and nodded. "It makes sense."

"But how does it make sense to figure out total communication with other people while you're *alone*?" Esme pressed.

"Eventually, once we've figured out IC completely, it won't have to be this way. But for now, we have to start over. Go back to the beginning. To ourselves. Can't you see that?"

Baron nodded, but Esme shook her head. Ren brought his hands together in front of him, then said thoughtfully, "Try thinking about some time in your life you've been hurt by someone. Now, what if that hurt had never happened? How much better would it be?"

Before she could stop it, Esme's mind leapt to Aunt Stevie. She remembered the feeling of being constantly let down, of being abandoned, and a familiar weight settled in her chest. What would it have been like never to feel that? Then, suddenly, Esme remembered the cake.

She looked up at Ren, her voice firm. "You're wrong," she said.

"Oh please, Es," Baron said, and laughed. "You can't really argue it's better to be hurt than not."

"I'm not saying that," Esme said deliberately. "But just listen for a minute. Last year, on my birthday, I woke up sad. I was sad because I was absolutely sure my aunt wasn't going to remember. I was positive. Because she never remembered *anything* that had to do with me. She forgot to pick me up all the time. She never came to my track meets. Never left me money to get lunch. So all the—" Esme paused, surprised at the term from science class that had popped into her head. "All the *empirical evidence* told me that she would forget my birthday, too. But just as I was about to walk out the door that morning, my aunt bursts out of her bedroom holding a cake. She'd made it the night before, after I'd gone to bed, and kept it in her room so I would be surprised. It was chocolate with white frosting and my name was written across it in purple icing." Closing her eyes, Esme smiled to herself. "And I can't remember a single moment before or since when I've ever been so happy."

"I'm not arguing that good things don't happen," said Ren, unimpressed. "I understand that happiness occurs, too."

Esme's eyes snapped open, and she leaned forward eagerly. "But what I don't think you understand is that the cake wouldn't have been so good—that I probably wouldn't have even *remembered* the cake to tell you about it now—if not for every disappointment that came before it."

"I don't—" Ren stammered. "I don't know if I—"

"It was the hurt that made that sort of happiness possible," Esme said urgently. "The hurts, they all run together. But the cake, that single moment of happiness, I'll remember forever."

"But the pain," Ren said weakly. "All the sadness."

Esme stepped toward Ren. "You asked me to remember my hurt. But now I'm asking you: do you remember the happiness? The last time you felt that way?"

Ren remained where he stood, looking anywhere but at her face. Something in him had wavered, though—there was a small shift in his posture, a relaxing of his shoulders and neck. It was enough to make Esme feel bold enough to ask what seemed like a ridiculous question. One she knew she wouldn't regret.

"Ren, do you want to come with us? Away from here, I mean. On our ship."

Baron turned to Esme and laughed. "Come on, he'll never—"

"Yes," said Ren.

45

"YOU DO?" ASKED Baron, incredulous.

"Yes," Ren repeated.

"Yes!" Esme cried, raising a fist in the air. Then, before Ren could change his mind, she started clomping forward, tearing at the thick vines blocking her path, while Baron chuckled, shaking his head.

"You're going the wrong way, Es," he called out after her.

"Actually, she's not," said Ren.

Baron looked at him, puzzled. "We definitely came from the north."

Ren nodded. "But there's a shortcut that way." He lifted a long arm in Esme's direction. "The camp's about a mile off, just across the creek."

"Oh. Okay, well then—" All of a sudden, Baron went stiff. "There's a creek?"

Ren nodded.

"A freshwater creek?"

Again, Ren nodded.

"Hey!" Esme called back to the boys. "What's the holdup?"

Just then, a tall clump of bushes ahead began to stir. A boy in a white tunic emerged before them.

"Devon!" Esme called out in surprise.

But Devon did not look at her; his focused was fixed on Ren, who now seemed to be shrinking into himself.

"I see you made a friend," Devon said flatly. Esme took a step closer to the Outlier. Devon gave her a hard glare, then turned his attention back to the taller boy.

"What are you doing, Ren?"

Ren's head was bowed so low it looked like his spine was made of something more flexible than bone. Esme didn't understand exactly what was going on between them, but she didn't like Devon's tone. She took another sideways step toward Ren and crossed her arms.

"He's decided to come with us," Esme said, a bit louder than she intended. Devon still didn't look at her, but now he cracked a small smile.

"I don't think that's going to happen. Ren wants to maintain IC. He believes IC is the purest way to communicate. The only way to communicate, really. And he can't do that if he goes with you. Right, Ren?"

Ren nodded sadly.

"You see?" Devon said, still staring at Ren. "He wants to stay."

"No, he doesn't!" Esme cried. Without thinking, she grabbed hold of Ren's arm. The boy immediately recoiled, and Esme leapt back, shaken.

"Ren," she said softly. "You don't have to stay here. He can't make you."

Ren shook his head. "I need to maintain IC."

"You got confused," Devon said, his voice gentle now. "That's what happens when you don't use IC. It's okay. Perfectly understandable. Now you can go back to your station and resume your work."

Ren was beginning to take a few steps back into the jungle when Esme called out his name. She moved to go after him, but Devon yanked her back, hard.

"Don't," he said, still gripping her arm. Esme shook herself free and glared at him. At that moment a crackling buzz sounded, and the blue light in Devon's ear began to wink. He glanced at Baron and Esme, then turned away and touched the blinking light.

"Devon here. Yes, yes, I found them. We're heading back now."

Esme felt the blood pulse in her face. She rubbed angrily at the splotch at her neck, not quite believing this turn of events. This wasn't right! She watched as Devon continued talking to whoever it was back at camp, no longer hearing his words. Then, before she could stop herself, she lunged forward, ripped the 3-tak from Devon's ear, and hurled it as far as she could into the jungle.

"You stupid girl!" Devon spat, whirling toward her. Esme ducked her head, cowering against the blow, but it never came—Devon was hurled back hard onto the ground, felled by a swipe from Baron's sturdy forearm. Esme stared, astonished. She'd never seen Baron hit anyone.

Baron seemed just as surprised as she was. He looked down as Devon struggled back onto his feet, then stood rigid for a moment, shoulders heaving, before beginning, methodically, to wipe the dirt and leaves from his pants. When he looked up, his face was still, his voice deathly calm. "Your crew is leaving the island," he said.

"I'm sorry," Baron started. "I didn't mean to—"

"It has nothing to do with that," Devon said. "I came to tell you that you're leaving. Our water systems were designed for the exact number of people in our group. We don't have the technology to support anyone else."

Baron looked at Esme and shook his head. He turned back to Devon.

"But what about—" he began, before Devon cut him off.

"It's already been decided," the boy said, glancing back at Ren. Then he turned to Esme and looked hard into her face. "Let's go."

Esme didn't budge. "I want to say goodbye to Ren."

Devon narrowed his eyes. "So say it."

"I want to say goodbye *alone*." Esme drew out the last word as long as she could. Devon moved to argue, but when Baron took a step forward, he relented.

"Fine," Devon said. "Make it fast."

Baron watched as Esme picked her way over to Ren, who had retreated a few yards into the jungle. The tall boy still didn't look at her, but after a minute he seemed to be doing most of the talking. Baron looked over to where Devon was crawling through the bushes nearby, searching in vain for his 3-tak. He decided it was time to say something.

"We know about the creek," he announced.

Devon let go of a branch and turned around. "Excuse me?"

"The creek," Baron repeated. "I'm just saying we know about it. You said we had to leave because of the water shortage. But the creek is freshwater. So I know you could let us stay."

In the darkness of the jungle, the whites of Devon's eyes seemed to glow. "It's not as simple as it seems."

"Seems pretty simple to me," said Baron.

Devon looked hard into Baron's face. "You tried to disrupt our work, and the work of the Outliers. I won't let you destroy everything. It's too important."

Esme was making her way over to Baron now. The curious part of him wanted to press Devon, to find out exactly what was happening out here, but a bigger part of him sensed the danger hanging heavy in the thick jungle air. No one else knew where they were. As Esme came up alongside him, Baron put a hand on her shoulder.

"We need to go," he said.

Esme nodded, and Baron looked away, trying not to see the pained look on the girl's face. She was staring back at the black-barked tree— staring at the spot where Ren had already vanished.

46

ROSE WENT FIRST.

"If I were home right now," she started.

"What would you do?" the crew called back in unison.

"If I were home right now, I would be walking through Union Square with my mom. We'd both be eating chocolate ice cream. No—chocolate chip. I'd look in all the big department store windows. My mom would take me inside one to buy a dress—a green one, with a zipper down the front and a red pocket on each side. Then we'd go to a movie. And I'd get popcorn." Rose sighed, smiling out across the shimmering blue water. It seemed to stretch on forever.

The ship swayed against the gentle waves, back and forth and back again, lulling the crew through the late afternoon. Butterball clouds puffed above them, the setting sun tinting their borders a soft, rosy hue. It had been two weeks since they'd left the last island.

They'd all felt a keen sense of discouragement, at first, disappointed by yet another failure to find a place to stop and stay. But as the days passed and the familiar rhythms of life aboard the *Defiant* returned, the crew settled into an unusual calm. They'd added a new chore to their daily routine, as well—where they used to throw back the rubbery green plants that tangled in the fishing line, now they dried the seaweed out on the deck in long ribbons. Quincy and Baron had come up with the system together. At first no one besides Quincy much liked the taste, but after a week they all got used to it. Now everyone was snacking on dried seaweed throughout the day, happy to have an alternative to fish jerky.

Of course, no one had stopped scanning the water for glimpses of green. It was a habit too deeply entrenched in them, after all the months at sea.

Only one crewmember still seemed troubled—still pulled by some mysterious, dark weight. Gabriel knew Esme was prone to gloomy patches, but this one didn't seem to be lifting even a bit.

"Es?" he called across the deck to where the girl stood alone at the helm, gazing out at the sunset. Esme didn't reply. She made no indication that she'd even heard him. Gabriel took in her stooped shoulders, her slightly bowed head, and called her name again. Esme still didn't turn, but this time she replied with a far-off "Hm?"

"What would you be doing if you were home right now?"

"Oh," she replied absently. "I don't know, really."

Gabriel exchanged a brief look with Baron, who raised his brows in reply. This wasn't right. No one liked to play If I Were Home Right

Now more than Esme. Without a word, the two boys picked themselves up off the deck and walked over.

Gabriel tried first. "Is something wrong?" he asked gently.

Esme shook her head.

"C'mon, Es," Baron followed. "You can tell us. It's *us*."

Esme shrugged, keeping her face turned away from the boys, not trusting herself not to cry. She knew what was bothering her—she'd just hoped it'd go away on its own. But as the days went on, as much as she tried to contain it, the sadness only grew heavier. Now it was clear that it was leaking out. She swallowed hard.

"I can't stop thinking about that boy we left."

Gabriel was confused. When had they left a boy?

"Ren," Baron said, understanding immediately.

"Yeah." Esme looked at the boys now, her green eyes two watery pools. "He's so alone out there. All by himself in the jungle. And he wanted to come with us." She stopped, hearing the quiver in her voice.

Baron took off his smudgy glasses, polished them with the edge of his shirt, and put them back on. Putting his chin in his hands, he thought a moment, then said, "Well, he did and he didn't."

"What do you mean?" Esme sniffed.

Baron sat down, his round face tensed in concentration. "I've thought a lot about him, too. That boy Ren. Ever since we left the island. And at first, I felt sad, too. But then I thought more about it. It's true that he *did* want to come with us, and be around people. But a part of him also didn't." Baron paused thoughtfully. "He was like a porcupine in the winter."

"Sorry, what?" Gabriel laughed.

"A porcupine," Baron said seriously. "In the winter, porcupines huddle together to stay warm. But as soon as they get close, they prick each other with their quills and scoot away. But then, as soon as they separate—"

"They get cold again," Esme finished.

"Exactly!" Baron exclaimed. "They risk freezing to death, so they have to get close again, and of course, they end up getting pricked. I think Ren was sort of like that. He didn't like being alone, but when he got close to people it didn't feel very good, either."

Baron looked back and forth between Gabriel and Esme, eager for them to agree. But they both seemed lost in their own thoughts.

"It's just a theory, anyway," he muttered, annoyed. He didn't need them to agree—*he* considered it to be a pretty dead-on comparison. Porcupines! Baron looked to the far end of the deck, where Quincy sat tossing bits of rotting driftwood over the rail and into the water. Quincy will appreciate this, Baron thought, walking over to him. Just then, a fat, cold raindrop splashed against his forehead.

Baron looked up to find the wispy, rose-colored clouds turned a deep charcoal grey. *Plonk, plonk-plonk.* The rain was coming down faster now, darkening the wooden deck. Esme and Gabriel scrambled to their feet.

"Call the crew," Gabriel instructed, turning his face to the sky.

Within the hour, the storm was pouring over them, casting the *Defiant* into a heavy darkness. The crew struggled to batten down the hatches while a hard wind whipped across the deck, pelting rain into their eyes.

White-capped waves battered the ancient ship. The *Defiant* rocked side to side, moaning with the strain.

"Hold on!" Gabriel shouted.

There was a loud *THWACK THWACK THWACK* from above them, and Gabriel looked up to see the mainsail flapping wildly in the wind.

"Mainsail's luffing!" he called out.

"No," Esme said, and shook her head, squinting upward. "That's not it. Something's caught up there, I think."

"I'm on it!" Quincy called back, and before anyone could argue he was shimmying up the ladder to the crow's nest.

As he climbed up and up, Quincy commanded himself not to look down. He'd never been comfortable with heights, had never really liked having to go up to the nest. But his crew needed him now, and he would do his part to help.

The wind ripped past his ears. The rain stung his eyes like angry wasps, so that he could barely see his hands before him. He looked up, and though he couldn't see the basket, he could just make out the bits of silver streamer flailing in the wind. Using them as his marker, Quincy kept climbing, higher and higher, until he reached the tiny basket and tumbled in.

Far below, Quincy heard shouting. He popped his head out and looked down, struggling to see the crew. His first thought was that he'd messed something up. But then he understood—they were cheering him on! Quincy clasped his hands above his head and shook them triumphantly. Suddenly the boat lurched, heeling sharply. Quincy grabbed tight to the rim of the basket, stifling a scream. When the ship righted itself again, his legs were shaking so hard he didn't know if he could stand. He had almost fallen out of the basket entirely. He didn't care about fixing the line now; he cared only about getting back down. But just as his foot found the first rung of the ladder, something made his whole body go numb.

Back on the deck, Gabriel saw Quincy stop mid-step. What was holding him up? The rain had let up a little, so Gabriel could see that Quincy was looking out at the dark pitching water. Peering into the murk, Gabriel tried to figure out what the other boy was staring at, but he couldn't see much. Then the black blanket covering the moon shifted. The water around them was lit with a cold white light.

Gabriel froze. There, in the chopping waters ahead, was the angry dagger of a red sail, as unmistakable as blood in the water.

47

"ARE WE GOING to die?" Carlos whispered.

Gabriel felt a current rip through him. The smaller boy was pulling at his arm, his tiny face twisted with terror. Gabriel had spent hours planning what he would do when the red-sailed ship returned, but now he felt himself struggling to move or think.

Crouching down, he brought his face level with Carlos's.

"No," he said firmly.

Gabriel straightened and turned to where the rest of his petrified crew stood together. "No," he called across the deck. "We are not going to die."

"Why aren't we turning?" Baron cried out. "We can outsail them. We can—"

"There isn't time," Esme said darkly. "They're too close now."

"But what are we going to do?" Rose whimpered.

Gabriel didn't answer. The crew watched as Angelica's ship sliced toward them through the water. They were close enough now to make out the ghost kids lined in a row along one edge of the ship, just as before, their white hair glowing against the tar-black sky. And there, directly in the middle, was Angelica. The white bird stood motionless on her shoulder.

Reaching into his pocket, Gabriel ran his thumb across the cool, hard edge of the tusk knife. He had prepared for this, practicing with the knife whenever he could, and yet now he couldn't ignore the knot tightening in his throat. What if he missed? As the white blur of Angelica clarified in the distance, he began to doubt that he could do it. He had hated her, had wished her harm more times than he could remember— she had tried to kill his crew, to take from him the only family he had. But just picturing the knife between Angelica's eyes made him shiver.

A deafening rumble shook the ship. The black clouds ripped open, spilling down icy rain. The darkness had doubled, the moon hidden behind the thunderheads, but the crew could still see the red sail carving toward them. The other ship would overtake them in a matter of minutes. This couldn't be it, Gabriel thought. There had to be another way out. Maybe he could reason with her, give her the Codex, even. But if she attacked them anyway—could he do it? Could he really hurt Angelica? He knew how terrified his crew must be, huddled together, crying and helpless, beside themselves with fear. It was his responsibility to protect them. He was their captain. He opened his eyes and turned to face his friends.

Standing shoulder to shoulder, backs straight, eyes dry and clear, the crew of the *Defiant* waited for their captain to give them their orders. Gabriel looked at them in amazement. Baron, Esme, Carlos, and Rose, his brave crew—and high above, Quincy in the crow's nest, risking his life for their sake. In that moment, Gabriel finally understood that it wasn't just up to him. They would save themselves together, or they would all fail, together. Gabriel felt the weight of the tusk knife against his leg and reached for it. He knew then that he would do everything he could to fight for their survival.

In the next moment a blaze of light tore through the darkness, a bright pink streak jagging crazily across the sky. Before anyone could react, a second crooked bolt ripped through the black night, forking in two and connecting with the highest points on the water: the masts of the red-sailed ship and the *Defiant*. Instantly, both ships were ablaze in a shower of fiery white sparks. The *Defiant* shuddered, and the sparks cascaded down over the crew, catching the wood in a burst of white flames. Gabriel, stunned, watched as fire licked along the mast above. Bits of flaming sail showered down upon the deck. For a moment, he thought that they looked beautiful. Then he thought: where was Quincy? And at that moment a ribbon of fire ripped through his belly.

The red-sailed ship, mast aflame, was still bearing down upon the *Defiant*.

Gabriel doubled over, clutching his stomach, just getting a glimpse of Angelica hovering at the edge of the other ship's deck, holding an object over the rail. At his side, his fingers met something sticky, hot blood and something else, something hard. The pain was blinding, but he forced himself to yank out the thing lodged in his gut. His eyes flooded with tears, but Gabriel swiped them away and held the bloody shard out before him, turning it over in his hand. It took him a moment to realize what it was: a shark's tooth, a long one, easily three inches, serrated on either side. His knees buckled, and he grabbed a high hanging rope for support, struggling to stay standing as blood pulsed through the gash in his side. It was too much. Gabriel staggered again and started to fall.

Before he could hit the deck, Esme shot forward and caught his arm. Shoving her shoulder underneath him, she eased him down onto the deck.

"Gabe? Can you hear me?" Esme cried.

Gabriel looked back at her, his eyes wild with panic and pain. Esme pressed her shirt into his stomach, trying to staunch the gush of blood, but there was too much coming, and too fast.

"Esme!" Rose screamed, pointing out at the waters ahead.

Esme untangled herself from Gabriel and stood up. The red-sailed ship was almost upon them, close enough that Esme could see the slingshot Angelica held in her hands. All the ghost kids had them, she realized now. They were going to die. Esme closed her eyes against the night, against the bleeding boy on the deck, against the ship ready to attack, against the white-haired girl who laughed and laughed and raised her slingshot to take aim.

Crumpled on the deck, holding the slash in his gut, Gabriel knew there was nothing left to do. No plan. No hope. He couldn't speak and he couldn't move. Something essential was draining out of him. He let the darkness settle, preparing himself to finally, finally let go.

Then he heard it. That terrible laugh echoing across the water.

Instantly, through the awful, unbearable pain, something began spinning in Gabriel's chest. His fists tightened. The white-hot anger spun and gathered and grew, whirling faster and faster inside him. He threw everything he had into it, fed it with all his pain and sadness and fear, until the sheer force of it lifted him up onto his feet. When he saw Angelica release her shot he sprang forward, hurling himself at Esme and knocking her onto the hard deck below.

Keeping her body still, Esme willed her eyes to open. Very carefully, she began moving her legs. She touched her chest, her arms, her head.

"Esme?"

The voice calling her name was so small, so out of sorts with everything happening around her, that it almost made her laugh. She sat up and saw Gabriel lying unconscious on the deck beside her, his entire midsection red with blood.

"Esme?" There was that voice again. Esme looked up to find Rose standing above her. Strange, Esme thought. She keeps saying my name, but not looking at me. Instead, Rose's eyes were cast upward, into the sky. Esme followed her gaze, mesmerized by the flames flickering along the mast. She followed their trail until, with a start that knocked the air from her, Esme realized what Rose was staring at. It was the crow's nest— the place where Quincy should have been.

"Where's Quincy?" Esme stammered. "Where'd he go?"

Rose didn't answer. Somewhere far off, Carlos was wailing. Esme understood she needed to move, but she couldn't seem to figure out how to do it. Smoke billowed down from the blaze above. Maybe she could just lie here beside Gabriel for a while. It would be so nice to close her eyes.

Someone was shaking her.

"Esme!" Baron cried, his face inches from hers. "We have to get to the rowboat!"

Esme looked down at Gabriel. His face was a gruesome yellow-white, and she could smell the blood flowing from his wound. "I don't think we can move him," she said.

Baron grabbed Esme's arm and looked fiercely into her eyes. "We don't have a choice."

Esme watched as he slung Gabriel's arm around his shoulder and began half-lifting, half-dragging him along the deck.

The wind whipped around them as Esme, Rose, and Carlos crawled along the deck after Baron. They stumbled into the rowboat and began to loosen the fist-thick knots that secured it to the ship. The waves beneath them continued to gather and swell, rocking the flaming ship toward the water. The rowboat gave a hard lurch down, and Baron cried out as the ropes ripped through his hands, searing them like hot metal. The crew held tight as they plummeted toward the thrashing waters below.

48

THEY HIT THE water with a splintering crash. The waves beat against the boat, icy spray flaying the bare arms of the crew as they grabbed for the oars and swiped desperately at the sea. They were bobbing directly beneath the *Defiant*, and with each rising wave, the rowboat threatened to smash against it. The ocean seemed intent on pushing the boat back toward the blazing ship. The fire was licking up the mainsail now, consuming itself and then shooting upward in ever more powerful bursts. The water was so dark that they seemed to be suspended by nothing, floating alone beside the flames.

The next wave brought the red-sailed ship into view, though it was less ship now than raging swell of flames and smoke. Its mainsail was completely engulfed, and despite the rain, flames had started sweeping across its deck. Billowing black smoke rose up into the night, blocking out the stars. Glints of white were streaking from the red-sailed ship into the water.

"What is that?" Carlos whispered.

Baron gasped. "Oh, God." He closed his eyes. "They're jumping."

A tremor shook Esme's body. "We have to help them!" she cried.

Baron shook his head sadly. "There's no room in the boat."

"And they tried to kill us!" Rose cried.

Esme looked at Gabriel, unconscious and bleeding at her feet. She knew what he would do. Gripping the seat beneath her, Esme raised herself on trembling legs and faced the battered crew.

"We are the crew of the *Defiant*, and we will all die here tonight before we let another group of kids drown while we do nothing."

For a moment, nobody spoke. Then Baron picked up his oar and placed it in the water. Rose and Carlos did the same.

With their last bit of strength, the crew threw their bodies against the wooden oars. They tore against the waves until their hands were ripped and bleeding, but they barely felt the pain. Every second that passed meant another ghost kid drowned. Through the rain, Rose scanned the water, searching desperately.

"I don't see anything!" she cried.

"Keep rowing!" Baron hollered back.

They continued to pull against the pounding waves, the sea crashing against their tiny boat. But it was hopeless. They could barely make out anything through the downpour. Esme was about to give the order to pull the oars in when a white flash in the water ahead caught her eye.

"There!" she cried, pointing.

A few yards off, a small girl clung to a length of plank wood. The

waves bore down, her tiny raft threatening to tip at any moment. She wouldn't be able to keep her grip much longer.

On the floor of the rowboat, Gabriel was coming to. Now he raised his head to see the white flapping wings of a bird, clutching the girl's arm.

"Angelica!" he called out weakly. There was no reply, just the steady sound of rain against water. Then a swelling wave swept the rowboat forward. Angelica's plank was no more than a few feet from them.

"Angelica!" Gabriel tried again.

Now the girl turned, her eyes locking with his. The desperate fear there made Gabriel's breath catch.

"Baron," he gasped, clutching the wound at his side. "Reach an oar out to her!"

Baron complied, stretching his oar out as far as he could manage, until he was almost touching the tiny plank. Terror marred the girl's face as she tried to raise a hand to the oar without losing her hold. The plank tipped, and Angelica clung tight to it again, Rodney flapping madly on her arm. Gabriel watched, sickened. He could not let her drown again.

"Angelica!" Gabriel cried. "You have to try!"

But something had replaced the fear in her eyes. Her face was twisted now, pinched tightly, gleaming with what he recognized as pure hatred. Angelica lifted a hand to her shoulder. With one smooth movement, she scooped the white bird down, tucking it securely beneath her arm, its feathers glowing white against the blackness of the water. Then she shifted her weight and gripped the plank. She was close enough now that Gabriel could see her chest swell as she drew in a great breath. When she spoke, her voice was clear.

"I don't need *you*."

"No!" Gabriel screamed, but there was nothing he could do. Angelica jerked her body to one side, flipping the plank over. Before they could pursue her, a battering wave swept the rowboat away.

"Where is she?" Gabriel cried.

They struggled against the rough sea, pulling at the oars. Angelica had disappeared into the dark water. After a moment they collapsed against the edges of the tiny boat.

Behind them, two flaming ships lit the night. The crew could only stare as the *Defiant* sank lower and lower, its deck consumed. High above, the clouds continued to swirl, hard rain falling into the rowboat. Between occasional gusts of heat from the ships, the crew shivered in stunned silence. They were beaten and scared, tattered and bloody. They had not been able to save even one of the ghost kids. They had lost their ship, and seemed about to lose their captain. And Quincy was really gone.

Rose reached for Carlos's hand. He looked at her, and when he saw her trembling chin, he crumpled into sobs. He lay his head in Esme's lap. Above him, hot tears flowed down the older girl's cheeks. She buried her face in Baron's shoulder. Wrapped tightly together, the crew of the *Defiant* wept.

When they had emptied themselves completely, they sat in silence, rocking back and forth on the waters that had finally begun to calm. Later, they would reflect on how strange it was that the storm had stopped almost the instant after the sea had swallowed the red-sailed ship, as if it had gotten what it had come for. But at the time, they were too stunned to consider anything much beyond that they were a crew without a ship, lost at sea, with absolutely no chance of survival.

49

IN THE LONG days that followed, as the rowboat drifted aimlessly across the vast empty waters, the crew sat quietly and waited to die.

Nobody said aloud that this was what they were doing, but without food or water, everyone understood that there was no hope left. A thick blanket of clouds had covered the sky; they had no idea where they were, no ship, no supplies. They hadn't seen any land for weeks. They were beyond desperation. This was the end.

The funny thing was, the sea had never been calmer or more beautiful. It was seventeen shades of blue: cerulean and sapphire, navy and turquoise. But the crew barely noticed the beauty. Hunger and thirst wrapped themselves around every moment.

Esme knew she should be trying to come up with a plan. But as they drifted along, one hour bleeding into the next, she couldn't clear her mind enough to think. Gabriel would have figured out something by now, she thought, looking down at the boy lying unconscious on the floor of the boat. His wound was seeping still, coating his shirt in a deep red bloom. She had tried her best to treat the gash, to clean it out with seawater and cover it with a piece of cloth ripped from her own shirt, but there was just so little she could do. And Gabriel would not wake up.

Esme tried to put herself in his place—to imagine what he, as their captain, would say or do to make things better. But it was no help. She was paralyzed. They all were. And now that the shock of the storm had passed, they were all able to fully feel the deep, awful sadness of Quincy's death. His absence seemed to yawn wider and wider, enveloping them.

We never even got to say goodbye, Esme thought sadly.

"Or tell him how much he—"

Before she even realized it was happening, she was speaking aloud.

"He had the greatest laugh," she said softly.

The crew looked at her, puzzled, as she continued. "You know how it would seem to start in his belly and sort of rise up and spill out of him? I loved that about Quincy, his laugh."

A few of them nodded thoughtfully, remembering.

"He let me play with his hair sometimes," Rose whispered. "He let me braid it." The crew waited for her to go on, but instead she dropped her face into her hands. Baron picked up the thread.

"He was so stubborn. But it was because he had conviction."

Carlos sniffled. "What's conviction?"

"It means he believed in what he believed," Baron replied. "And he was loyal. He was rough sometimes, sure, but he was a loyal friend." Baron's voice cracked. "I never told you guys about this," he continued, "but back on Seal Island, Carrick and some other guys were giving me a hard time because I didn't want to play football. Carrick called me a wimp, and Quincy got right up in his face and told him to shut up."

"He said that to Carrick?" Esme said, and laughed.

Baron nodded. "He told him to shut up, and that I was smarter than all of them put together. You should have seen Carrick's face." Baron smiled sadly. Rose put her good arm around him, and he dropped his head to her tiny shoulder.

"And he was the best swimmer!" Carlos cried out, then quickly looked away. They all did. No one wanted to think about Quincy struggling in the water.

Esme looked around at the crew. These were the people who had kept her alive over the last few months—the people she had kept alive. She put a hand to her forehead, felt the heat pulsing there, and thought about the pink flash, on that first day, and about what Devon had said, about the wrong energy that had come to exist between the adults. She thought of what Ren had said to her, out of the others' hearing, when they'd left him behind. The radio signals coming from the mainland, the chatter he'd picked up—always young voices. They were trying to find each other, trying to figure out where to go, what had happened. They'd said that the lightning had turned inside out. They'd said it was God. They'd said the sky had split open, that the connections between things had all gone wrong.

A series of images flashed through Esme's mind: the first tuna they had caught, with the smaller pink fish stuck inside it. The bright white freckles on the girl Outlier's face. The pink sand on the blue-light island.

The pink skin connecting those thin girls at the elbow. The white hair of the ghost kids. The pink flash. Bad energy.

"Esme?"

Carlos had been watching her for a few minutes now, and was frightened by the faraway look spreading across her face. His voice quavered as he spoke.

"How do we fix this?"

"I don't know," Esme said.

"Why are we here?" Carlos whimpered. "Why did this happen to us?"

"I don't know," Esme repeated, her face worn and blank.

"Es!" Carlos cried out.

"What?" Esme stared back at him, startled. "Why would you think I'd know that now?"

"I don't know," Carlos said quietly, looking away. "I guess it's because it's the end." He turned back and gave Esme a searching look. "Aren't you supposed to know in the end?"

Esme watched Carlos's face crumple, and for a moment, she thought she might lie—tell him it wasn't the end, that they'd find land soon. That they'd be okay. It would have been a kindness. But not the truth.

"No," Esme said softly. "No, I don't think that actually happens much. I think you mostly never really know. Not even in the end."

Wrapping his arms around his chest, Carlos lowered his head. He stayed that way a long while, curled up, hugging himself. But just as Esme reached out to touch him, she saw his head begin to nod, up and down, up and down.

Across the small boat, Rose had been half-listening to the conversation, feeling little more than idle curiosity. It was hard to summon up any strong feelings, now. The immense hunger and thirst made it seem as if she was somehow outside her body. Besides, if she was going to muster energy for anything, it would be to point out the thing in the water.

She had been watching it bob there for a while now, but no one else seemed to see it. She figured it was just another hallucination. But the thing wasn't going away. It was getting bigger, in fact. And from what she could make out, it looked very much like a body.

50

"HEY. GUYS," Rose croaked.

Her throat was painfully dry, but she swallowed hard and tried again. "Do you see that?"

The crew looked to where Rose was pointing. It was difficult to make out at first——just a tiny sliver of black against the blue water. But it was definitely real. Esme picked up an oar, and together they pulled the rowboat forward. They could see it now: a large plank of wood, square in shape, charred black on all sides. And on top of the plank, splayed out across its length, was a boy. He was asleep or unconscious, but not dead—they could all see his bare chest rise and fall. Maybe it was the days without food, or delirium from the heat, but it wasn't until the rowboat was nearly upon him that the crew realized who they were looking at.

"Quincy!" Baron cried, and before anyone could stop him, he jumped into the water and started swimming toward their friend. He reached the plank quickly but stopped just in front of it, treading water, unsure of what to do next. He wanted to touch Quincy, to wake him up, but he didn't want to end up rolling the boy into the water. Instead, Baron took firm hold of one edge of the plank and, with great effort, began to swim back to the rowboat, dragging the plank behind him.

"Quincy!" Carlos cried, jumping up and down. "He's alive!"

"But he's not in good shape," Baron said gravely.

Together, the crew lifted the boy up off the plank, then pulled Baron in after him. They circled around and leaned in close. They saw the chafed and bleeding lips, the tiny white blisters and burns that covered their friend's frail body, the spongy hair ringing the familiar feline face. His breathing, initially so encouraging, now seemed dangerously shallow. Esme put her hand to Quincy's forehead and flinched at the heat.

"Is Quincy going to die again?" Carlos whimpered.

"No," Baron said sternly. "He's not. But we need to cool him down."

He carefully rose to his feet and positioned himself just behind the other boy. Then, looping his arms beneath Quincy's armpits, Baron lifted him into a standing position. He kept lifting until the tips of Quincy's toes hovered inches above the floor of the boat. Silently, Esme took hold of the boy's feet and pulled them to her, until the limp body was stretched horizontally between them. Then, moving cautiously, they lifted their friend over the side of the boat and slowly lowered him into the cool water below.

Esme let go of Quincy's feet and repositioned herself beside Baron. Quincy's head lolled forward, threatening to plunge into the water, but Esme caught it and held him steady. She peered into his face, this face she knew so well. Without the crooked smile, the mischievous eyes, he looked like a stranger.

Esme took a breath and felt her resolve take root. Even if they were all about to die anyway, right now she was going to save him. Still holding his head upright, Esme slid onto her belly and bent her body over the side of the boat until her face was just inches from Quincy's.

"Quincy," she started, her voice firm. "You need to wake up."

The crew held their breath and watched. Nothing happened.

"Wake up!" Esme tried again, louder this time.

"Wake up, Quincy!" Carlos echoed, his tiny voice pleading.

"C'mon, Quincy, you can do it!" Rose shouted. "Open your eyes!"

They kept on like this, shouting encouragements, urging their friend to come back to them. But despite their pleas, despite the cold seawater rising up to his neck, Quincy would not wake up.

Esme slumped down into the boat, defeated. They had just gotten Quincy back, and now they had lost him all over again.

"It's no use," Esme said dully. "He's too far gone."

"He is not," Baron said evenly.

"Come on," Esme sighed. "Pull him back in. It's over."

"We'll see," Baron replied. And then he plunged Quincy deep below the water.

"What are you doing!" Esme cried, leaping to her feet. Baron didn't reply. He kept his eyes fixed on the boy he held in his hands.

"Pull him up!" Rose screamed.

"If Quincy's going to die," Baron muttered, "he's going to die fighting."

Esme leaped onto Baron's back, scratching at his thick arms. The rowboat tipped dangerously, threatening to dump them all overboard. But Baron held on. His focus never left the spot where he had plunged Quincy down.

"Baron, please," Esme whimpered, though she knew it was no use now.

Suddenly, a long skinny arm shot out of the water. In one fluid motion, Baron sprang from his crouch and onto his feet, catapulting the sputtering boy out of the water and onto the floor of the boat. He flipped Quincy onto his stomach, and the nearly drowned castaway pushed himself up onto all fours, retching up what seemed like a gallon of seawater. He coughed so hard it seemed like his back might snap in two. Quincy was alive.

The crew took turns patting and rubbing his back, exchanging wild-eyed grins. After a time, his coughing slowed, and Quincy collapsed onto his stomach. He lay there, not moving, his head to one side, his eyes closed.

"Should we just leave him like that?" Rose asked.

Esme had no idea. She glanced at Gabriel, who sat propped against the side of the boat. Her eyes fell on the black festering wound at his stomach, and she forced herself to look at his face instead. His eyes were closed, as they were all the time now. She knew it wasn't his fault he was hurt and sick, but she still couldn't help feeling like he had abandoned her when she needed him most. He didn't even know they had rescued Quincy. Who else could help her now? Without Gabriel, how did they have any hope of saving themselves?

All at once, something sparked in Esme's brain. Dropping to her knees, she put her mouth to Quincy's ear.

"Quincy?" she whispered.

A moment passed.

"Quincy," Esme tried again, a little louder this time. "Can you hear me?"

Slowly, just barely, Quincy's right eye slid open.

"It's me," Esme said. "And Baron's here, too. And Gabriel and Carlos and Rose. We found you. You're safe now."

Esme pulled back and watched as the corners of Quincy's mouth curled up. It was the smallest of smiles, but there it was. Esme leaned back down.

"I have to ask you something important. We need your help, okay?"

The crew leaned in as Quincy's cracked lips parted. He winced. Then a sound, barely audible, escaped from him. It was a thin, wet gurgle, like water from a spigot, followed by a low, throaty croak. Esme put her ear close to Quincy's mouth, placing a hand on his back to steady him. She could feel his lips struggling to move.

"Quincy, listen," Esme said. "This is important. When you were floating out there, did you see any land?"

She moved her ear so that it was almost touching Quincy's lips again. He swallowed, coughed, and closed his eyes. Esme waited a full minute. Then another. The world around her seemed to stop; she no longer felt the waves rocking the boat beneath her, no longer heard the ragged breathing of her crew. Her whole being was focused on just one thing, one sound, that airy, rusty creak.

After three full minutes of silence, when Quincy spoke the word that would save them, his voice rang clear and deep, vibrating like a bell in an empty church.

"East."

51

THROUGH THE LONG, dark night, the crew of the *Defiant* rowed their small boat east. Their stomachs were empty, their bodies wretched and weak. They rowed through their weariness and through their fear, through their hunger and through their pain. Something inside them had been lit up again. It was the flame of hope.

As night gave way to dawn, a fiery sun rose from the waters. A few high stars still flickered above them, their light barely visible against the periwinkle blue. It was a color that promised a clear day ahead.

The only sounds were the clean splashes the rowers made as they traveled on, each pull of the oar bringing the crew closer to the ribbon of green land they had been watching unfurl. It was just ahead of them now.

When the sun began to fall again, Esme set down her oar. The green swath before her continued to grow and take shape. She let out a long breath. They were going to make it. She looked across the boat, taking in her crew. *Her crew.* Without exchanging a word, they had all recognized that she was in charge now; Esme was their captain. But she didn't linger long on this thought, because a more urgent one was circling back through her mind: Gabriel.

When she reached the sleeping boy, she paused a moment, taking in his long arms and flattened nose, the way his hair fell in a black curtain over his eyes. His wound had closed, at least for now. If she could keep it relatively clean, he might still have a chance to recover. Esme reached down and touched his cheek. He still burned with fever and she didn't want to wake him, but she also knew that it was time. He had slept long enough.

"Gabriel," Esme called out softly.

The boy groaned. His eyelids darted and danced, but would not open. He didn't want to wake from his dreams, where everything was right and whole and safe. But someone was calling his name, urging him back. He was needed.

Gabriel's eyes flickered open.

He blinked once, twice, and then once more as his gaze settled on the face of the girl crouching before him. He smiled.

"Esme."

"Hey there," Esme said, and smiled, brushing the hair from his eyes.

Gabriel gave a yawn and stretched his long arms high in the air above him. "How long have I been asleep?"

"A long time."

She watched as Gabriel struggled to keep his eyes from closing. Eventually, when it proved too difficult, he shut them against the bright sunlight.

"Hey," Esme said, giving him a nudge. "I have something to tell you."

"Mm," Gabriel murmured, eyes still closed. "What's that?"

"We found land, Gabriel."

"Land?"

Esme nodded. "A new shore." She took Gabriel's nodding head in her hands and turned his face to hers, and as she did this he opened his eyes once more.

"Hey, Es," he mumbled dreamily.

"Yes?"

"Are there people on the land? Other kids, like us?"

High above them, a seabird cawed, and Esme looked up to see white wings spread and fall, beating against the warm currents of wind that swirled around the tiny boat. She kept watching as the bird hovered above their heads, playing with the wind that kept pushing it higher and higher, until it was just a pale blur against the dusky blue sky. When she looked back down, she saw that Gabriel was on the verge of drifting off again.

Slowly she raised herself up. Shielding her eyes against the setting sun, Esme gazed across the shimmering water, the waves turning in ribbons, and answered the sleeping boy's question.

"I have no idea," Esme said, smiling as the stretch of green continued to grow before her, just ahead and to the east. "Let's go find out."

THE END

ACKNOWLEDGMENTS

Jordan Bass
Dan McKinley
Dave Eggers
Lauren Hall
Brian McMullen
Ethan Nosowsky
Andi Winnette
Eli Horowitz
Namwali Serpell
Yana Garcia
Lily Padula
Leo Beckerman
Matt & Carla Quint

This book would have not been possible without
your brilliant advice and unwavering support.
Endless thanks.

ABOUT THE AUTHOR

M. Quint is a writer living in San Francisco.

ABOUT THE ILLUSTRATOR

Lily Padula is a Brooklyn-based illustrator from a
small beach town outside of New York City.